AL ONE
THE

TERRY GRIMWOOD

For Debra –
the love of my life and inspiration for this book and so much more

CHAPTER ONE (2016)

Jack called her.

Her name was Louise and they had met while rehearsing the lead roles in an amateur production of *Brief Encounter*.

Now there was an irony.

Jack had managed to secure tickets for an early screening of the movie version back in 1945, on his late wife Marion's birthday. How long ago was it now? Jack performed a swift mental calculation. Seventy-one years. She was forty-five that day. The same age as Jack, but then he had always been forty-five.

He was still forty-five and, as far as he knew, would remain that way until....

Until it ended.

Marion's birthday outing had taken place late on a November afternoon, much like this one. Perhaps that was why this day seemed so charged, so alive with some delicious energy that had reawakened emotions he believed to be long buried.

As the phone's ringtone warbled in his ear, Jack knew that this would be a precursor to hurt and heartbreak, but at that moment, he didn't care. Jack Smith was tired of loneliness. He had endured it for as long as he had been able. There were times when he had embraced it, but not anymore. Selfish? Yes, cruel even, but surely he deserved something that resembled happiness, if only for the briefest of moments.

Jack was out on the balcony of his first floor flat. The air was cold and clean despite its bonfire tang. November always smelled of smoke. The light was fading. Streetlamps came on. He should go in. He wore only a shirt and chinos.

The flat was in Stevenage. The town was, for some reason Jack could never fathom, the butt of many a joke. He had found it to be pleasant enough, a place of trees surrounded by soft, rolling countryside.

Better still, it wasn't London. He had, long ago, had his fill of the capital.

He stayed where he was. His phone uttered its repetitive electronic tone. Louise wasn't going to pick up. He had misjudged the connection between them as more than friendship. It was hard to pinpoint exactly when Jack's feelings toward her had changed. He had noticed her on the evening she turned up for the first reading of the play. He found her strikingly attractive, well dressed, smart even, though her outfit was casual. When she was given the part of Laura and Jack was given Alec, he found himself looking forward to working with her. There would, of course, be some mild flirting, but little more.

A few weeks in, mild flirting had been transformed into glances, touches, and a growing awareness of Louise's presence that stayed with Jack long after their allotted rehearsal time.

Jack made no move. There was a truth to deal with, the truth of who, and *what*, he was, and of the impossibility of a future. Logic was a poor competitor to feelings, however. Louise's spirit, her *self*, was relentlessly vivid in his mind. It made him nervous. It exhausted him. He wanted to believe that their nascent relationship teetered on the threshold. One invitation, for a drink, a coffee, dinner, and they would both fall. Now that the play was over, performances complete, set broken, and applause an echo through Jack's capacious memory, there was no longer an excuse to see Louise. Time with her required affirmative action.

Jack cut the call.

For the best. There were too many reasons to turn away from this.

Christ, he was lonely.

Restless now, he went back into the flat and drew the big curtains over the French doors. He crossed to the standard lamp and switched it on. The light was comfortable, cozy even. He picked up the television remote. He had films recorded and saved. He had books to read. He had music to listen to. The radio, perhaps. Things he enjoyed.

He switched on the television. Saturday night programming was noisy and brightly coloured. He disliked its garishness. There was nothing wrong with it, just the sort of harmless entertainment he had seen all his life, just not to his liking.

He flicked onto his saved shows and found a film; *A Night to Remember*, the sinking of the *Titanic*, made even more poignant by monochrome softness and associated memory. Jack was unsurprised by a stab of emotion as he remembered the first time he had seen this film, again, with Marion, on some far-off night at a long-demolished cinema.

He remembered too much because he remembered everything.

A baby cried.

Louise Martin started and turned sharply away from the cafe window to scan the customers packed inside for their post-shopping coffee. Yes, there, bundled into his pusher, an infant of about six months, face screwed up into a mask of rage and frustration. His mother crouched down in front of him and blanked Louise's view. The cries faded into a resentful grizzle as the mother hauled the child from its prison and onto her lap.

Someone else snagged Louise's attention. A man, middle-aged, heavy set and broad, wearing a large overcoat and Homberg hat. The brim of the hat was pulled down low and hid his eyes. He was watching her though, his gaze, intense and discomforting. After a moment, he raised his coffee cup as if in greeting, then got to his feet and headed for the door.

Shaken, Louise went back to her drink and book. The baby's cries had put her on edge and turned the man into someone sinister. She forced herself to concentrate on what she was reading. She was resigned to the fact that some wounds would never heal. She was also aware that she was something of a cliché at that moment; a single, lonely woman, sipping her cappuccino as she watched the darkening world go by. A paperback lay on the table in front of her, face down and open at the page she had reached. It was a Penguin edition of F Scott Fitzgerald's *The Beautiful and the Damned*. It was a great book and the latest in the long line of classics she had set herself to read over the past ten years. Suddenly, however, she was not in the mood for reading.

The New Town was still crowded, despite the nearness of shop-closing time. Couples and families mostly. It was one of those days. What Louise Martin had come to call her Lonely Days. No one to talk to. No one to have a night out with. All her friends and acquaintances at home with their partners and children. Here she was, alone like a friendless teenager, thinking far too much and too often about the only partner-less and family-free friend she had.

Jack Smith.

She could call him, of course.

But no, it would seem—what was the current term for it?—needy. Although she *was* needy. What was wrong with that? Everyone *needed* in some way. Tonight, she needed company. Perfectly natural for a human being.

She was lying to herself, of course. This was more than a simple desire for the presence of another human being in her life.

But surely Jack would have asked her out by now if he was really interested. And was it a good idea for her to become involved with someone? She was broken. She was fragile. It couldn't last. So, why couldn't she stop thinking about him? Why had the thought of rehearsal nights excited and unnerved her so much? Why did Jack's oh-so-casual "See you around" after *Brief Encounter's* final performance make her feel bleak and empty?

She shook her head and muttered "Jesus, what a mess."

She drained her cup, closed her book then grabbed her coat from the back of the chair and her shopping bag off the floor. Perhaps there was a film at the local multiplex worth seeing. Anything that would prevent her from going home.

Her phone warbled.

No, she told it silently as she picked it up off the table, I do not have PPI and I was in no recent accident.

She looked down. The caller was Jack.

She ignored it. Relationships were trouble. Her life was too complicated. Everything was complicated.

The warbling stopped. Good. Bad. Oh shit, she didn't know what it was. Her skin prickled. She was hot, a little panicked.

No. Go. She fumbled herself into her coat and walked quickly from the cafe. It was better outside, in a street, still busy despite the nearness to its shops' closing time. Cold, clear. Busy.

Bloody hell. Louise stopped, drew her phone from her handbag and opened its *recent calls* screen.

CHAPTER TWO (1916)

He *was.*

There was nothing, he was nothing, and suddenly there was noise and light and the brutal shockwave of some huge, raging monstrosity that careered past at the very moment he came to *be*. It pummelled him with the sheer fury of its passing and ripped away every one of his fledgling thoughts. It was flashing light. A roar and clatter. A metallic thunder that shook the whole world. He screamed, mewled, shivered, and curled tightly. The noise was terrible. It battered and beat him until he could no longer breathe.

Then it was gone, replaced by darkness.

He lay on the rough, cold floor, not daring to move. The noise had become a rumble then a vibration, fed to him through the walls and the shattered, hot air of the place. He became aware of smells now, the odour of dampness, and the staleness of trapped, stagnant air. Animal musk broke through, pungent and warm. He heard scrabbling and skittering noises. The place was alive. It thrummed with the energies of beating hearts and crackling nerves. He felt other disturbances, humming through the tangled skeins of matter and energy from which this world was formed. They were voices, distant, brief snatches of fear, joy, and anger.

The man twisted about to press himself against the wall that curved up behind and then above him. The bricks still dripped gold-white light. It seeped from the pores in the masonry and mortar. It dripped onto him from the roof. It was the amniotic fluid in which he had been nestled as he was formed and given life. His womb was still meshed into the brickwork, weaved between its molecules. The thought of it made him lonely. He wanted to go back to it, but there could be no return.

The need to venture outside forced him up. He used the wall to support and guide him as he took a careful step. Its texture was rough and uneven, as was the floor beneath his bare feet.

There was a hint of light ahead of him. Then more mechanical noise, distant vibrations both in the ground beneath him and in the air itself. He felt the electric sting of molecules, the scrape of minute dust particles. He felt the cold impact of photons.

The glow grew brighter. It seeped into the dark and revealed long metal rails that snaked away into the tunnel. It also revealed that the walls glistened with moisture and were slimed with primitive plant growth. The air was warm and stale, although there was movement, a slight stir that alarmed him. The vibrations that were the mechanisms of this world increased and became physical. The rails under his feet trembled. The monster was coming back.

He stopped and turned in the direction of the sound. It grew louder. He felt a wash of warm air. He sensed the brutal metallic fist behind the light, the solidity and sheer physicality of its presence. The lines hummed and vibrated beneath his feet. The noise of the thing bounced from the walls. He turned and ran. He stumbled over the lines. He gasped for breath which was stale and coal laden. He could feel the thing bearing down on him. The rails and sleepers battered his bare feet. The grime and grit ground into his sweat-slicked skin. There was little time.

The tunnel widened. The brightness of the light confused him as did the smooth, white-tiled walls. He saw a low cliff-face. People stood on its summit. Many of the men wore uniforms of a greenish colour. They had backpacks, long, heavy-looking rifles. The women's bodies were covered by their jackets and ankle-length skirts, only their hands, heads and feet showed and, even then, many wore gloves as well as hats to cover their tightly tied hair.

A blast of hot wind. He threw himself at the wall of the platform and hauled himself upward. There was a roar. His feet scrabbled for purchase. He struggled against gravity and the weakness thrown over him by panic. He heard cries, screams, and shouts. He was hoisted upward just as the world behind him was torn open by the beast as it squealed and rattled into the station and shrieked to a halt in a chaotic flicker and clatter of light and metal.

There was a moment of chaos, of voices and hands. Faces were thrust at him, the women's pasted with oils, the men's with sweat and dirt. Many of them were pockmarked, grimed, and lined. Their combined breath was smoke-laden, in many cases foul with food smells and the perfumes of disease. He sensed anger, shock, scorn. There were too many. It overwhelmed and confused him. He struggled free and stumbled back into yet more of them. People swarmed from the train; others tried to get in.

"Are you a mad man?" The speaker's face was red and webbed with broken blood vessels. He exhaled a mix of smoke and alcohol. A thick moustache bristled under his bulbous nose. "Where are your clothes?" he demanded. "Speak up. Where the devil are your clothes? You can't run around in the altogether, you fool. There're women and children here. It's not decent."

"You a German?" someone else shouted, a woman, this time, her voice harsh with spite. "An 'Un? A baby murderer?"

"'E's a bloody 'Un spy, that's what he is!" Another man, one of those in uniform.

Others began shouting. The crowd shifted around him. He was buffeted, people grabbed at him. The men in uniforms moved closer. They looked angry, as if they wanted to perpetrate violence. Some of the women covered their eyes and those of their young. He heard laughter, outrage.

Then the train was in motion and all other sound was drowned by its clank and rumble, all sense by the flicker of its lights as it sped-up and dived, wormlike, into its tunnel. The cacophony of its awakening and departure seemed to add momentary confusion to the crowd's agitation and the man used that moment to break free. He saw a set of steep moving stairs. He bounded upward, barged past the people who were riding the device, desperate, now to get to the top and out.

Until the instant of life a few minutes ago he had been nowhere, yet the names of things, the processes and structures of this place were all clear to him. Wall, steps, a coat, a pipe, a lamp. Knowledge planted within him, enough to survive and function.

Entrance hall. More people, more steps. Then outside into the madness of the street.

Where there was no relief. The confusion, the noise and movement and colour were even more intense than they had been down in the tunnel. Everything was bigger, louder, and faster. Structures loomed over him, endless cliff faces pocked with grubby windows, floor upon floor, their frontages ornate and dirty. Horses clattered by, dragging carriages and wagons behind them. Bells clanged as trams rumbled past sucking sustenance from wires that webbed the space above the streets. Omnibuses and motor cars weaved through the chaos. It was a mad dance of machinery into which walkers often rushed in a lethal dash to the far side of the street.

The smell clawed at Jack's stomach; animal, dung, sweat, tobacco smoke, perfume wetness and alcohol tang, fumes, organic waste, food....

Jack ran, cold in his nakedness, stared at, shouted at, sworn at, and shoved. He was kicked by a lanky young man who danced off balance as he snapped out his leg and bruised Jack's buttock with his filthy shoe.

But that was only the surface. Blazing through the chaos around him was The Fabric; the shimmering, thrumming threads from which the universe was woven. Each face he saw was merely a mask, each building a façade, each vehicle a shell that contained a complex noisy, foul-smelling collection of components.

The man clamped his hands over his ears against the din. His eyes were screwed against the maddening kaleidoscope of colour and image. It was unendurable.

More whistles, Shouts. He was being pursued. He did not look back but forged on through the oncoming tide of human flesh. He lurched out into the street and weaved his way through the vehicles and horses. There were harsh horn sounds. Horses reared and whinnied. More curses and threats.

He saw the entrance to a side street, plunged through and found himself in a quieter, cooler lane. There were fewer people here, many standing and talking in the doorways of shops and houses. They watched him. Some shocked, some laughing. He felt the presence of the other pursuers. He heard whistles again, and shouts.

Another turn. Another narrow street.

Another.

His body ached now. He had to rest, or his heart would stop. He felt it. He felt every beat of it.

An alley way.

A house that caught his attention.

It was a ruin that stood between two other badly damaged buildings. The brickwork was stained black, and its windows were vacant holes. The roof was shattered. Its surviving tiles clung to fire-blackened skeletons of wood. This house had been devastated by some awful force. Without further thought, Jack stepped into the ruined entrance. He climbed over the partial barrier created by a pile of rubble and into a dark, fire-stinking hallway. The ceiling was intact, the walls too, but the building was broken and precarious.

A stairway stretched upward from where he stood. The treads were burnt-black, the walls scorched. There was dust and rubble everywhere. He mounted the stairs, his senses electric with the swirling torrent of impressions he picked up from The Fabric. Its threads thrummed violently from the aftershock of what had happened to this building and this street.

He reached the landing. One wall was missing, transformed into a vast landslide of wood and rubble that filled the tiny back yard. To his left was an open doorframe. He went through into what he understood to be a bedroom. Indeed, the bed was still in place, dusty, dirty, and dishevelled.

Clothes were scattered about the room. Jack crouched down and picked at them. These were skirts, trousers, shirts, a jacket, a nightgown.

There was even a wardrobe, incongruous in the devastation. He opened the doors. More garments. He drew them out and spilled them onto the floor. So many. So much to choose from. So much information. He dropped to his haunches, covered his ears, closed his eyes, and found himself deep in the threads of The Fabric. They shimmered and vibrated about him as the catastrophe that had occurred here began to make itself known.

Something had come in the night. Six or seven weeks ago, a gigantic vessel had flown over the city. It had crawled noisily through the darkness to rain destruction onto this and several other houses. For what reason? There was an air of something in this city. The Fabric was filled with grief, fear, and anger. There was war here. He dived even deeper into The Fabric and tried to follow the trembling threads to their source, but it was too chaotic. He tried to make sense of what he found. No sense was forthcoming.

Why this house?

No answer.

Only echoes of terror and pain. A sudden roar, heat, smoke, destruction.

Grief.

Loss.

Jack opened his eyes. The Fabric was dimming now, and it no longer dominated his senses. The city sounds were a dull roar in the background. He reached for a pair of trousers and a shirt and attempted to put them on. They were confusing at first, too small and tight, but he persevered because he knew that he would not be accepted if he did not clothe himself. As he fumbled with the buttons on the shirt, he wondered what had become of the people who owned these clothes. He could smell them in the material, beneath the stench of smoke and burning.

He found a jacket. Again tight, but wearable. He needed a hat. All men wore hats in this place. He went to the wardrobe and found nothing. Tired, he climbed to the bed and lay down on the ruffled, dusty sheets and blankets. The bed creaked as he climbed onto it. He lay still and it was a relief. He looked up at the ceiling. The plaster was cracked and a patch of it had fallen.

He found pictures among the clothes. They had been thrown off the wall and showed a young man and woman, she in a white gown, the man in formal looking clothes. The man looked uncomfortable; his head held stiffly in place by the high collar of his shirt. Their arms were linked. There was another of a slightly older couple. The same people. This picture was newer and not so faded; black, white, and grey, no colours. The man grinned, his eyes bright with mischief. The woman too smiled happily. She sat on a chair; the man stood behind her with his hand on her shoulder.

Jack examined the muddle of images, sounds, and smells he had experienced. He tried to comprehend what it all meant. He was in a city. The city was swarming with people just like him and yet, not like him at all. There was a conflict in progress and this city was part of it, although not directly. Other than this house, the place appeared intact. There was no sense of impending doom, only a vague constant tension.

He closed his eyes and let himself fall toward the comfortable shadowland of sleep. He wondered about the people in the picture. The people who had lived here. Had they been in this bed when it happened?

No, something… a crying child. The throb of engines overhead. The thud of explosions. The woman…getting out of bed and going to her children, who slept in the room across the landing, the room that no longer existed.

"Hello, Jack."

Jack? His name was Jack?

He started and sat up quickly. His heart hammered. He was afraid. It was dark now. The darkness pressed in on him, disorientating and cloying. There was someone here, in the black. Someone who knew his name.

"Who are you?" His voice seemed smothered and made small by the dark.

A light flared halfway between the bed and the doorframe, small and brief and scented by a hint of sulphur. A large, square looking face was revealed. Much of it was shadowed by the brim of a fedora. The light died and was replaced by a red pinpoint glow. Jack smelled tobacco.

"It's all right," the visitor said. His voice was deep and authoritative. "My name is Lyle. I'm your friend." The man perched himself on the side of the bed, which sank under his weight. Jack could see him now as a silhouette against the black. "I'm here to welcome you and explain why you exist." He chuckled, a heavy, rasping sound. "Which is more than the creatures who live and die on this planet are ever told." The man held out a large brown envelope. "First, the somewhat mundane side to life on Earth. There are papers in here, a birth certificate and so forth. They will serve you for a few years but will need to be replaced now and then. Leave that to me. You'll see that you are forty-five. Too old to serve in the army. Those who don't volunteer for the slaughter without good reason suffer badly. Your age will protect you from abuse and violence."

"You said you would explain why I exist?" Jack asked. He was nervous. The man's presence seemed to consume the air in the room. It spread out like a shroud and deepened the darkness.

"Ah yes, of course. You are an observer and a collector. You are here to absorb the minutiae; the small and personal. You're fortunate that your coming to *be* is in the heart of such tumultuous times."

"Why?"

Another chuckle. "How many times have humans taken up that cry? We've watched this world, *our* world, unfold like a flower at its birth and in its infancy, and then mourned when it was ruined. Perhaps we should have simply swept it away and begun again, but something stayed our hand. There are moments when we witness things that give us hope. It is those moments that cloud our certainty that this should all be broken down and remade. Is this world of ours a thing of beauty or a distorted, deformed monstrosity, fit only for eradication? We need to be sure. We need to *know* the human. We need to observe and collect. That is your meaning, Jack."

"I don't understand. What am I? Am I—?"

- human?

The question went unanswered. He was alone.

Hunger and thirst eventually drove him from the sanctuary of the bomb-ruined house and back into the city. There were still people around. There was loud laughter, shouts, and occasional snatches of song. The sound spilled from noisy, well-lit establishments. Men lounged around the doors or staggered out as if dazed. Occasionally, Jack saw a fight. Others cheered from the shadows as men threw wild and erratic punches at each other or grabbed at their opponent's clothes and rolled on the filthy cobbles.

Some of the men were in uniform and as rowdy as the rest.

The stink of alcohol hung about these places.

He stopped. He was dressed now. He could enter one of them and obtain drink. He paused, nervous. Up until now his only experience of human beings was of their violent rejection of him. Gathering his courage, he made for the open door of the next pub he found, identified by a battered and weatherworn sign as "The Duke of York." A couple of men in uniform stood outside, talking softly. They watched Jack approach and he passed between them without incident. The Fabric shivered with their terror of what they were soon to face. It was so intense, Jack had to reach out to the door frame for support.

"Had a few already?" one of the soldiers said. They both laughed.

"No. Not yet," Jack said.

He realised that it was the first time he had spoken to anyone here. His conversation with Lyle in the derelict house had not been verbal. There had been an *exchange*, their voices an illusion. The sound of his own voice was odd and the vibration it made in his throat not unpleasant.

The men were laughing.

"Well, yer better hurry up, mate, they're closing soon."

Jack nodded and formed his lips into what he understood to be a smile.

Then he stepped inside.

The light was yellow and grimy, provided by flickering, wall-mounted lamps. He could feel electricity in the town around him, but many buildings, like this one, still used gas. The noise in here was almost unendurable. Nearly everyone was male. Two women sat over in the corner, close with a pair of men. There was touching and stares. Intensity. The women's faces were caked in creams and powders. Beneath, their skin was grubby and lined. One of them had a disease. At that point, Jack wanted The Fabric to fade away completely. He wanted to see only what his eyes saw and hear only what his ears heard. The physical din and chaos in here spiralled in on him. The sub-physical din was even louder.

Jack moved carefully through the bodies. He apologized and practiced his smile. Most of the men ignored him or moved just enough for him to get through.

The air was drenched in the smell of alcohol and hazy with smoke. Tobacco exhaust curled from the pipes and cigarettes every person in here had clamped between their lips. The smoke made him dizzy.

He reached the bar. The wood was dark and wet with spilled drink. One of the bartenders caught his attention. He was a tall, broad man with a fierce-looking moustache and an even fiercer glint in his eyes. He wore an apron and a shirt that was clamped at the elbows.

"Well?" he said. There was hostility in his tone.

"A drink," Jack said. "I would like a drink."

"You've come to the right place, my friend. And what sort of drink would you like?"

"I'm thirsty. What do you recommend?"

The barman smiled a smile that held little mirth or friendliness. "Some light ale, perhaps?"

"Yes, please."

The barman smirked, grabbed a glass that did not look particularly clean and placed it under one of the pump handles.

"That'll be tuppence," the barman said as he placed the drink on the bar.

"Tuppence?"

"Yes. Tuppence." The smile had turned into a snarl.

"I don't understand."

"Oh, you don't understand. I am very sorry to hear that, but you can't have this drink until you give me tuppence. Two pennies. You know, money. You foreign or something?"

Jack frowned, trying to make sense of what he was being told. He shoved his hands into the pockets of his stolen jacket. They were empty of anything but grit and dust.

"'Ere, I'll treat yer." His benefactor's voice was slurred and loud in Jack's ear. The man who was huge and drenched in sweat, slammed two coins on the bar, grabbed the drink then thrust it at Jack. "All the best to yer. I'm celebrating tonight, see. Me boy's been wounded and 'e's comin' home." There was a loud cheer that all-but deafened Jack. Glasses were raised. "'E's done 'is bit and now 'e's safe an' sound."

"Thank you," Jack said. "You are a kind person."

"You 'ear that, you lot?" the man shouted. "'E says I'm a kind person."

The comment was met with a wave of overpowering laughter.

As Jack sipped at the pale ale, he pondered the man's happiness. His son had been injured. Possibly disfigured or suffering the loss of a limb, but his father was happy. That meant the danger the young man had been in was so great that even a wound was better than remaining there. The war must be terrible.

He sipped again. The drink was warm and had a bitter taste, but it slaked his thirst well enough. A few more sips and he felt dizzy. Alcohol obviously had other effects. He needed to be careful. He stood in the crowd of men by the bar. Singing began, raucous and of poor quality. There were songs about dillying and dallying, old bulls and bushes, and riding bicycles made for two. Then came one that boasted about how Britannia ruled the waves. Which was sung even more loudly than the rest and even caused some of the men to weep.

The noise, heat, and sheer intensity of human presence melded with the increasing effects of the pale ale were becoming unpleasant.

Jack placed the glass on the bar and set off for the door just as the Britannia song ended and Jack's benefactor lifted his glass high and shouted, "To the King, God Bless 'im."

Most of the others joined in.

Then someone began to sing about God saving the King. Again, all joined in and there was intense emotion in the rendition, ugly and ragged as it was. Jack continued toward the door.

"Oi! Don't you have no respect?" The benefactor sounded angry. Jack paused and turned back, puzzled.

A strange silence had fallen. It felt as if everyone, including the two painted women were staring at him. The threads of The Fabric thrummed with violence.

"I'm sorry, I don't understand." Jack said.

"Oh, I think it's very easy to understand." A man in a khaki uniform stepped forward. He was thin and hard looking. His stare seemed to tear into Jack's soul. "Everyone stands for the National Anthem. What are you, some sort of conchie? Is that it?"

"No…A conchie? I'm sorry?"

"Or a spy. Is that what you are? A fucking Hun spy?"

Was that a joke? It made no sense to Jack. He shook his head. Confusion outweighed his ability to compute the information he was receiving.

"I am an observer," he said. "Is that what you mean?"

"An observer, eh?" the soldier said. Jack noticed three vees on the arm of his tunic. They must mean something. The man's features were raw, like granite. There was tension in his body. His fists were clenched. "And what are you observing then, sonny? Troop movements, armaments factories?"

"Leave 'im alone," Jack's portly benefactor shouted suddenly. "'E's not right in the 'ead. 'E can't 'elp it. He don't know nuffink'."

The soldier wasn't listening. Jack stumbled back as the man moved in and lashed out with his fist. There was an explosion of pain as it crushed his nose. His already muddled senses shattered into confusion. The Fabric flared bright. Jack almost fell but felt hands on him, pushing him back up onto his feet. There was cheering and jeering now.

Someone shouted a startled; "There's no blood. Look at his nose...there's no blood."

What did that mean? No blood?

No one else appeared to be interested. They had a fight to entertain them.

The soldier's eyes burned and there was something resembling fierce joy in his face. Jack found balance as the soldier came in again. He saw muscles tense in the man's left arm. He saw the direction from which the punch was coming and when it did, he was able to feint left and step aside, out of danger. The soldier, meanwhile, drunk and driven forward by the momentum of the punch staggered into a nearby table. Glasses fell and beer spilled. He ended up crouched over the tabletop, hands bleeding from broken glass. The three men who had been sitting there were on their feet, as angry as he was.

The soldier pushed himself upright and came at Jack again, swinging wildly. Jack dodged and ducked. He felt the shockwave of each blow as they hurtled past but managed to avoid each one. His own head was ringing, he felt nauseous, but some instinct had been energized within him that kept him out of harm's way.

The soldier finally dropped to his knees, exhausted and raving. His comrades had him now. As they dragged him to the door, one of them glared at Jack, while another of them stared at him with something resembling fear. There was a hush once more in the pub.

Until Jack's benefactor said, "I ain't seen nuffink like that before. Beat the bastard and never laid an 'and on 'im. That deserves another pint."

The barman did not look pleased but took the benefactor's money and passed another glass of gold-coloured drink over the wet shining bar. Jack didn't want it, but it seemed to be part of the ritual here. He was not sure what he had done to deserve this praise.

"Now listen," said the benefactor, his voice as slurred as that of the soldier now. "When we sings the National Anthem. You've got to stand still and to attention, see?"

Jack nodded. "I will next time. Thank you."

He drank the ale, sang along with the other men, and let the good feeling surge through him. Then suddenly, the nausea increased, and he felt the need to vomit. Amidst a storm of laughter, he stumbled outside and emptied his stomach onto the already filthy cobbles.

Recovered, Jack groped his way along the street and away from the pub. The Fabric was beginning to elude him, but he managed to find the threads that led him back to the ruined house. The city was quieter now. Most of the people who lived here were asleep, at rest from their cares and fears. Some, he could feel, were awake and staring into the darkness, unable to rest.

His hand went to his nose. It had been broken but now there no was pain or injury there at all.

No blood.

The lone voice in the pub was right, Jack mused. The soldier had cut himself on the glass broken by his fall and he had bled. Jack's body had healed itself. The realisation was reassuring, but it also brought loneliness. He was different.

He was *empty.*

CHAPTER THREE (2016)

Louise lived in a cottage in the village of Walkern, a couple of miles out of town. The house was old and quaint. Its front nudged at the edge of the lane on which it sat; its rear looked over a large expanse of lawn and garden.

A moment. Jack tried to calm his nerves then gave up and climbed out of his own car. He had been here before because Louise, like most members of Gravely Amateur Theatricals, regularly hosted play readings and lines rehearsals. This was different. Once more, that November smokiness hung in the air. There was a heavy stillness. His footsteps were loud and felt like an imposition.

He pressed the doorbell. then stepped back, not wanting to be up-close when the door opened. Another lurch of his heart. So familiar, those sensations. The door opened.

For rehearsals, Louise dressed casually, a jumper perhaps, jeans or trousers, a neat blouse, and that was how Jack was used to seeing her. Tonight, Louise wore a fur coat, open to reveal a dark blue dress of a simple cut.

Jack was jolted by a vivid flare of memory that erupted, complete and painfully bright, from the millions of moments that filled his mind.

Marion.

Marion; blonde, fiery in her opinions, free-spirited yet damaged. He saw her wrapped in a fur coat, always elegantly and expensively dressed, even at home, even during the ordinary. Her small, manicured hands hidden in soft, kid gloves, her hair lacquered and perfect.

Odd how the past seemed so close tonight.

Jack caught himself staring at Louise and looked away. He was tongue-tied, briefly stunned and exhausted by the memory, which brought with it that familiar bitter-sweet wash of loss.

"Hi," said Louise.

"Hi," Jack answered. He winced as a sudden pain lanced through his temples. It faded as quickly as it had come.

Louise's smile was shy. Jack stepped back to let her past.

"You look lovely," he said. The words felt clumsy.

The smile broadened. "Thank you. You look good too."

They walked to his car. He held the door open for her and as Louise climbed in, Jack was suddenly conscious of the scruffiness of the vehicle. Dusty on the inside, grubby on the outside. When Jack turned the key, classical music poured loudly from the CD player. He reached for the off button, muttering "sorry" as he did so.

"It's all right. I like this."

Sibelius's second symphony, not the most accessible music ever written. Jack turned the volume down a little.

"Do you fancy Indian or Chinese?" he asked.

"Thai."

He liked her decisiveness.

"Thai it is. I know just the place." Now he had a purpose, a destination. Stevenage Old Town. The Jade Elephant restaurant.

"Had a good day?" Louise asked him. She sounded as nervous as he felt.

"Not bad. Quiet." Sitting in his flat and thinking of nothing but Louise Martin and why he shouldn't ask her out on a date. "You?" All so formal, all so stilted, the game to be played, as part of the transformation from the relaxed relationship to…what? Lovers?

Louise began to talk about the play, about the rehearsals and how she had struggled to learn her lines. She said that she found it harder and harder with each play she was in. "Getting old, I suppose." She chuckled ruefully.

"Yeah, that's what it is."

"That's not the right answer, Mr Smith."

They laughed. Tension broken.

The meal was perfect. The food, the lighting, the ambience. Louise talked easily about her work as a sales manager for a company that made and supplied plumbing parts. Not the most interesting career perhaps. She told him that she had been a teacher once but preferred this less stress-inducing career. She was blessed with a sharp wit and a seemingly bottomless store of funny anecdotes.

There was a gracefulness to her movements, which Jack found steadily more alluring as the evening progressed and he was increasingly overcome with his need for her. It was the way she pushed her hair behind her ear, the way she glanced down at the end of every story, the way she raised her brows just before she laughed. They were simple, human gestures and expressions, yet, right now, something much more, something that was uniquely *her*.

But there was also immense sadness, there, in her eyes. In the barely discernible lines that landscaped her face and in that wonderful voice of hers. He could hear it, he could feel it and wished he couldn't.

"Are you alright?" he asked. The question came out of nowhere, unbidden, and unwanted.

Jack was a good-looking devil, Louise decided. He had worn well for his forty-five years. He was smart, dark suit, open-necked white shirt. He seemed relaxed, although there had been a trace of nerves earlier, and a moment by her front door, when he had seemed to lose himself, a moment when he had stared at her, yet not seen her. It had passed, as suddenly as it came. She dismissed it, shyness, perhaps, stage-fright.

She talked, he listened, so many clichés in one day, the lonely coffee-sipping woman in the cafe and now the caring, listening man. There was one aspect of this she did find troubling, however. He had told her very little about himself. Not always a bad thing where men were concerned, but the lack of flesh on the bones of his existence didn't seem natural. Surely, he had a job and a history. An attractive man like that must have had women in his past, possibly a marriage—or two.

Louise didn't know how to ask him, or what to ask. And did it matter? No doubt he would tell her at some point. Deliver an anecdote, a funny story. Explain just how important *his* job was.

Then he asked her if she was all right.

"Yes, why wouldn't I be?" She was startled by her own sudden anger. A part of her retreated from the question.

"I'm sorry," he said. "I didn't mean to upset you."

"I know, but…." But what? The question was perfectly reasonable, wasn't it? Yet it had disturbed her. It had dug into her and found something she didn't want discovered. "It's okay. I'm just…."

She wanted to go home.

Because he knew. He had found it, her secret.

Which was ridiculous.

But it felt that way. It felt as if he could read her. It felt as if he could feel what she felt and had reached right in, taken the lid off the already fragile box of her pain.

"Would you like another drink?" Jack said.

"No, I think…."

He looked bleak and crestfallen, and she wanted to lift him again, but she couldn't. She had to get out of here, away from him.

"I'll get the bill then we can…."

Louise got to her feet. "I'll take a taxi home. I'm sorry Jack. I just need to be on my own." No, she didn't. She needed to be here, with this man. But he had frightened her too much for her to be able to stay.

Later, she was in that taxi she had preferred. She sat in the back. The driver tried to engage her in conversation, but she couldn't trust herself to speak, so had given the sort of single-syllable answers that were as close to telling him to leave her alone as she could manage politely. She struggled to keep the demons locked inside her and that required all her energy. The wounds she had spent the last six years carefully stitching together were beginning to break open again. Memories, that odd mixture of good and bad that always framed past heartbreak, were seeping through the cracks.

The journey wore on, anonymous residential streets, lights showing in most of the houses. It was still early for a Saturday night. Louise didn't want to go home, yet could think of nowhere safer. She bit down on self-pity. Why did this happen every time she opened her heart, even the barest crack?

Heart open, eyes shut.

That's how it had started, wasn't it?

Love, an odd thing, a many-faceted, hard-to-pin-down feeling, emotion, concept.

Richard, that was his name. She had met him while Christmas shopping, six years ago...Six years? God, that long? The mall café had been full, seating only available if you were prepared to sit opposite a stranger. Freshly divorced, Louise had not been looking for anyone. She had experienced a passing admiration for the somewhat chiselled-looking character in a business suit who nodded, smiled, and said, "Feel free," when she had asked permission to sit at his table. She had not, however, looked any deeper than that.

"Christmas shopping?" he asked after a moment.

She glanced up from the paperback she was trying, but failing, to read. Dostoevsky's *The Idiot* was not the easiest text to digest while sitting in a noisy shopping centre.

"Yes, but all done now." Her pickings were slim because a complete family had been removed from her list. When Aaron walked out, his nearest and dearest had immediately closed ranks and turned their collective backs on Louise. Aaron's infidelity was, it seemed, her fault.

"You?" A stupid question seeing as her coffee table companion obviously had no shopping bag on or near him.

A smile, easy and charming. "Lunch break, and I'm a man, so I do mine on Christmas Eve." His voice was middle-class correct, but his tone warm and deep. "I always come in here for my lunch. I need to get out of that office. Mind you, it isn't that pleasant in here at this time of the year."

"No, no I suppose not."

"What do you do?"

"Teacher."

"You have my admiration. I couldn't do that. I haven't got the patience." Stock answer, but she found that she didn't mind it this time. She was flattered by his admiration, generic though it might be. "Richard," he said and held out his hand. Louise glimpsed an expensive-looking watch and a shirt cuff secured with an equally shiny cuff link. No ring though.

"Louise."

"What do you teach?" That question, interest in what she did and was. Something Aaron had seldom ever showed, even on their first date.

"English language and literature, at a high school."

"High school? That appeals to me even less."

His stare held her, and she knew, even after this exchange of uninspiring sentences, that she would become involved with this man. This Richard. At some point during their brief conversation, they exchanged telephone numbers.

Three nights later, he phoned her and asked her out for a drink. Old-fashioned, reliable but lovely. He drove her home. He came in and they slept together. It was comforting, dark, and warm. It was a sweet-smelling, night-shrouded thing that wrapped itself about her. She abandoned herself to it, suppressing the knowledge that there would be hurt further up the line. Now was all that mattered to her, the glorious, endless, and fantastical now.

The fantasy lasted three months. Three months during which Louise could think of little else other than her time with Richard. Her life and routines revolved about him and, she believed, his about hers. They met four nights a week. On Tuesdays he came to spend the night at her flat. On Fridays and over the weekend, she stayed at his cottage. Routine, one of the foundations on which relationships eventually come to rest.

Richard's house, located just outside the village of Walkern, was small, ancient, and crooked. It creaked and stirred at night as if the generations who had lived and died there had never really left. Louise loved the place and its eccentricities and was convinced that it really did have a ghost, although she had never seen it.

It was there that she discovered the truth behind the square-jawed man in the suit. That man was a front, an avatar sent out into the world of business and money to finance the quieter, close-to-the-earth life he lived. Richard's first love (second love now, Louise hoped) was his organic garden. He was a different character out there, self-contained, gentle, funny, patient and, yes, rugged, heroic almost, like some idealized male off the front cover of a romance paperback. No matter the weather, he would join himself to the soil. Louise helped as much as she could. She found that she didn't care about the cold, or the rain. Anyway, there was always the pub down the road in the evening, or better still, the cottage itself.

Three months of bliss, then they had their first argument. Ridiculous really. It was a weekend, and when Louise turned up at his door, Friday night-tired, he had not greeted her with his usual enthusiasm and seemed in an odd mood. He was morose, disinterested in what she had to say, or suggested they do. Louise tried to get him to tell her what was wrong. He wouldn't. He told her he was tired. He told her he wasn't feeling well. He told her to bloody well leave him alone.

She did. She grabbed her coat and suitcase and left. She tried not to cry but halfway home she gave in. It didn't make her feel better. A good cry, she had long ago discovered, seldom did.

She waited for him to call her. He didn't. The weekend passed without any attempt at communication on his behalf. On Monday, Louise faltered in her resolve. Her own stubbornness in the matter began to seem childish. She should phone him. She was growing concerned; she was worried, angry, jealous, then worried again. There could be a dozen reasons why he hadn't phoned, not least that he was being as bloody-minded about it, as she was. She tried to resist the temptation, but on Tuesday evening her bloody-mindedness failed her.

He answered the phone just before she hung up.

"Yeah?"

"Are you alright?"

A moment. Silence. Why silence?

"Richard?"

"I'm sorry." His voice was…dark and gravelled, the voice of someone who was ill. "I feel…don't feel like…."

"What's wrong?"

This is it. Over. Done.

"Richard? Are you still there?"

Nothing. He had hung up.

His cottage was virtually in darkness. The only light was the metallic blue and grey of a television screen visible through the sitting room window. The curtains were open, which was odd because Richard liked to make his house welcoming and comfortable. He always closed the curtains.

There was a moment of fear, of wondering if something awful had happened, some unthinkable catastrophe. It couldn't be, of course. Things like that didn't happen to the ordinary, the quiet and invisible. Even so, Louise was frightened by the time she got to the front door. She rapped the old-fashioned knocker. The noise was too loud. It was a physical thing that cracked into the night silence.

No answer.

Louise tried the handle and was startled when the door opened. Richard was careful. He never left the door unlocked. Louise called his name as she stepped into the tiny hall. She fumbled for the light switch. The light came on, its yellow hue somehow distasteful and redolent with decay. It lit the way but offered bleakness rather than warmth.

She heard the television coming from behind the sitting room door, muffled voices, a snatch of music. She went in. There was a moment of confusion, of jagged hard-to-process images, all caught in the flicker of the screen. Richard was seated on the floor, in front of the television, head down, arms about his knees.

He wore a tee shirt and tracksuit bottoms. His normally neat hair was dishevelled. The room's coldness was damp and established. The heating was off and had been for some time.

"Richard?" Louise said. She crouched down and placed a hand on his shoulder, which felt oddly bony and fragile, like an old man's. "Richard, it's me, Louise."

He stirred and lifted his head to look at her, eyes wide and bemused.

"I'm sorry," he said. His voice was rough. It sounded as if his vocal chords had been dried out.

"What's wrong?" Louise said.

Richard shook his head. "It…it's like this sometimes. I should have warned you…."

"What is this? I don't understand." Louise remained gentle, despite her rising panic.

"You should go home."

"I'm staying here."

"I felt it coming, a couple of days ago, when you were here. I know the signs. That's why I didn't phone you. I couldn't. It's like…like a dark cloud."

"Depression?"

A nod. "Black dog, the blues." It sounded as if the words caused him physical pain. "I'm clinically depressed. That's the diagnosis anyway. I'm on medication; I see a psychiatrist. It helps keep things at bay, but sometimes, nothing can stop it. Something comes for me out of the dark and I have to let it come."

"Does anything trigger it?"

Richard shrugged. "You, I think."

"Me?" Louise couldn't keep the hurt out of her voice.

"Not anything you've said or done." Richard sighed, shook his head then, with obvious effort, went on; "I don't want you to have to cope with this, but…." He grabbed her hand, his grip painfully tight. "I don't want to lose you either. You will go away in the end. You won't want to handle this."

"How do you know?" Louise answered, more sharply than she had intended. "What do you know about me that makes you think I can't cope?"

He began to shake, the tremors rhythmic and fierce. It took a moment for Louise to realise that he was crying.

"Sometimes," he said in a chopped-up, gasping voice. "I don't know who I am."

"You're not this."

"This is real, the rest…. The rest is a mask. The person you love, is the person the drugs create."

"I don't think so. This isn't you. I think it's the medication that lets the real you come through."

When she kissed him, Louise realised that it was the first time in her life she had tasted a man's tears.

The taxi slid to a halt. Louise handed over the fare and was suddenly out in the dry, brutal cold. She gathered her strength and headed the few yards back to her front door. There were lights on in the houses on either side. The cottage was in darkness.

Jack sat in his own car, astounded by the depth of disappointment he felt. He should shrug his shoulders. The whole thing had been a mistake, surely that was why he had been so indecisive about it in the first place. He had known that it would end in tears. He should have followed his instinct.

Oh, come on, it wasn't that simple. This had nothing to do with right and wrong, wise, and unwise. This was emotion and feeling and desire. A lethal combination in which there was little sense or logic.

And Louise's sudden change of mood, her hasty exit?

Are you alright?

It wasn't the question. It wasn't the four words. It was obviously something a lot deeper. She had been happy until then. The transformation had been almost instant. And he had seen, at that moment, something hideous rush up from her subconscious, the unfurling of a toxic cloud of pain, triggered by a simple expression of concern. There was nothing to be done about it now, so he started the car and set off for his flat.

The Old Town was busy. This was where all the pubs and restaurants could be found. The original High Street. It had the air of a village about it these days, complete with its own small green and war memorial. The Remembrance Parade had taken place there last weekend. Jack attended. He always did. He had a lot to remember, not least his time at The Front in 1918 and as an ARP Warden during the Blitz. Each year, the emotional impact of the experience was intensified by the fact that even the oldest of the men in their British Legion uniforms, and the most frail and aged onlooker, had been unborn when Jack Smith came to *be*.

As he drove out along a country route, taking a more leisurely ride homeward, he examined his thoughts and tried to understand them. He had known many women. He had experienced many things and surely his heart should be calloused, but it wasn't. Instead, it seemed to grow increasingly tender and soft with the passing of each decade. Perhaps he had seen too much.

And Marion, why had she come back to him with such force? Lizzy too. The two women who had meant the most to him, were suddenly vivid in his mind, the memory of them painful and raw, as if he only just lost them.

He wanted to turn the car round and drive back to Louise's cottage and pound the door until she came out to him. No use playing any games now. Suddenly, the whole thing had lurched from pleasant interlude to something akin to desperation.

A wave of pain cut the thought in two. It blanked everything in a sizzling white haze. The car kicked and shuddered as it drove against the grassy bank and the steering wheel was wrenched from his grasp. Headlights burst out of the darkness and a horn blared. Jack's car staggered into a stall and was then rocked by the shockwave of the other vehicle's passage.

The pain was like fire. It burst outward from inside his skull, igniting nerve endings and sending muscles into spasm. He sat with his head back, hands over his face, clawing for breath. The pain turned white.

CHAPTER FOUR (1916)

It was dark now, yet there were a surprising number of people outside. They milled around, agitated. Many looked upward, at the sky, which was a narrow strip of velvet darkness that ran between the tall houses. Light poured from windows and streetlamps and painted restless shadows.

Then more people poured in from side streets, running, shouting, and crying.

Another sound cut through the babble and confusion. Jack saw a police officer on a bicycle, whistle clenched between his teeth. The constable lurched to a halt, leapt from the machine, and shouted at Jack, who could smell the sweat of exertion on him, and something else…fear.

Jack had not returned to the bomb-shattered house in which he had found refuge on his first day in the world, but had slept under bridges, in shop doorways and anywhere else he could rest, undisturbed. He had foraged for food, begged, as he had seen others do. This new life of his was uncomfortable, sometimes made miserable by rain or a chill night breeze, but he knew nothing else or how to attain any sort of real home. There were moments of relief when he found a Salvation Army soup kitchen and sometimes a bed for a night in one of their hostels.

What puzzled him most were the number of soldiers amongst the homeless, men who had returned, wounded, from the war, and now had nothing. What sort of reward for their sacrifice was this?

"Get off the road yer bloody fool!" the constable shouted. "An' 'urry up about it!"

Jack tried to comply, but it wasn't easy. Too many people. Too much noise. It disorientated him. He stumbled and grabbed at the constable's arm.

"'ere, gerroff. C'mon, leggo, before I arrest yer for assault. You 'ear me?"

"Yes…yes I hear you." Jack released him. The constable muttered something else then leaped onto his bicycle and tore off down the street, blowing his whistle again and again.

There was another sound, faint but somehow ominous that drew Jack's gaze upward. Suddenly there were more lights, long beams that reached up to probe the blackness. Searchlights.

"Please… help me please…Ellen, I can't find Ellen."

The shout brought his attention back to the street, where people were still running, their terror, a vibration in the chill dark air. One of them looked wildly around. A woman, bundled into a long dress. She had a shawl clutched about herself. Her searching gestures grew frantic. She called a name, voice shriller with each cry. "Ellen! Ellen!"

Jack stood where he was and watched her. This was fear, yes, but it was deeper and more primal than the terror expressed by the others out here. They were frightened for themselves. This woman was frightened for someone else. This was desperation, love, and dread of loss. The woman called across the street to him, but he couldn't understand or hear what she said. She broke into to an awkward run, hampered by her clothes and the swirls of frightened people who streamed along the road, and blundered to a halt a few feet from where Jack stood.

"Have you seen Ellen…My daughter…Have you seen her?"

He shook his head. "No."

"I have to find her before that bastard starts dropping bombs on us."

"Who?" he said. "Who do we have to find?"

"Ellen, my little girl." The woman's voice seemed on the verge of breaking. "The Germans, the bloody Germans. There's a Zeppelin up there. We have to get indoors somewhere. But I can't, I have to find my daughter!"

"Where did you lose her?"

"What?"

"Where did you lose your daughter?"

She paused, hesitated then pointed back along the street. "Down there. We was walking home from me mother's. She was frightened and wriggled free of me. I couldn't hold onto her and now I can't find her and they're going to drop bombs on her and—"

Jack grabbed her arms and held her, tightly. It felt right and natural and seemed to restore some of her strength.

"I'll find her," he said.

"Please…."

All this time, the sound of the approaching Zeppelin had grown louder. The noise of its motors pulsed down from the sky. Their vibration stirred the air and strummed the threads of The Fabric. Jack smelled diesel fumes, molecules of the chemical scattered by the craft's exhausts. He felt its vastness and steady, relentless approach.

Its nearness drove some of the crowd into a frantic scramble for shelter. Others stood still and gazed upward, their dread a shimmering vibration. It was as if their terror had transformed into an awful fascination with the invisible monster they could hear high above them.

"We should go back and see if she's where you left her."

The woman went quiet, as if the idea had never occurred to her. "Yes, I suppose…."

Jack set off down the street. There was no time to wait for her to follow him. He glanced up as he ran and saw the lights again, now converged on a huge object. Jack could see its long, tubular body, made small by its altitude, yet obviously immense. It moved slowly, but there was threat in that patient progress.

Jack ran. There was a side street, a well of darkness. The woman screamed at him but didn't look back. Instead, he concentrated on finding the child.

Another sound, a bit like the noise of the constable's whistle. It was tiny and distant but grew steadily louder. Something was falling from the sky. Jack called out the child's name. "Ellen!"

No answer. The whistling grew louder, louder, then stopped, for a moment, a brief fragment of time. And in that moment of stillness, Jack felt her. He felt the whisper of her breath, a small disturbance in The Fabric, a tiny wave of fear.

The explosion was a cataclysmic eruption of light and noise, several hundred yards away. It hurled the buffeting storm of its shockwave into the street and almost knocked Jack from his feet. Lights came on, people spilled from doors, or peered out from open windows.

Jack found the entrance to an alleyway, which was narrow and stank of human waste. Water splashed under his feet. He shouted to the child again and heard the whistle of a second bomb. Then a whimper. A soft, child's cry.

"She's here," Jack shouted, but the sound of his own voice was torn away by the detonation of the second bomb. He saw the flash then the ground bucked beneath him and threw him onto his back. The air tasted of grit and smoke and there was shouting and screaming. The bombs appeared to have no pattern other than the direction in which the Zeppelin flew. It destroyed and killed anything and anyone over which it passed. Its crew did not care.

His head ringing with the noise of the blasts, Jack moved carefully toward the source of the tiny crying sound. The air was heavy with smoke now. He coughed. He felt the heat of a fire.

Jack saw movement. He felt breath, a scattering of molecules against his skin. Then he saw her, the child, a dark shape crammed into the shadows behind a dustbin. The bin was full and overflowing, the ground around its base filthy with its spill. Jack reached out.

"Ellen?" He saw her shrink back. She was afraid of him, which was unsurprising. His beard and his hair were thick and matted. He was dirty and he stank.

Another bomb was on its way.

He reached out and grabbed the child. His hand closed over hers. She murmured in fright, but that didn't matter. He had to get her to her mother. He pulled her out.

"I have her!" he shouted. He saw the mother, running, an image frozen in a sudden and brief glare as a gout of flame reared over the houses on the opposite side of the street.

The noise of the explosion punched at his ears. There was a sudden hail of debris, ripped up from the heart of the blast and hurled down onto the surrounding streets; tiles, glass, and burning fragments of wood. The night was splintered by a dance of light and dark, fire and smoke.

"What happened to you?" the man in the chair demanded. He coughed as soon as he had spoken the sentence. He was thin, pale, and obviously struggled for breath. He leaned close to the fireplace by which he sat, as if to grasp at every scrap of the meagre warmth it gave out. "The state of you, woman." He nodded towards Jack. "And who's he?"

"He found Ellen when she was lost," said the woman, whose name, it turned out, was Lizzy Reid. "And God knows what would have happened to her if he hadn't. Them bombs were too close for my liking." She seemed to have recovered from her earlier panic and distress, because now she sounded belligerent rather than frightened.

Jack, meanwhile, stood awkwardly in the doorway to Lizzy's kitchen. Her gratitude to him for saving her daughter's life had been overwhelming. She asked him where he lived so that she could send him some gift. When he told her that he had nowhere, she insisted that he come home with her.

"Bombs?" The pale man was suddenly appalled. "You were under that Zeppelin?"

Lizzie was brusque, as if offended by the suggestion that she had been in any danger. "We're all right, a bit dusty and smoky that's all. No harm's come of it."

"What's your name?" The man's regard was now fixed on Jack.

"His name is Jack Smith, and he has nowhere to live," Lizzy said. "We owe him a favour. He can lodge here. We could do with the money."

"Have you gone mad? He stinks. He's a tramp. I can't believe you've brought a tramp into the house. Is he drunk?" He raised his voice and switched his stare to Jack. "Are you drunk?"

"No, he's not drunk," Lizzy snapped, again before Jack could answer.

The man sniffed and shrugged. "It's your house." He returned his attention to the fire. "But make sure he has a wash and a shave. We don't want fleas and lice in here." He returned his attention to Lizzie. "And you and Ellen could do with a scrub-up as well."

"This is my brother, Arnold," Lizzy said to Jack. "I'm sorry he's so rude."

Despite his obvious respiratory illness, Arnold produced a pipe, which he proceeded to light. It scented the air with a delicious, smoky smell. There was a glass and dark bottle on the floor beside Arnold's chair. The fire burning in the grate threw out a further, dense smoky odour. A gas lamp hissed and cast a dismal yellowish light from its wall bracket.

For the first time since they had met, Jack saw Lizzy clearly. She was a small woman and pleasing to Jack's eyes. He pondered why a woman's face and the way she talked and moved should make him feel this way. There seemed to be no logical reason for it. But the dark softness of her eyes, that face and that hair, revealed when she removed her hat, all sent an odd electricity through his nerves and made it hard to speak or act. There was something strange about her skin though. The tear tracks that had meandered through the dust and soot on her cheeks revealed a yellowish hue which did not look natural or healthy. Not that many of the people who lived in this city were particularly healthy anyway, but this, surely, was a sign of some disease.

The child, Ellen, stood behind her mother, clutching at her long, worn-looking coat. Ellen, Jack saw, was younger than he had imagined when he found her in that alleyway. He was not sure how old. He had no experience with children. He was not sure how fast they grew.

"You can have Ellen's room," Lizzy said. "She can come in with me. Arnold sleeps down here. The stairs are too much for him these days."

"Thank you."

"The rent will be...."

"Seven and six a week," said Arnold.

"All right," Jack said.

"In advance."

Jack noticed that Arnold was holding out his hand. It shook slightly. No doubt because of his respiratory illness.

"I don't understand," Jack said.

"The rent, Lizzy's too soft, that's why I have to look after her. You have to give us the money now, the first week's rent."

"I don't have any money."

"I thought so." Arnold turned to glare at his sister. "You brought some beggar here and expect—"

"He saved Ellen's life, so you can shut your mouth, Arnold. It's my house and I will make the rules." She turned to Jack. "You can pay at the end of the week. They always want people to work at the factory. You can come with me tomorrow."

There was a tiny yard at the back of the house, hemmed in by three high brick walls and dominated by a coal shed and privy. Jack filled a pair of buckets from a standing pump on the corner of the street and washed as best he could. There was little room or opportunity for modesty, which seemed important here, but it was dark and although neighbouring houses overlooked the yard, no one seemed interested enough to watch. Lizzy had also given him a set of clean clothes, promising to launder the ones he had been wearing when they met.

When he had washed and dressed, Lizzy, who had obviously cleaned herself up indoors, came out with an oil lamp, a chair and sheet and told him to sit. He did as he was told and Lizzy set about cutting his hair, which was still wet from washing.

He noticed that her hands trembled.

"Are you all right, Lizzy?"

"What? Oh, just a little shook up due to that bomb. My ears are ringing a bit too. Sounds like Bow Bells in there." She chuckled but her mirth sounded false.

"You don't have to do this—"

"I am perfectly fine, thank you very much. We wasn't killed and nor was Ellen so we should count ourselves lucky."

"Yes. I suppose we should."

Jack relaxed, enjoying the experience. Lizzy stood close to him, and her proximity was startlingly pleasurable.

"Besides, giving you a haircut will take my mind off it. I'm not good at it, though. You'll need to get to a barber to have it done proper, but anything's better than looking like a gorilla."

"A what?"

"A gorilla, you know, a big monkey that's as tall as a man."

Jack chuckled. Laughter was another unexpected pleasure. He had not experienced it often. "No, I don't know."

"Well, they're as mad and evil as they come," Lizzy continued. "Arnold read about them. He likes to read, not stories, but facts, you know history, that sort of thing. He ain't got much else, has he? He can't work, not with his chest. He gets to *The Queen Victoria* for a pint sometimes, but only when he feels up to it, so he reads all the time. I know he can be a bit rude, but he is my brother."

Jack let Lizzy's voice soothe him. He liked the way she moved easily from subject to subject.

When he went back indoors, Lizzy indicated the second armchair by the fire. Jack sat down. Arnold scowled at him as he sipped his drink and puffed at his pipe. Never taking her eyes off Jack, Ellen went over to Arnold, and he hoisted her onto his lap. She curled up against him and looked as if she was about to go to sleep.

"See that," Arnold said. He coughed as he spoke then waved toward the mantelpiece. There was an image in a small frame. The image was grey and white and showed a man in a uniform. He stared into the camera, looking both proud and nervous. "That's Russell, Lizzy's husband. Do you understand what I'm telling you? Her *husband*."

"I understand." Jack was puzzled and leaned forward the better to see the portrait.

"He's out in France serving his King and Country, so don't get any funny ideas about my sister, all right? Not that she'd look twice at you. How old are you?"

"Forty-five." He was much younger than that, of course. Younger than the child, although he knew that there would be no use in trying to explain that to Arnold.

"You sure? You don't look it."

"I'm sure."

"Some people lie about their age to get into the army, others to get out of doing their duty."

"I have a birth certificate."

"All right, all right, I believe you. What were you doing out there roaming the streets anyway? You're not…" Arnold leaned even closer, so close, Jack could hear his laboured breathing and the movement of fluid in his lungs, "…a lunatic? Some madman from the asylum?"

"No, I'm not a lunatic. I have all my faculties."

"Faculties? Oh, listen to you. Like long words do you, think they make you sound superior to people like us?"

"What do you mean? Why would I want to sound superior?"

"Don't mind him," Lizzy said. "My brother never did have no manners."

Arnold scoffed and sat back. He played with his pipe and relit it with a match. He puffed at it furiously then collapsed into a fit of coughing, violent enough for Ellen to jump from his lap and return to her mother. Arnold wiped at his lips with a grubby looking piece of cloth and Jack noticed that there were specks of blood.

Lizzy returned with a plate of bread and cheese. There was also a mug of tea. It tasted good. Jack was hungry.

"That's your husband." He nodded toward the picture.

"Yes," Lizzy sounded sad again.

"He's fighting for his King and Country."

"He volunteered as soon as it started. He didn't have to, not so soon, seeing as we was married and everything, but that's Russell for you."

"I wish I could have gone," Arnold said. "Even Lizzy's doing her bit. She works all hours at that factory, making shells for the fellas at The Front. And look what it's doing to her."

"Arnold, please. It's a job. We need the money...."

"Look at her face. It's turning yellow. That's why women like her are called canaries because the chemicals affect their skin. God knows what it's doing to the rest of her."

"It isn't doing anything.," Lizzy's voice had softened into weariness. "And it's a sacrifice we have to make. There's nothing wrong with me that a bit of powder and some fresh air won't cure."

Jack was awoken by Lizzy's shout from the landing outside the bedroom. It was dark. He had not slept well and was still exhausted. The night had been troubled by thoughts of Lizzy, of how lovely she was, of how he wanted to see her and hear her talk, and simply be near her. Also, he was not used to sleeping on a mattress, or being warm under clean blankets and sheets.

Downstairs, in the parlour, Lizzie had made tea. There was more bread with butter and a small dab of marmalade then fried potatoes, mixed with scraps of cabbage and onion. It was bland, but filling.

Arnold was asleep in the armchair. He was pale and his breathing noisy and irregular. He didn't stir as they sat and ate the breakfast Lizzy had prepared. Ellen was still in bed. Arnold, Lizzy said, usually took good care of her and would walk her to the school around the corner if he was feeling strong enough. When he wasn't, like yesterday, he'd send her to their mother's.

There was little warmth in the air as Lizzy and Jack set off to the nearest tram stop. The darkness had turned grey. The rising sun was bright and orange-red when glimpsed between houses. The journey to Stannard and Long's Engineering works in Hackney Wick, was a long and complicated one; three changes of tram and omnibus, endless streets, shop fronts and houses. Despite the Zeppelin raid, there seemed to be little damage. People looked to be getting on with their lives.

There was, however, an air of grimness. Men in uniform strolled about the streets and rode the omnibus. Jack saw, in their faces, a tightness, a closed door which no one would ever open. Some shook, their tremors given away when they lit themselves a cigarette or pipe. The soldiers he saw looked pale and thin. They were men who had suffered and were suffering still. Several of them walked on crutches, or were pushed in wheelchairs, others had one uniform sleeve pinned-up and empty.

These men had, at least, escaped the war, but their escape had not been complete.

Stannard and Long's was a hell of noise and smells. Jack sensed that some of the odours were from the dangerous chemicals that had affected Lizzy's complexion. When he walked in with Lizzy, he saw from the great clock that hung on the far wall of the shop floor, that it was a quarter past seven in the morning.

Lizzy took Jack to a small office that overlooked the inferno of the factory floor. She knocked on the door and Jack noticed that she barely lifted her eyes when a man with too much fat on his body and an unhealthy-looking red face came to the door.

"Yes? What do you want? Shouldn't you be at your work?"

"Sorry, Mr. Geils, it's just that this gentleman is looking for a job, if there are any going."

Geils swung his gaze round at Jack. "Oh yeah? And what can you do? Shouldn't you be in uniform?"

"I'm forty-five."

"Well, I suppose you're healthy enough." Geils raised his bushy eyebrows, appeared to think for a moment, then said; "All right, I do need more brawn. Women can't lift heavy things and most of the young fellas are out serving their Country." He grunted and made to go back into his office. When he next spoke, it was over his shoulder to

Lizzy, just before he slammed the door shut. "Take him to Harris and tell him he can set him to work on anything that needs doing. Then bloody well get to work yourself." Jack heard a final, muttered, "Lazy little sow. Any excuse," through the door as it slammed shut.

They headed for what Lizzy told him were the changing rooms. "We have to wear overalls," she said. "And we have to wear wooden clogs because of the sparks." The woman, Jack noticed, also wore hair nets. "We'll have to find a spare set for you."

Jack pushed carts through the factory. The place was a relentless storm of noise, hammers, drills, the clang of metal and shouts and cries of the workers. He was quickly tired, and the day seemed to stretch out forever.

His task was to transport giant shells over to where Lizzy worked. He hoisted the shells from the cart using a pulley and chains and stood them upright on the floor. Lizzy was part of a gang who worked on each shell individually. The work was repetitive and seemed to be a long process. Jack watched her, intrigued by the ritual she performed. Her small body was quick, her movements fluid and easy. She looked at him and frowned. "You mustn't be caught standing around. You'll get the sack."

"What are you doing?"

"Putting in the exploders," she answered. She didn't stop as she talked. Jack watched her drill a hole into the nose of the shell with a huge brace-and-bit then pour in the explosive mixture. Next, she dropped in the detonator and rammed it home with a mallet and metal rod. Finally, she screwed the percussion cap onto the shell's nose. That done, she moved onto the next one.

She wiped her forehead with her arm. Jack found that he liked the gesture. He tried to understand why. She was merely wiping sweat from her face. But everything she did, the way she spoke, the way she moved, all pleased him and made him want to stay near to her.

CHAPTER FIVE (2016)

Louise woke and for a moment enjoyed the neutral, warm nothing that preceded full awareness. It was a brief, untroubled blank, too quickly washed away by an incoming tide of memories and feelings.

Last night.

Walking out on Jack, distressed by a simple question.

She rolled onto her back and closed her eyes, which was no help at all. She wanted him and the intensity of it frightened her and was, no doubt, the reason she had run.

Restless, she sat up. Jack didn't live that far away. A short car journey. It wouldn't take much.

She got up and headed for the bathroom. She had to get out of the cottage, but not to Jack's flat, not into more heartache. She had been burned twice. She was not about to be burnt again.

There was Richard. Always Richard.

And on his heels came a loss that could never be negated, no matter the outcome of either of her dilemmas. "Where are you, Richard?" she whispered to him. "Why don't you come home? It wasn't your fault. It wasn't anyone's fault."

A few miles away, Jack came to and found himself slumped in the driver's seat of his car. A dazzling autumn sun shone directly into his sore, puffy eyes. He was cold. His mouth tasted foul, and he was nauseous. At least his head no longer ached, although the attack had left a scraped-out, damaged sensation in its wake.

And fear.

He had witnessed such a headache before, and it had preceded the end for someone just like him.

The end. Oh God, his time. The *end*.

He remembered Josephine Anderson again. The memory brought on another wave of debilitating fear.

He shuffled upright and grasped the steering wheel. The sky was a rich blue and almost cloudless. The ground outside was white with frost. There was an odd motionlessness about everything. It was as if the scene was a photograph. Jack shivered and reached for the keys. He needed to get home.

And what of Louise? Was this fair to her? If the headache was what he feared it to be, then his days here were numbered. He knew it was best to leave her alone. He didn't want to. He wanted to see her, hear her voice, anything but this icy silence.

A silence as white and unbroken as the pain had been.

He had hoped that, when he eventually arrived home at his flat, Louise would be waiting for him outside. She wasn't, of course. Why should she be? And it was best that she kept away from him. Jack experienced a pang of disappointment, nonetheless.

The end was going to be a lonely place.

Tired now, he got out of the car and made for the building's entrance then climbed the stairs.

And there she was.

Louise stood by the door to his flat, bundled into a parka, hood up against the bitter cold which had penetrated the building. Jack's resolve crumbled at the sight of her.

"I'm sorry," Louise said.

Jack shrugged. "It's okay." And it was.

They stood, awkward, for a moment. He should send her home.

"Coming in?" he said.

She nodded.

There was delight in simply having her near him, as she waited for him to unlock his door, as they stepped inside and he offered her coffee or tea, in the way the flat suddenly changed when she was inside. Small, simple things. Foolish things. Yet, each one redolent with feeling.

She sat on an armchair. He on the sofa.

"I'm not being fair to you." Louise stayed where she was while she spoke. She still wore the parka and clutched the coffee mug in both hands as she stared out through the French doors. "I'm struggling with this."

"This? We went out for an evening, that's all. There's no pressure on you, Louise."

She turned to look at him. "Yes, there is. We've become more than friends."

"I know," Jack said. "But if you can't…if there is something in the way…." He shrugged, maddened by the impossibility of simply saying what needed to be said. He had learned long ago that communication was a series of games and puzzles. The unsaid often meant more than the spoken.

"This has to be slow. I can't rush into anything. I couldn't cope with that."

"I understand." Slow? Did he have enough time left for slow? But she was here, wasn't she? She was the present and that was nothing but good.

"I wasn't expecting this," Louise said. "I didn't think it would happen to me again."

The *again* brought an unexpected pang of jealousy.

"I'd like to go for a walk" she said, another distraction, a welcome one this time.

Jack found a thick denim shirt and a parka of his own then drove them a few miles out of town. They walked down a disused railway track, preserved for hiking. The track was bordered by high banks and trees. The walk was awkward. The tension was back. Their arms brushed and they sometimes bumped against each other as they moved aside for other walkers or cyclists. None of it transformed into anything more than self-conscious contact. Then Jack had an idea.

"There's a blues club, in London, they have an open mic on Sunday afternoons. I was going to play there today."

"Play? Guitar?"

"No, harmonica. I sing too, well, I growl, actually."

Another collision with the past. France, 1918; Wally, handing him that Hohner mouth organ.

And the wounded German soldier who didn't bleed.

The club was actually a pub. Called the *Aint Nothin' But the Blues* bar, hidden halfway down Kingly Street. As they emerged from Oxford Circus station Louise finally slid her arm through Jack's and drew close to him. The contact sent that familiar old electric shock through him.

The jam had already started when they arrived. The house band was in the closing stages of its half-hour warm-up set.

The place was dark and carefully blues-tacky. A neon sign, the shape of a beer bottle hung at the back of the stage, the legend "Blues" glowing from where its label would have been. There were a couple of loops of multi-coloured lights. The walls were plastered with aging posters and flyers for ancient blues greats. A dozen or so guitar cases and bags leaned against one wall. Jack went over to the clipboard on the bar and entered his name and instrument.

They found a couple of chairs at one of the few tables set out near the stage. Jack drank a pint, Louise, red wine. A few people said hello, hands were shaken. There were shouted introductions for Louise. She leaned close and said, "I like this place." Her breath was hot against Jack's cheek, and it was monumentally erotic. He resisted an urge to kiss her deeply and hard. That, it seemed, would come later.

Barry Jackson, the emcee, introduced the house band's final song. It was a slow, mean, and dirty twelve-bar that throbbed out of the speakers like a dying heartbeat. Music then, the pulse that ran through humanity's veins, from the primitive beat of drums to the complexities of a full symphony. Jack had seen, listened to, and danced to, countless variations of this heartbeat. He had sat in hushed reverence before a hundred orchestras, and he had waltzed and performed foxtrot and quick step at countless parties and in countless dance halls. He had joined the surging sweating masses as they worshipped at the feet of such giants as The Rolling Stones, The Who, and Led Zeppelin. Big Bands, hip-and-cool jazz combos, choirs, folk singers, country singers, the avant-garde, and the traditional. He had tasted them all.

This music had a complexity and passion all its own. It was primitive, soulful, and raw, but salted with technicalities and flair. These songs were primal cries of basic human passion.

"Welcome to the Sunday afternoon blues jam," Barry said when the song ended, and the applause had died down. "And that's exactly what it is, a jam. If you want to play, put your name down on the clipboard on the bar and I will use the list to create a series of fifteen-minute bands. Now, let's have Billy on the drums, Billy on the drums please, Tony and Guido on guitars, Tony and Guido, please, and Damo on bass."

Away they went. Jack felt the first electric shock of nerves. He wondered at the feeling. He had been coming to this place for five years, once a month, religiously. He had been on that cramped little stage countless times, but still, the fear came.

And what of the real terrors he had faced; homelessness and hunger, the war-torn fields of France and the burning buildings of a Blitz-torn city? The memories of them were still in place, vivid and within easy reach, but locked away. Those were other lives. That was how his existence felt to him; a series of complete lifetimes, with only the most tenuous of linkages to connect them.

"You alright?" Louise said. Again, her breath was warm on the side of his face, again that immense surge of need. Jack smiled and nodded in return.

He was called up for the third open mic set. Nerves dissolved into heart pounding excitement as he wrestled his way through the press of punters and up onto the stage.

The musicians settled in . There was a fury of plugging-in and tuning-up. Jack waited patiently behind the mike.

"*Roadhouse Blues*," said Jack. "In E."

Nods all around.

The drummer counted in and the riff was underway.

Jack brought the harmonica to his lips.

And was slammed back by a sudden wave of pain that opened like a fiery flower in the very centre of his brain. White hot streaks of agony shot outwards, burning his eyes, roaring in his ears. He grabbed at the microphone stand and hung on. The lights, dim as they were, seemed unbearably bright. Around him the fifteen-minute band chugged into the song. He sensed their puzzlement when he failed to take his cue.

The pain eased a little. He took a deep breath and started. It was okay. He was singing, although it hurt. He had to get through this. It was an act of defiance he barely understood. A need to ignore *their* call, to carry on and be human in this human world.

Verse, chorus, second verse then harmonica solo. The pain in his skull throbbed in time to the song's beat.

Someone was watching him. Okay, there were a lot of people watching him in this room, but there was someone else whose regard was deep and penetrating. As he forced his music through the fog of pain, Jack tried to see who it was. The punters were too indistinct in the half light. They were faces, heads, and shoulders. They were forms with no detail.

Nothing he could do about it. Jack played on, then stood back to allow the guitars to come through for what turned out to be a pair of blistering solos. The crowd broke into applause and then he was back at the mic, singing the last verse and chorus and after a final harp solo the song clattered to its end.

The audience seemed happy enough with the performance. They clapped and cheered enthusiastically.

"What's next?" the bass player asked.

"*Love in Vain*," Jack said without thinking of the significance or what Louise might feel when he sang such sad lyrics of lost love.

He closed his eyes. The dark turned deep red and the red swirled blood-like, dancing with every beat that sliced through his head. He sang and again it hurt, the slightest effort, a brutal self-inflicted wound. He blew the harp again and now the harsh, metallic sound of it scraped away at his skull and was all-but unbearable. He closed his eyes against the confusion of light and shadow. The music pounded out its slow blues-march and he pressed on. He felt his stomach churn.

Last verse.

He cut in across the first guitar solo, sang the lyrics then turned to the axemen and indicated to them to take over the song and play it to a close. Then he lurched off the stage—no time to scoop up his harmonica case—and ploughed through the audience. He pushed and shoved his way toward the door that led to the toilets.

There was a steep, narrow staircase beyond the door. Black-and-white portraits of blues stars had been drawn on the walls in the tiny lobby at the bottom. Jack burst through the toilet door and into a cubicle. He made it with moments to spare. When he was done, he struggled to his feet and flushed the pan then shoved the door open and stumbled to the sink. He washed his face then put his mouth under the tap to swill it out. The pain had eased a little. He sweated. He felt aches all over his body. He straightened and became aware that someone else was in the cramped little room.

Jack did not turn around when his name was spoken.

"Who are you?" Jack said, eyes fixed on the murky mirror above the sink. There was no reflection in the glass, apart from his own. Jack wasn't surprised.

"It doesn't matter, names are irrelevant to me/us. It's nearly time, Jack." The voice sounded kind.

Now Jack turned. The figure was indistinct, even though it was close. It was more absence than physicality. Jack saw a familiar, human-shaped hole, through which stars shone. He felt a tingle spread over his skin, like static electricity. The figure shifted and flickered but was more than a simple hologram or projection. It was here, a few inches from Jack's face. He realised that what he saw was only part of it. Like a hand reaching down to him from on high.

"I don't… I don't want to go," Jack answered.

"I understand," it said. "But you don't have a choice. Get ready, Jack."

Then it was gone, the disconnection, a sudden electric snap.

"You look terrible," Louise said to him as they stepped out of the pub and into the sharp, cold night air of Kingly Street.

"Migraine." Jack answered. His head still ached, but not with the same ferocity as before. He felt hollow, his mouth foul-tasting and dry. His hands trembled.

"I think we should go home," Louise said.

"Don't you want to eat?"

"Have you got any food?"

"A little."

Just like that, she was coming back to his flat. She intended to cook for him and look after him. A cliché, but at that moment he was happy to live the cliché.

Louise tucked her arm through his and drew close. He liked that closeness. She was Lizzy, Marion, all of them and none of them, uniquely *her*. Oh, he had felt it before, but this time, it was precious, fragile, something that he needed to cling to.

The flat was cold and unwelcoming when they arrived. Jack switched on the heating while Louise searched the fridge and cupboards. Jack dealt with the table, found a pair of ancient but serviceable candles, and put *Kind of Blue* onto his ancient deck. Perfect album, perfect mood. He had seen Miles Davis perform, in London, 1959, 1960? Whenever it was, it was at a time when this album was fresh and new. The music was a smooth sea of glass whose undercurrent was a fury of innovation and energy. Davis himself was a genius and yet appeared to treat the audience with utter contempt. No one minded; the applause was loud.

Because it was small, the flat warmed quickly. Jack sat and waited for whatever meal Louise was creating out of the disparate material in his fridge and cupboards. He was glad to sit. The journey home had been gruelling, though he had tried hard not to show it. He was weak and his skin was oddly sore, as if burned by the being he had encountered.

Jack's mood switched instantly from contentment to unease.

The expanse of glass that formed the French door and adjacent window became a portal to oblivion. The darkness out there was vast and deep. He felt its infinity. He felt the presence of the creators behind it. He felt their approach. He wanted to get up and close the curtains but was held in his chair by a fear that his silhouette would be clearly seen, which was ridiculous, because they would find him when they wanted him.

What was going to happen? Was it death? Jack tore his gaze from the darkened windows and felt the panic return. He didn't want an end. He wanted Louise. He wanted to stay in this world.

He should send Louise home now. He was about to be *recovered* (wasn't that what Lyle had called it?). He would fight, but in the end they would win. So, what did he do? Sit here and wait? Or live?

He surged to his feet, wrenched the curtains closed and stood by them, head down, trying to slow his breath.

"Come on, eat up."

He started and turned to see Louise placing two plates of food on the table.

They ate in relative silence. Jack wanted to be content but was too uneasy. He glanced constantly at the curtained French doors, the action more tic than necessity.

"What happened in that pub?" Louise asked. "And don't say migraine. It was more than that, you looked frightened."

"Frightened?"

"On stage, your face. You looked as if you had seen a ghost."

"You wouldn't understand."

"A bit patronising."

"I'm sorry, yes it was. I just don't know how to tell you."

"Try."

"Not now, please. I promise I will, but not at this moment."

Louise looked at him then appeared to come to a decision. "Okay, but if we're going to...I need to know, all right? You intrigue me, but you also frighten me a little."

"Frighten you?"

"I haven't felt like this since…for a long time." She looked down at her plate, worked at her food. "There's a blank, Jack. You never talk about yourself. I don't know anything about you other than what I see now and what I've seen since I met you."

"There's nothing to tell."

"I don't accept that."

Jack sighed and felt his grip loosen on the fragment of peace he had managed to salvage.

"What is it you want to know?" He could tell her everything, of course, every memory, every moment of his life.

"Anything." Louise sounded frustrated, not overtly so, but there was an edge to her voice. "I know you work in construction. I know you live here and that you are one hell of an actor." She chuckled and there was, thankfully, humour in the sound. "Perhaps that's why I've fallen for you because I'm Laura falling in love with Dr. Alec Harvey. But not a brief encounter, I hope."

The pun lightened the mood a little.

"It's more than that."

"Then give me something, Jack."

I was born in an underground tunnel, Louise. And do you know when that was? 1916, a hundred years ago. I was forty-five at that moment and I've been forty-five ever since. From those first few minutes, I have been scooping up every single instant of my existence and storing it away so that someone can rip me open and judge you—

There it was.

Judgement.

This world and its people were to be judged on the evidence that he had gathered. Isn't that what Lyle had told him? A judgement based on two millennia of observation and gathering.

And if this world was found wanting?

Jack became aware of his name being called from a distance. He snapped back into the now.

"It happened again." Louise sounded worried. "You went away, Jack."

"I'm sorry," he said.

He felt her hand tighten about his. Her eyes were soft, in that way of hers that was immediately erotic. Jack poured more wine, drained the bottle, and handed Louise a glass. "Last bottle, I'm afraid. Shame, I should have picked up a few more."

"Probably for the best. I have work in the morning."

He looked at Louise and realised that she was beautiful. She smiled. "What are you staring at?" Her voice was hoarse. Jack lifted her hand to his lips. The taste of it was sweet and warm. He heard Louise's indrawn breath. He stood and held her, tightly. Her body was strong, yet somehow fragile. He had to take this moment and the moment was filled with this woman. He crushed her and she him, and it was as if he held the only person who could keep him from drowning.

He kissed her. The act was sudden and impulsive, but also driven by his fear. Louise responded, eagerly, her mouth soft and her breath scalding. He drew her to himself, and they surged to their feet, bodies pressed hard against one another. He felt and absorbed every curve, every texture of her, the softness of her hair, her sweater, the smoothness of her skin, the taste of lipstick, the overwhelming scent of her perfume.

He laid her on his bed and Louise reached up to pull him down. She wanted to kiss him and be drawn into him. She needed to feel him, to taste him and be overwhelmed by him. He was warmth in her arms. He was a need. She felt her heat rise and her own body move against him as if it was an urgent, animal thing detached from her and yet absolutely her. She strained herself toward him, hating the infinitesimal gap between them. She wanted to be inside him, shrouded in his flesh and able to fold herself about his soul.

Sometime later, she woke from a half-stupor and there was the blank, empty core of this. It stole her breath. It was a physical hurt and it almost drove her out of the bed.

There had been an impenetrable darkness at the core of Richard's soul. She couldn't handle another. She couldn't face whatever hid within Jack's darkness. She needed to know who and what he was, and until she did, there could be no more of this. She clung to the sheets on either side of her, as if the bed was about to upend and dump her into a well of darkness. The moment passed and she rolled over and slid her arms about the sleeping Jack. She kissed the back of his neck and tasted the salt of his sweat. He murmured and stirred. She was calm now.

CHAPTER SIX (1916)

The first day became the second then the third. After that, the days began to merge, each one starting in the earliest hours; the tram, the omnibus, the hell of the factory and endless, backbreaking labour. At first, Jack spoke to only Lizzie, but, after a while, found himself chatting with some of the other men, two in particular. One was tall, gaunt-faced, and possessed of a shock of jet-black, curly hair and a moustache; the other was a clean shaven, slight-built, energetic character, who was nearing retirement. It was the dark-haired man, Sam Brightwell, who said, "What about a pint, after work eh? Down at the *Hammer and Nails*. How about it?"

"A drink?"

"A pint," Sam explained. "Don't tell me you've never had a pint of beer. Bloody hell mate. Where you been, on a South Sea Island?"

"Or are you a retired clergyman?" the other man, Bernie, said. "Or one what's been unfrocked."

"I have drunk beer before. Pale ale." Jack found that he was nervous about going to a pub again, after his first brush with one of those places.

"Well, that's all right then. You can have as much pale ale as you can swallow tonight. We have to celebrate getting our wages don't we, Bernie."

"We do indeed, Sam. We do indeed. It is Saturday after all. We need to make sure we quench our raging thirst before our missuses gets their hands on our hard-earned pay."

That night he told Lizzie he wouldn't be coming home straight away.

"Oh yeah?" she said. "And where are you off to then? Got some lady friend to see, have you?" She was smiling, teasing him, Jack knew, but there was something else in her voice and in her eyes. It was as if she didn't want him to see a "lady friend."

"No," Jack said. "It's all right. I'm going to the pub with Sam and Bernie."

"It isn't none of my business where you go or who you go with, is it?" That odd brusqueness was back. A sort of pained dignity she drew about herself when she was angry, sad, or even frightened.

"No…I suppose not." Jack was puzzled. Why was she upset?

"But you be careful Jack Smith. Bernie and Sam are a pair of drunken fools when they have a pint or two inside them. Don't let them get you into any trouble."

The *Hammer and Nails* wasn't far from the factory. Like the first pub he had visited after coming to *be*, it was fogged with cigarette smoke and redolent with the scent of beer and the body smells of the customers. There was laughter and loud voices. Some of the customers were in uniform, the khaki of soldiers and the dark blue of sailors. A piano tinkled in the background.

The night was long. The haze produced by the beer seemed to detach him from reality. He became a true observer, couched in a fog of wellbeing, watching and cheering arguments and fights, joining in loudly and raucously when a song broke out. He even remembered to get to his feet when the patrons sang to God to save their King.

He didn't go home to Lizzy's that night but slept in an alleyway. He had no idea how to get to her house anyway and was unable to walk any distance without collapsing. The world heaved and spun about him. There was no relief from the spiralling, raging storm of it, even when he closed his eyes. So, he lay down on the filthy ground, curled into a foetal position and hoped for unconsciousness. There was an odd sense of coming home in the act. When he awoke, he was cold and damp and his head felt as if someone was trying to tear it in half. He didn't move for many hours and when he did, it was to wander aimlessly through the streets. He couldn't eat. At least it was Sunday. There was no work for him today.

Eventually, he managed to find his way home. Lizzy was angry with him. Arnold appeared to enjoy her fury and Jack's humiliation. Jack stared at her as she berated him and saw something strange. It lay behind her anger and harsh words. She was almost crying. There was a catch in her voice, a desperation that cut through the torrent of hard words. He was startled and confused and oddly pleased, despite the lingering nausea and pain in his head.

Ellen peered at Jack from behind her mother's skirts. She had lost her apparent fear of him over the last few days, but suddenly he was an object of terror to her once more.

When it was done, Jack went up to bed.

As he lay on top of the blankets, he tried to understand how this worked. The drink made you feel good but left you weak and ill. The drink also seemed to be a spark for arguments. Women, it appeared, did not like men to drink beer.

He closed his eyes.

When he woke, it was dusk, and he felt a little better. The house was quiet, but there was another sound, the deep throb of engines.

Zeppelin.

He got out of bed, went to the window, and peered through the curtains. A distant searchlight probed the sky. Puffs of anti-aircraft fire blossomed against the twilight purple. Then he saw two of the monsters, grey-white blurs, pinned by the lights.

A flash lit up part of the city, threw roofs, chimneys, and a church tower, into momentary silhouette. The flash resolved into a restless orange glow that pulsed, shifted, and painted the underside of its own smoke. The bomb had fallen about a mile away. The detonations from the anti-aircraft shells and the bombs took five seconds to reach him and came as deep, heavy thuds followed by a rumble of echo. The window shook.

There was another effect, a tremor through The Fabric. It had been a while since Jack had been this sensitive to the weft and weave of its energies. The tremor disturbed him. Fear, pain, a terror that flared bright then faded.

Someone had died, over there, in that inferno.

Suddenly it was worse.

One of the distant Zeppelins seemed to expand. It grew larger and brighter. It glowed, the light yellow-white then orange-tinged. The craft began to fall, slowly. It was on fire. Hit by a shell or damaged in an attack by one of the flimsy aeroplanes that Jack had occasionally seen flying over the capital.

The flames brightened.

The shockwaves came.

Human shockwaves; the combined terror of the Zeppelin's crew, raw, brutal, and hellish. The Fabric shuddered and twisted, and he heard them, felt them, screaming as their flesh blistered and their blood boiled, as they plunged from the sky, howling for release, but knowing only agony and unspeakable fear.

Jack gasped. He fought for breath. He leaned forward, fingers splayed on the windowsill, his forehead pressed against the glass. The horror came at him in waves. He felt the heat of it. He heard the roar of flames. He groaned in shared despair. There was no relief, no place to hide. The entire world burned and it was the most intense pain he had ever endured. Then finally, it began to subside and The Fabric settled once more. He felt pity, although he knew that he should feel none. The men in that craft had rained death on the people below them. Didn't they deserve to die?

But then what of the shells he helped manufacture; who were they destroying? How many fathers and sons, brothers and uncles were obliterated by the work of *his* hand? Didn't he deserve a fate like those aviators out there?

The questions were dissolved by a second, then third, bomb, widely spaced, each bringing waves of trauma through the fabric. The other Zeppelin was still intact and sowing its lethal seeds over the city. The blasts pounded at Jack's skull until he stumbled back and threw himself onto the bed, pillow held over his head, begging for it to stop.

It would never stop.

It was autumn. Another day ended and it was already dark when they walked out of the factory.

"I have to go somewhere before I come home," Lizzy said.

Jack was startled. He and Lizzy always went home together. He looked forward to walking beside her, talking to her. And there were the glances she gave him. The ones he sometimes caught and returned. He even liked the abrupt way she behaved with him sometimes. Signs, he was certain, that she was experiencing the same odd feelings as he was.

The thought of going home alone was oddly bleak. He felt unreasonable worry, and jealousy. It was the same when she talked about Russell, her husband, when she had told him what a good man he was, how he provided for her and was kind, in his way. He didn't look kind in the photograph. He looked angry. On the other hand, Jack couldn't believe that Lizzy would lie to him, so perhaps the photograph was not an accurate representation of Private Russell Reid. Nonetheless the presence of the man, albeit in the background, disturbed Jack and created many unpleasant emotions.

"Where are you going?" Jack asked Lizzy as they stood at the factory gate.

"Best you don't know."

"But I want to know. I don't want you to be hurt or get into trouble."

She looked at him for a moment. Her expression was a tender half-smile. She touched him, offered the merest, feather-light brush of her gloved hand against his cheek and then she was gone, lost in the crowd.

For a moment, Jack thought of following her, but he decided that she didn't want that, so he turned away and walked down the street toward the omnibus. She had seemed nervous. Whatever this thing was that she was going to do, it was important and it frightened her.

He climbed aboard the omnibus and found that he had to stand because it was too crowded for him to sit down. The child, Ellen, ran to him when he came through the door. She did that a lot now. She no longer seemed afraid of him, not that she had reason to be anyway, but neither did she have any reason to feel such affection toward him.

"Where's Lizzy?" Arnold asked. "You didn't leave her behind at the factory, did you?"

"No." Jack was puzzled by Arnold's tone. This was not his usual scorn. This was worry. "She said she had to do something."

"Oh God, she hasn't gone to one of those bloody meetings, has she?"

"What meetings?"

"She didn't tell you?" Arnold chuckled scornfully. "I thought she told you everything."

"I don't think she tells me everything."

Arnold shook his head. "Simple aren't you, simple in the head." He jammed a forefinger against his temple. "Or you pretend to be."

"Why would I pretend to be...simple?"

"To worm your way into her affections. Nothing a woman likes more than to look after a man."

"I don't believe that to be true."

"Don't you? How in heaven's name did you get to be your age and not know anything about women?"

Jack sensed that no answer was necessary. He was hungry and walked past the man and to the tiny pantry and helped himself to some bread and lard.

"Did she say what time she'd be home?" Arnold asked when Jack returned to the fireplace and sat down to eat and drink.

"She told me nothing," Jack answered.

Arnold grunted then coughed. The coughing had become worse. There were more blood spots on his grubby handkerchief. He looked even paler and weaker than before.

Jack picked up the newspaper that Arnold had long read and discarded. There were reports from The Front. The Great Offensive begun in June was yielding huge successes for the British army and her allies. The breathlessly optimistic report was followed by a frighteningly long list of casualties.

The knock on the door came many hours later and woke Jack from an awkward slumber in the armchair. He lifted his head, mumbled, then started awake. The fire was almost out. He looked across at Arnold who was also waking.

"Wassa time?" Arnold mumbled. Jack glanced at the clock. It was past midnight, almost one in the morning. "Is Lizzy home?"

The knock was repeated. It sounded urgent, desperate almost. Jack got to his feet and groggily made his way across to the back door. He opened it to find a woman standing there. She was wrapped in a shawl and looked nervous and cold.

"What's wrong?" he said. "Are you alright?"

"Yes, yes," she answered and stepped inside. "My name is Marjory Portman. I'm a ...a friend of Elizabeth's. I'm sorry to disturb you all." Her accent was correct, an educated accent, what Lizzy would call *proper*.

"What is it?" Jack said.

"It's about Elizabeth...are you her husband?"

"I'm the lodger, Jack Smith. This is her brother." Jack waved toward Arnold who stayed in his chair and mumbled a reluctant greeting.

"Is her husband here?"

"He's at The Front," Arnold said.

"Ah, right, yes, of course. Well, I'm afraid Elizabeth has been arrested—"

"By the police?" Jack's sleep-fog was gone in a moment.

"Who else do you think arrested her?" Arnold snapped from behind him. "Bloody simpleton."

Marjory bridled. "There is no need to be rude, Mr...."

"Jones," Jack added helpfully. "His name is Arnold Jones."

"Is it indeed." Marjory repaired her dignity and continued. "Anyway, Elizabeth is at the police station.

"Is she all right? Is she hurt?"

"No, no, Mr. Smith, please don't worry. She is uninjured, no thanks to the gentlemen in blue. They're not going to charge her, but she is frightened and needs someone to fetch her home. Unfortunately, I am in no position to aid her. I have to keep away from the police, at the moment."

"You're one of those bloody suffragettes, aren't you," Arnold called out.

"Yes," the woman said. "And so is your sister."

"I've told her over and over again to keep out of it. And now look what's happened. Stupid bloody cows, the lot of you."

"Arnold, please don't speak to her like that," Jack said.

"It's all right. I'm used to that sort of abusive language from men. Can you go and fetch her, do you think?"

"Of course." The idea of rescuing a frightened Lizzy from the clutches of the law was suddenly exciting. Jack was puzzled. He felt happy at the prospect of seeing her when he should be worried, afraid for her even.

The reception area of the police station was a hot, crowded, and noisy chaos of uniforms and dresses locked into what looked to be mortal combat. Jack stood in the doorway, uncertain as to what he should do. The sight of the police constables unnerved him. They shouted and grappled with their prisoners, who were, in turn shouting and struggling and in one or two cases, trying to sing. Many of the women wore sashes. Some of which were torn or stained with what looked like blood. A man with impressive mustachios and three chevron stripes on his sleeves yelled above the din.

Jack noticed that there were other men there too, not in uniform, some angry with the police, others with the women they were leading away, their wives or daughters presumably. One, a stocky, craggy-looking individual was shouting into his wife's face. Spittle sprayed from his mouth. The woman flinched away, her face riven with fear. Jack wanted to help her. He wanted to push the man away, drive his fist into that ugly, snarling visage, and feel his knuckles crack against bone. He wanted to see blood and fright in his eyes.

Appalled, Jack forced the sudden rage down into himself. This was something new and, he sensed, dangerous. The bully deserved a good hiding, but he was not the man to do it.

The next couple he saw were arm in arm. The woman, close to the man who was protecting her. Her dress was torn. She was hatless and her hair awry. They were hunched down as they emerged from the crowd. The man, her husband, presumably, wanted to get her home and safe. *There* was love.

Desperate to do the same for Lizzy, Jack plunged into the melee and made his way to the sergeant with some difficulty.

"What do you want?" the sergeant bawled at him,

"Lizzy Reid," Jack shouted back.

The sergeant looked up to give Jack his full attention. "Who?"

"Lizzy Reid, I've come to take her home."

"You her father?"

"No, lodger."

The sergeant's eyes widened then he frowned, sceptical. "She's in here somewhere. Just find her and get her out of here sharpish. I'm fed up with this lot and…" He turned to address the room in general. "…IF THEY ALL DON'T PIPE DOWN, I'LL THROW THE LOT OF THEM INTO THE CELLS!"

Jack made his way toward the far side of the reception area where more women waited quietly. He recognised none of them. Then he saw Lizzy seated, face covered by her hands. Jack touched her shoulder and she started. She looked up and he saw the bruises. A trickle of blood ran from her nose.

Without a word, she got to her feet and put her arm through his. He led her carefully through the struggling bodies, the fug of sweat and the mists of cigarette smoke, and out into the now-deserted street. The noise from the police station faded with distance. Lizzy did not remove her arm until he kissed her, on that nameless street, just as it started to rain. He kissed her and she kissed him back and the heat was fierce. He knew what he wanted to do with her and to her and he could sense that she knew too.

She pushed him away, breathing hard. "We…we mustn't."

This was not a rejection, this was fear. Jack stepped back and nodded. "Of course. I am sorry."

"It's all right," Lizzy said quietly. "Thank you for coming to get me, Jack."

He nodded, unsure how to reply. Lizzy put her arm through his once more and they continued walking.

Because the silence was almost impossible to bear, Jack asked; "Why were you arrested and why did they beat you?"

"I'm a suffragette. Men don't like us. They tell us we're unpatriotic and unchristian, although I'm not bothered by that. I don't feel patriotic because they keep sending our lads out to get killed and we don't seem no closer to winning. And I'm not a Christian no more. What God would let all those young fellas die out there? Why didn't He put a stop to it before it started?"

"There is no God," Jack said. "The creators are godlike, but they are not gods."

"And you would know, would you?"

"Yes." He was startled at his own certainty. No one had told him about the creators, other than allusions made by Lyle during that first encounter in the bombed house.

Lizzy stopped again and looked at him, then shook her head and chuckled. "You're an odd one, no mistake."

"What is a suffragette?"

A chuckle, which dried-up straight away. "You really don't know, do you?"

"No, I don't."

"We want votes for women."

"Women can't vote?"

"Course not."

"Why?"

"We're women, that's why. We're not clever enough to vote."

"That isn't true."

"I know that." Lizzy sounded agitated. She softened. "They've always wanted us to stay at home and do as we're told. But now they want us to go to work in factories and do the jobs that men do, because they've sent them all to The Front. Oh, they want us out of the home now, all right."

Jack tried to understand what Lizzy had told him. "I still don't see why it means that you have to be beaten by the police."

"We brought it on ourselves. Some of us have smashed windows and planted a bomb or two." Jack felt her arm tighten about his. She was angry. "They won't listen to us, see, so we have to do something."

"Were you planting bombs tonight?"

"Course not. Mrs. Pankhurst asked us to stop all that when the war broke out so we can support the country. And I've never even seen one of their bombs let alone set one off anywhere. We was just having a meeting, that's all. Just listening to a speaker who was telling us how the fight is going. One minute we was sitting around drinking tea and chatting, the next, the door burst open and the police were after us. Perhaps they was just bored or they'd been drinking beer down at the station and were in the mood for a fight. Anyway, they were on us, fists and truncheons, shouting and swearing at us and calling us everything under the sun."

Jack wondered at this need for the police to crush any dissent from the people who they were supposed to protect. This society was unfair and savage. He also felt his admiration and desire for this woman intensify. She was brave as well as beautiful. She had spirit and was as willing to fight for what she believed in as any of the soldiers at The Front, more so, probably. After all, how many of the men sent to die, fully understood why they were there, other than subscribing to the vague rabble-rousing platitudes about serving King and Country? Oh, and then there was the idea that they were doing battle with a race of monsters who raped the virtuous and slaughtered the innocent.

The latter was true, of course, the Zeppelin raids were proof of that. But if the British possessed such craft, would they hold back from bombing German cities? He doubted it.

"Do you miss Russell?" he asked and wondered where the question came from.

"A little." Lizzy shook her head and laughed ruefully. "If it wasn't for that photograph, I'd be hard put to remember what he looks like. Awful ain't it. After all, he is the man I fell in love with and married and who put a roof over my head and food on the table. There's a bit of me.... No, no it's not right to say it."

Jack experienced an odd quickening of his heartbeat.

"There's a bit of me...you won't tell no one, will you?"

"No, I promise."

"There's a bit of me what's not missed him at all. I like working at the factory. I like being with the other women. It's more of a lark than being in the house all day. I know Russell won't like it when he comes home. He'll want me to stop working..."

Home? Jack didn't want him to come home.

"...but I'm not going to. And I'm...."

Jack didn't ask her to finish the sentence. He sensed that she couldn't, anyway. Her tone of voice, the way she moved closer to him, made it unnecessary.

When they got home, they found Arnold asleep, snoring lightly, mouth open. Jack took Lizzy through to the kitchen and washed her face. He was gentle. She kept her eyes on him and he saw real fear this time. Not of him, no this was fear of herself and how she felt.

Eventually, she went up to bed, thanking him again for coming to fetch her from the police station, this time in a voice so quiet it was almost a whisper.

Jack sat in the kitchen until the last embers of the fire flickered out and it was utterly dark and cold.

When he finally made his way upstairs, he was stopped by her voice.

"Jack?"

He paused for a moment, heart drumming, mouth dry, then stepped into her bedroom.

Lizzy was gone by the time an exhausted Jack dragged himself from his bed the next morning. He was relieved. He had gone back to his own bed sometime in the early hours and was not sure how he could have faced her. He did not understand why he felt that way. Their lovemaking had been a wonder, something deeper and sweeter than anything he had so far experienced and yet he now felt awkward. He suspected that Lizzy's early start had been for the same reason.

Harsh truths boiled like clouds at the periphery of his warmth, however, but at this moment, too far away to concern him greatly.

"The police did her over then," Arnold said.

"It would appear so," Jack answered.

"Looked after her, though, didn't you."

There was something in Arnold's tone that Jack didn't like. He did not reply.

"You ought to be careful," Arnold continued. "And so does she. Getting herself mixed up with the likes of that Pankhurst will land her in prison."

"But why shouldn't women vote?" Jack said.

"Thin edge of the wedge," Arnold grumbled. "They're already taking men's jobs in the factories."

"But the men are...." Jack stopped. He was too tired to argue and he understood that such an argument could not be won.

He finished his cup of tea, then left for work. The day was autumn grey, wet and cold, which did little to lighten his mood. He wanted Lizzy. He wanted to be with her. He wanted to touch her. She was a source of warmth in the desolation. She was hope. He understood that it was dangerous and wrong because she was loved by another man and they were married and he was sacrificing everything for his country.

Lizzy was not at her usual task. Jack asked a woman he knew to be Nancy, where she might be.

"She's been sacked."

"Why would they do that? She's good at her job."

"Because she's one of *them* women, you know, a suffragette."

Jack dropped the handles of the barrow and strode toward the office. He was startled by the feeling he had now. It was almost as strong as the wildness he had experienced in the police station. It raged through him, red and fiery. He pounded up the stairs to hammer at Geils' door.

"What?" Geils shouted from within.

"I want to talk to you."

The door was thrown open. Geils glared at Jack. "Why aren't you at work?"

"Where's Lizzy?"

"Bugger off back to—"

"No."

"What?"

"Not until you tell me what happened to Lizzy and why she isn't here anymore."

Geils recoiled a little. This heat pouring through Jack made him strong and took away his fear. The foreman obviously sensed it too.

"I sacked her, not that it's any of your concern."

"Why?"

"Get back to work or I'll sack you as well."

"Why?" Jack wanted to strike him. His rage was molten. It exhilarated him.

"Because she's a bloody anarchist. I don't want her sort working here. Satisfied?"

"Why should I be satisfied at someone not being allowed free speech?"

"Free bloody speech? There's a war going on. Men are dying for their country and these whores think it's all right to smash things up, plant bombs, and kill the King's horse? Is that their right?"

Jack felt the rage dissipate. He struggled for an answer. Reason was breaking through. He must not be sacked because, with Lizzy out of a job, his money would be important now. Without another word he swung around and walked back down the steps and into the fury and heat of the factory floor.

Later, while Jack, Sam, and Bernie ate their lunch together as usual, Sam said; "They're looking for people to work at that TNT plant in Silvertown. She should try there."

Lizzy did not seem pleased to see him when he arrived home that night. She was brusque and would not look him in the eye. Ellen was more forthcoming, but then cowed when her mother snapped at her to sit at the table and mind her p's and q's. Lizzy's injuries seemed more livid now than when they were fresh. A bruise had formed around her left eye and her nose was swollen. There were grazes on her left cheek and on the backs of both of her hands.

Jack did not attempt to talk to her. The wall she had erected between them was too high and impenetrable. He would wait. Humans cycled through their moods with alarming regularity, traveling quickly, and often inexplicably, from light to darkness then back into the light again. He ate and he waited. He drank tea then retreated to his room as soon as the meal was finished. He had no stomach for sharing time with Arnold or treading softly around Lizzy's dangerous silence.

He would tell her about the TNT factory in good time. Perhaps even apply for work there himself.

He did not light his candle, but lay on the bed and let the night creep in. He didn't sleep. Instead, he searched through his memories and tried to understand this world. He tried to comprehend its enigmas and ambiguities, its confusions and beliefs and how none of them seemed consistent or even logical. He had some grasp of good and evil, of what was right and what was wrong, but even that was fluid. Each person seemed to have a different view of life and of morality.

He closed his eyes then opened them again when he heard her enter his room. Lizzy didn't speak but moved carefully across the small space to the bed. He heard the rustle of her nightgown. He smelled the scent of her and heard her soft breath. In a moment, she was in his arms and he held her tightly and whispered to her. He was barely aware of the words he uttered. She flinched back when he kissed her bruises and that was when he discovered that he knew how to be gentle, slow, and tender.

CHAPTER SEVEN (2016)

Jack woke the morning after the blues pub scare and gave thanks to he-knew-not-what that he was still alive and on Earth. His gratitude was intensified by the warm presence of Louise asleep beside him in the bed.

For a few moments, he felt the familiar euphoria of new love, but it was soon tainted with gnawing, dark guilt over the fact that he may be taken at any moment and that he was offering Louise a lie. That fact heightened his need for her. Selfish, yes, but he could not bear the thought of her not being there. He did not want to face the end alone, which was not fair to Louise. More than unfair. It was downright cruel.

He rolled over and drew her to himself. The act was defiant. Lost in her warmth, he didn't care.

And that was the waking of their first day.

Breakfast eaten, Jack pulled on his overalls and warm clothes, kissed Louise, held her tightly for a few moments then stepped out into the cold. The sky was dark and lowering, the air heavy with moisture. Traffic was relatively light. Even though Christmas was a month away, it was already being proclaimed by the flashing lights displayed over the frontages of some of the houses he passed. Jack had mixed feelings about Christmas. It was an odd time of year, marked with gluttony and materialism, but also an excuse for parties and family gatherings. Somewhere in the glitter and fury of the season, it was possible to catch the faintest nod toward its real meaning, which seemed to have little relevance to how Christmas was celebrated.

Since Marion's death, Jack had spent Christmas alone. He usually volunteered to help serve lunch at shelters or at nursing homes. The old, to whom Jack served those lunches, were a strange concept to him, stricken, as they were, by a weakness and vulnerability he could not imagine. Their one journey through life was almost at an end. Some of them talked of their past, believing that it was a time lived before Jack was born, unaware, of course, that he remembered those times well and had lived through them himself. It was they who had not been born when Jack Smith came to *be*.

And the people he had known then, many of them young and strong, were themselves old, or long gone. Lizzy's brother Arnold, Sam and Bernie, Mr. Geils, and Ellen. Lizzy's daughter, someone he remembered only as a small child, would be over one hundred years old, if she was still alive.

Marion, too, was long gone. She died in the brutal winter that bordered 1962 and 1963. She was 62 years old. Still beautiful. Facing the unthinkable with her usual stoicism and humour, she seemed to revert to the Marion he had first met, Ninety-one years ago.

She had described her cancer as beastly. The tiny helpings of hospital food she managed to eat, as perfectly horrid. During their last lucid conversation, she looked up at him from her pillow, a thin, ashen, skeletal thing and whispered that she did not really understand who or what he was, but that she loved him anyway because he had been kind to her and had stayed with her even as she aged and left him behind.

Outside the hospital, on that iron-grey afternoon, chilled by the brutal air and the frozen snow that had lingered for months now, Jack had taken his vow of solitude. He could not love and lose again. As the decades trundled along their allotted paths, he kept his promise. He watched. He listened and felt. He suffered the emotional shock of a president's assassination along with the rest of the world. Years later, he sat through a night, transfixed by his television, as men walked on the moon.

The world changed radically in the decade that followed Marion's death. It was wrenched out of shape in a way he had not seen before. The old deference was dispensed with.

But, slowly, Jack's need to absorb and taste and be part of the world slipped away from him. He was tired. He relished his solitude. He had friends. He always made friends, but each time he had to relinquish them when the truth began to make itself known. The cycle of meeting, enjoying, then retreating became tiresome. It hurt and sometimes broke his heart. The cruelty of his existence was made even more poignant by the arrival, once every twenty years of a brown envelope containing a new birth certificate. It always reached him, no matter where he lived. A recurring reminder of his otherness.

Better to be alone.

Jack Smith settled down to wait for the creators to come for him. It was a frightening prospect. He did not know what it meant. But it was inevitable and not to be fought against. Time and its passing lost much of its meaning.

Then he met Louise.

The job was a farmhouse renovation out of town. The house had been gutted, its internal layout completely altered from homely to luxury country dwelling for its new owners, neither of whom had ever gotten their hands anywhere near the soil. The farm itself was no longer a viable business. The land had been sold to an agricultural consortium and the farm buildings had either been demolished or were due to be converted into flats.

The other builders were already there when Jack arrived. Their truck was parked by the front door. An unattended cement mixer waited. There was a van beside the builders' truck. It belonged to Jerry, the plumber. The man himself appeared in the doorway as Jack climbed out of his vehicle. He crossed to his van and began untying a bundle of copper pipes from the roof rack. He was a big man, made menacing by his close-shaved scalp.

"Hiya, mate." Jerry had a deep, gruff voice.

"Morning," Jack answered.

"Bloody freezing,"

"Well, you'd better hurry up and get the central heating finished," Jack said. An awful joke, but it was the sort of wisecrack that went down well on construction sites. Jerry laughed then hoisted the pipes onto his considerable shoulder and headed into the house. Jack followed him.

And there it was, that smell: newly sawn wood, brick dust.

The assorted construction workers had set up a restroom-come-makeshift canteen in one of the empty bedrooms. Seating consisted of slabs of foam, commercial sized paint tins supporting lengths of board, and a couple of fold-up chairs the carpenters kept in their van. It was foam and floor for Jack.

He made for the corner of the room reserved for the kettle and mugs and made himself tea. Outside, the light faded as the already dense cloud thickened. Something wrong with that light, Jack decided, although, of course there wasn't.

There was a promise of snow.

One of the two bricklayers, a young, affable, and newly married giant named Nathan, was seated on the paint tin sofa. He muttered over the sport pages of *The Sun*. "Don't know why I read this shite," he grumbled.

"Nor do I," Jack said.

"What paper do you read?" Nathan asked. "*The Financial Times*? *Country Life*? *The Lady*?" He laughed gruffly at his own joke. His gym-inflated arms were heavily tattooed; a swirl of viciously thorned roses, Celtic symbols, and an extravagantly illuminated rendition of wife's name, Sophie.

"I get my news off the radio. The BBC."

"Radio Three, of course," Nathan said in a mock upper-class accent and grinned at the others.

"Sometimes."

"Radio Three?" Rhys the other carpenter said. "Really? All that fucking classical crap?" He was a slight-built, wiry character. He drank his coffee hot, black, and strong. The smell of it threatened to overwhelm the other odours in the place.

"I like all types of music."

"So do I, but I can't get my head around classical."

"There's nothing to get your head around. It's just music," Jack said. "Can you hear a tune?"

"Not if Nathan sings it, I can't."

"Fuck off."

Laughter.

"But yes, I can hear a tune. I'm Welsh, aren't I?"

"Then you can understand classical music. A symphony is simply a long piece, made up of a series of tunes."

"Never thought of that." Rhys looked round at the others, grinning. "You learn something from Jack the Smith every day."

"Of course you do. It's because he's not fucking Welsh," Nathan said.

Daniel folded his newspaper and with a wide, exaggerated yawn, got to his feet. "Time to rock and roll." He unpacked his trowel and spirit level and headed for the door, ready to carry on with the new supporting wall that would divide the enormous kitchen from the new dining room.

Jack drained his tea. His first job would be to start the cement mixer, which was outside, in the cold.

"I'll mix the first lot, Jack" Daniel said. "You can shift this," he waved toward the assorted seats and the tea-making equipment, "into the small bedroom at the end of the landing then hack the old plaster off these walls. Do the same in the other big bedroom as well, will you? I've got the plasterers coming on Wednesday and we aren't bloody ready for them yet. At least we can get them started up here."

Jack set to work, gathering up the mugs and kettle. A few minutes later the cement mixer trundled into life outside. He finished clearing the room then fetched a hammer and bolster from downstairs and began hacking into the powdery, loose plaster.

The task was mindless and hard. Exactly what he needed this morning.

Two hours in, his phone rang.

Louise was at her desk by eight-thirty, attempting to write out a list of her jobs and targets for the day. Claire, the company accountant had already commented on how happy Louise seemed and made it her business to extract the name of the man who must have caused this transformation from Louise's tightly sealed lips.

Louise wanted to tell her but was held back by an irrational belief that if she talked about Jack too intently, she would lose him.

He was stable, he was fun, and he was wise. She felt safe in his arms. She felt at peace. Even the blank secret place within him failed to disturb her for now. She knew that it would trouble her again and eat at her peace of mind, because beneath the euphoria there was fear. It had been like this with Richard, hadn't it? Weeks, months, of happiness, then the discovery of his dark cloud, the black dog that snapped at his heels.

Jack had a secret and it frightened her.

She heard voices in the showroom; the manager, Khalid Mehr, and someone else, male but unfamiliar. Probably a customer. Needing to see who it was, and not sure why, Louise leaned back so she could peer out through the office doorway.

The visitor was tall, broad, and wearing an expensive-looking fawn coat. He exuded an authority that was almost frightening. She recognised him. God, it was the man in the café. The unsettling character who had toasted her with his coffee cup. So? Coincidence. That was all.

The conversation was muted but Louise caught a name, spoken by Khalid.

"Let's talk, Mr. Lyle. I'm sure we can come to some arrangement."

"Thank you." Lyle's voice was deep and rich. As he made to follow Khalid, he glanced toward the office and caught Louise's eye. His expression remained neutral.

"Jack is not yours, Louise," he said quietly. "He's ours."

She struggled for breath. He had whispered the words in a busy, noisy office and she had heard them. He had whispered words he should not have uttered. How did he know about Jack? What did he mean by the comment? Was Jack married? Was he a criminal?

Or did this man know where Richard was?

If Richard was alive, then she was still married to him and had no right to go running after Jack Smith.

Her confusion, the shock, and something else, the weight of Lyle's words, the power behind his voice had shaken her badly. She felt the first breathless tightness of an anxiety attack. She was hot; she felt sick. She had to get out.

She was also furious.

Louise got to her feet and stormed toward the showroom in time to see Khalid and Mr Lyle making for the exit.

"What did you mean by that?" Louise demanded, unable to stop herself.

Khalid swung round, shocked then quickly angry. He snapped her name. She ignored him. Lyle turned also and stared at her but remained calm and impassive.

"Well?" Louise said. She held his eye, which was at once difficult and compelling. "What did you mean?"

"What I said. He belongs to us." His voice was kind. Deep. One that demanded attention and obedience, but Louise was in no mood to obey.

"And who the hell are you?"

"It doesn't matter, Louise," Lyle said.

"How do you know my name? Are you some sort of policeman?"

"Let Jack go. Please." He sounded tired now.

Without another word or even a goodbye to Khalid, Lyle stepped outside. As the doors closed, Louise was sure that he had disappeared.

"Louise." Khalid sounded furious. "My office, now."

Khalid's reprimand was lost on Louise whose mind was in turmoil. Jack was in trouble. They, whoever *they* were, wanted him. God, he might be a criminal. Lyle might be one of the good guys and Jack the psychopath, the burglar, the rapist, the traitor. Christ, she didn't know and she needed to. She loved him. She had to see him. Now.

Midway through Khalid's tirade she walked out and back to her desk. His voice followed her, volume and pitch increasing with his wrath. How dare she walk out. How dare she turn her back on him. How dare she insult a customer.

Louise grabbed her handbag and coat and left the office. When she stepped into the showroom, she expected to see Lyle waiting for her. But the showroom was empty except for its idealized bathroom and kitchen mock-ups. No one had followed her out of the office. She suspected that her days with this company were over. Well, so be it. She did not care.

Outside, the air was bitterly cold. She climbed into her car and stabbed Jack's number into her phone. No reply. She tried again and again until, frustrated, she threw the phone down onto the seat and let the anger take over. He had lied to her. That blank space of Jack's was a dark one. He was in trouble and he *was* trouble. Whether the people to whom he belonged were on the right or wrong side of the law, she had stepped into some sort of viper's nest. She had opened her heart. She had risked her wounded feelings and now he wouldn't even fucking well answer his phone.

She yelled and hammered the steering wheel with her fists. Then reached across to plunge her hand down into her handbag. She punched it through the bag's contents, make-up case, purse, Oyster Card in its neat plastic folder. And there, at the bottom, the hard circle of the ring. She drew it out. It was gold, decorated with a delicate filigree carved into its edges. She reached into her bag again and, after a few seconds, produced the engagement ring; a simple thin band on which a sapphire was mounted, cheap, simple, but the one she had fallen for and wanted despite Richard's surprise and the jeweller's obvious disappointment.

She placed her handbag on the floor, picked up the rings and slipped them onto her finger. They were still a perfect fit.

She did it because it hurt and brought a moment of pain. Pain was good. Pain tore open the carefully sealed boxes locked away in her heart, one by one. Each held the seeds of her destruction, which increased in potency with each box she opened.

It started and ended with the silence...

...It was that silence that Louise would never forget.

Their wedding day was a joy of bright sunshine, blue sky, and a registry office. As guests, they had invited a few friends from Walkern. Afterward, they went to a pub restaurant where they had a table booked and champagne on ice. There were no speeches, just laughter and warmth.

Then there was a brief honeymoon in East Anglia, where they hid themselves in Woodbridge, a quaint market town by the River Deben. They travelled, explored, laughed, loved, and Louise was content. Each evening ended with a walk along the river, to a tree-shrouded place called Kyson Point, where the footpath terminated in a tiny beach by a lonely cottage. A worn-looking wooden ramp projected from the beach into the river. Presumably, it was for launching boats.

One evening, on an impulse, Louise stepped onto the ramp and walked carefully out over the weed-clogged shallows to where the river turned dark and deep. She looked down and felt a moment of vertigo. She was exposed out there. One false step and she would be lost. Then she felt Richard's presence behind her. His hands closed gently about her arms. Now she was safe.

"This is our Garden of Eden," he whispered and kissed her neck. "Our ghosts are going to live here when we die."

Louise believed that she had Richard's black dog at bay and she was not going to let it savage what they had. She closed her eyes and remembered the other side of the dream, the darkness behind the dazzling sunlight.

When the honeymoon was over, she watched him, as she had grown accustomed to ever since she had moved into his cottage. She had learned the signs; a steady retreat into himself, short temper, impatience, then silence and a need to be away from her and everyone else. It happened every now and then, sometimes in clusters, sometimes several months would go by between them.

They lived in the cottage as they had done prior to their marriage. They tended the garden and met with friends and went to work. In the evenings Louise prepared lessons and marked essays. Richard read. There was a fire in the grate during the winter nights, wine in the garden on the summer evenings.

Then there was a child.

The call was from Louise. "I need to see you, now. I know you can't but...."

"Where are you?"

"I'll be in Costa, in the Old Town. I can't work. I've been sent home sick."

"Okay. I'm on my way."

"Please hurry."

Jack cut the connection, dropped his phone back into his overalls pocket and hurried downstairs, where he found Daniel the foreman.

"I need to go home for a couple of hours," he said. "I'm sorry. I wouldn't normally but...."

Daniel studied him, then nodded. "A couple of hours, okay, but let me know if you can't get back here."

It was raining again, the light grey and dismal. He left the farmhouse, saw Jerry's van and the builders' truck. *Sorry lads*, Jack told them silently, *my days as a construction worker are nearly done.*

My days are nearly done, full stop.

Not yet. He could fight them. Josephine had, for a long time. He felt a dull ache, an iron bar tight about his head. He tried to ignore it. He drove through a small village. He noticed everything. He drank it in and fed off it, because he was afraid that this would be his last taste.

The rain was heavy by the time he reached Stevenage. It lashed the windscreen and blurred the scenery.

Louise was already in the coffee shop, at a table by the window. There was a large cup of tea ready for him. Jack made to kiss her. She turned away, offering her cheek rather than her lips.

"I hope it isn't cold," she said, an innocuous enough greeting. She was pale and her eyes were crying-red.

Jack noticed a marriage and an engagement ring together on the appropriate finger. He had never seen them before.

"Thanks." He sipped the drink, grateful for it. ""Warm enough."

"I haven't been here long." Louise's hair was dry. She wore her "smart" coat, black, well-cut. An umbrella leaned against the wall by the window. "I like this table." she said. "I was sitting here when you phoned me and asked me out."

"Do you regret saying yes? Is that why you need to talk to me?"

Louise shook her head and her smile, wistful as it was, faded.

"The rings," Jack said. "Why are you wearing them? I suppose it has something to do with this."

"Yes. I'm married."

"Separated, or very good at organising your adultery?" It was meant as a lightener, but the moment he said it, Jack regretted the comment. "I'm sorry, that wasn't funny."

"It's okay."

A pause. Jack waited. He had to let her take her time. Whatever she wanted to say it was obviously not going to be easy for her.

"We had a child. Her name was Esther..."

...Pregnancy began with sickness, unrelenting nausea that plagued her every waking moment and left her exhausted. It passed and the next few months stretched into an eternity of steadily growing discomfort and tiredness, but also contentment, a secret joy which Richard tried hard to share in, but which was all her own.

Richard was the consummate expectant father. He went to classes with her. He looked after her, massaged her, cooked, cleaned, did everything right. Then, when The Night came, complete with rain and darkness and the mad drive to the Lister Hospital, he was calm and stalwart and stayed with her to the bitter screaming, bloody, and pain-wracked end.

Louise watched him take the tiny, squalling human in his hands and saw the joy in his face. It was as if the sun had risen from behind the clouds in his soul.

A baby, tiny yet deafening and as demanding as a dictator. She was selfish, dirty, and endlessly hungry. A succubus that drained the life from both her parents, reduced them to pale, tremulous, dazed wrecks, but they were happy beneath the trauma. There was peace here, and completeness. Richard seemed anchored by the relentless cycle of feed, change, bathe, sleep (if you were lucky), and then feed again. It was as if Esther drew him out of himself and smothered the darkness with her demands and his obedience to them.

Then, a month-and-a-half after the birth, deep in the night, came the silence,

It woke Louise from the heavy sleep she had come to enjoy between feeds, nappy changes, and exhausted pace-and-shush sessions.

It woke her with its nothingness. It wrenched her from the darkness and dumped her into confusion and dread. Richard was still asleep. She didn't wake him, but climbed out of bed, slowly, carefully then padded across to the cot. The night light glowed red from its 13A socket and created shadow from every shape and form in the room.

Louise leaned over to peer into the cot. It was from there that the silence emanated.

The reality was like an impact, wave upon wave of blood-red that slammed into Louise's mind. It wasn't real. it was unfair, ridiculous, horrible.

She unleashed her grief as a long, primal animal howl and collapsed to her knees. She clutched the lifeless child to herself and never wanted to let her go.

Months passed. Louise felt so damaged, she was convinced she would never be fully repaired. This had been a chance, a briefly opened door that Richard had followed her through.

Louise retreated into the fortress of her grief and was only vaguely aware of the new silence. Richard was suddenly reduced from husband and lover to a human being who inhabited the same house as she did. There was little connection between them.

She grew afraid of his ghostlike presence. They both drank, and fought, formless battles that meandered into emotional oblivion as exhaustion and alcohol took their toll. Richard's depression rose up like a dark tsunami and swamped not only his soul but Louise's as well. She had no strength to guide her husband out of the pit. There was no one there to take her hand either. It wasn't his fault. He had been broken long before the silence came.

Half a year slid by, a perpetual twilight that finally dissolved into a pale, bitterly cold dawn. Louise began to claw her way toward the light. She returned to work, although the classroom was all but unbearable now. She brought work home because its mind-numbing monotony was every bit as effective as the grape.

Then the second silence came.

Louise knew, even before she stepped into the cottage, perhaps even before she was out of her car. She was home from work and she was tired. There was a pile of marking on the seat beside her. It was dark, winter, now raining. There was a light on in the sitting room, visible through a chink in the curtain. But as she climbed out, swearing under her breath at the cold rain, she knew. Perhaps it was the worn-through remains of the psychic link, the kind that grows between couples. She felt her panic rise. There was a stillness about the house. There was a deadness, and emptiness. She hurried up the short path, trying to hold onto the marking and keep her handbag from sliding from her shoulder. She fumbled the key into the lock, opened the door, and called his name.

There was no reply.

As she stepped into the sitting room, Louise saw that the television was off. She saw that the room was empty. There was furniture of course, even a half-drunk cup of tea from this morning. There was a harsh glow from the single ceiling light, but no softer glow from the standard and table lamps.

There was no breath in her. There was no sound, no scent or vibration or feel of another person, nothing but the rattle of rain on the window. She dropped the paperwork onto the sofa and began her search of the cottage.

Richard was gone.

So, she phoned him again and again and again. Voicemail each time. No answer. No one there and there never would be again….

"My God, Louise. I'm so sorry. I don't know what to say. I understand loss, the first woman I…." He almost told her then, the impossible crazed story, of Lizzy. "I've lost people too but nothing like that. And then to be abandoned."

"I don't know where he is. I don't even know if he is alive."

"What makes you think that he might not be?"

"He walked out on me. He suffered…*suffers* from depression. I mean, serious clinical depression, the type that could drive you to suicide."

"When did this happen?"

"Four years ago."

"Louise, even if he is alive, he's made no attempt to contact you."

"You're right, he hasn't, but it isn't that simple. There are feelings involved. I thought I was over it. I'd managed to make myself see that he's cut himself off from me, that I'm dead, to him."

Jack made to hold her hand, an instinctive action. Louise drew away.

"So, I've told you a secret. Now you need to tell me one."

"What do you mean?"

"Who is Lyle?" she continued.

Jack recoiled. "Lyle?"

"He seems to know who you are Jack. He told me that you belong to him."

"When did you see him?"

"Today, he came into our office. He was meeting with my boss, but I think he really came to see me. Who is he, Jack?"

"I'm sorry, Louise…I can't tell you."

"What do you mean? What are you saying?"

Jack wanted to confess all to her, but he couldn't. The truth was too difficult. He took a breath.

"I can't see you anymore, Louise."

"Because of this Lyle? Is that why? I don't understand. Make me understand. Are you in trouble, Jack? I'll stand by you. I'll—"

Jack shook his head. This had been a mistake. Now, both of them were brutally hurt. He took her hands in his. "You can't help me. I'm sorry. You have to go now."

Louise glared at him for a moment then wrenched her hands free, stood, and walked out. She left her umbrella behind.

CHAPTER EIGHT (1916)

A week later Lizzy found a job at Silvertown. It felt strange to Jack, setting off to work on a different omnibus and travelling alone. He grew accustomed to it, but the journeys remained lonely.

Each night they would arrive home, Jack first, Lizzy two hours later. There would be tea, which Jack prepared, and a few hours by the fire, the newspaper and the clack of Lizzy's knitting needles. There were nights when the whistle sounded out the warning of an air raid, Zeppelins mostly, although large German aeroplanes, Gothas by name, had occasionally appeared in the daytime sky like ugly black insects. More terror. More destruction. It was usually a false alarm, but every so often they would hear the drone of a faraway aeroengine, the crump of anti-aircraft guns and the deeper thud of bombs. And each time Jack felt the vibrations humming through The Fabric, the only time he felt any connection with it now. He wanted it that way. It was too intense to feel everything.

Once the evening was done, Jack would go up the stairs to his bed and a little while later, when all was quiet and dark, Lizzy would join him. These were the moments when the bleakness and tragedy turned to joy and light.

Christmas loomed, though it would be a quiet one. Yuletide celebration had been made sombre by the grief of war. The weather turned cold. The days were short. The factory was due to close for one day only. Jack was looking forward to it.

Five days before Christmas, Jack arrived home late. He was cold. The weather was wet. From the moment he stepped inside, he knew that something had happened.

Arnold looked up at him and sneered, then returned his attention to the fire. Lizzy was seated at the table. There was a piece of paper in her hand. She was ashen and didn't move when Jack said her name. He repeated it and slowly, she turned to look at him. Her eyes were rimmed in red. Her cheeks streaked with tears.

"Russell," she said.

"What about him?" Jack asked as gently as he could. "What about Russell?"

"He's been killed."

The room seemed to dim. The air became too thick to breathe. Jack wanted to sit down. He wanted to put his arm about Lizzy's shoulders and comfort her. He wanted to take her upstairs and hold her while she cried. At least she had him now. They could live openly as lovers—

"You have to go," Lizzy said.

"What do you mean?"

"You have to leave. You can't stay here, not now I'm a widow. It wouldn't look right." Her voice was suddenly hard and cold. She had been hard with him before, many times, but this was different. This was final.

"You heard her," Arnold growled from his seat by the fire. "You should get your belongings and—"

"You can stay tonight," Lizzy said. "But you have to go in the morning."

He wanted to argue, to plead and beg, but he knew it would be no use.

Jack spent the night alone. He waited, for Lizzy's resolve to break, for her grief to overcome her coldness and for her need for comfort to win through. The door remained shut tight and all he heard was her soft weeping, far away in the dark. He felt her grief as a faint thrum through The Fabric. Ebbing and flowing, waxing and waning as she collapsed into exhausted sleep, only to wake again an hour later, then cry herself once more into unconsciousness.

Jack felt a grief of his own, not for the man she loved, because he was a stranger Jack had never met. No, the grief was for himself. The loss of this woman was another darkness he would have to learn to understand and survive. His strength was gone, his will dissolved. Tomorrow night he would go to the public house he often visited with Sam and Bernie, and he would drink until no shred of memory remained.

In the morning, he found a battered-looking suitcase on the landing. Jack picked it up, took it into his bedroom and opened its lid. There was a note inside, which Jack unfolded and read. Lizzy's handwriting was neat and small.

> *My Dearest Jack. I am sorry to throw you out. I cannot have a man staying here when I am a respectable widow. It isn't right. But I will always treasure you in my heart. I nearly fell in love with you and that would have been terrible because we could never have got married. Perhaps we will one day. But it can't be yet. I think Russell was killed because I have sinned with you. I think it is God showing me that it was wrong and that I have to be punished. Giving you up is the worst punishment I could ever have. This is the address of an old couple I know who are looking for a lodger. You should go and see them. You can have this suitcase for your things. All my heart, Lizzy.*

One day. The thought was a sliver of light, a tiny, vain hope. One day when the war was ended and memories of Russell cleaned away.

"You've got to understand. It isn't right for a woman on her own to have a gentleman staying at her house," Arnold said when Jack finally went downstairs. There was an uncharacteristic hint of sympathy in his voice.

"Why not?" Jack asked.

Arnold shook his head, scornful again. "You really are a queer one." He became serious. "Don't think I don't know what's been going on. I only didn't write and tell Russell because Lizzy begged me not to. He would have murdered the both of you if he'd come home on leave."

Jack left the house, on his way to work, suitcase in hand. He didn't look back.

The new lodgings were pleasant enough, plain, a little dusty and grimy, perhaps, but better than the streets. The couple who owned the house, Edward and Alice, were a cheerful pair. Jack was comfortable there.

Comfortable, but lonely.

He took to visiting a nearby pub in the evenings, a noisy, rough-edged place called *The King's Head*. There were often fights, although Jack could never work out what they were about. An insult perhaps, a chance remark, spilled beer. Soldiers frequented the place and often ended up battling each other. One regiment apparently better than the other and to prove it, a punch would be thrown.

Despite the roughness of the place, Jack found friendship there. A group of older men who played cards at a beer-stained table had welcomed him into their circle. There were two younger men as well, one missing his left arm, the other with his face distorted by burns and a wound that appeared to have torn away a chunk of his cheek.

Jack drank too much. Alcohol was an anaesthetic which was too effective to resist. It soothed away the tiredness from his days at the factory and it soothed away the pain of missing Lizzy. Often, when last orders had been called, he found himself staggering toward the streets where she lived, and stopped himself, appalled at what he was doing. He had to keep away. He had to wait until enough time passed for them to marry.

Hope, a ridiculous, flickering little flame, but a flame, nonetheless.

A Friday, one of the first in this new year of 1917. He would work tomorrow morning then the time was his own until Monday. Perhaps he would go to a dance on Saturday night. He had never been to one, but it was considered great fun and, no doubt, people would teach him the techniques required.

The day was long and he was relieved when the whistle finally blew to mark its end. He changed out of his overalls quickly, eager to get home, then out to enjoy the dubious delights of a Friday night at *The Kings Head*. He joined the rush to the factory gates. It was early evening, January-dark. There was a smell of snow in the air.

He wasn't sure what had happened at first. He felt it as a sudden, violent disturbance in The Fabric. It froze him in place, barely aware of the crowds of workers streaming past and around him. The sensation faded, a tremor that shuddered through him, then dissolved. Jack shook his head to clear it and re-joined the exodus.

The sound came a few moments later. It was a vast, dull thud. It was the stamp of a god's foot on the earth. Many of the people around Jack stopped and looked upward. It had become instinctive, any detonation was associated with the sky, Zeppelins, aeroplanes, bombs. The sky was blank, an indigo canvas washed out by the lights from the city below.

No, not quite a blank. A glow unfurled against the eastern sky. It shifted and shimmered and Jack knew that it was an immense fire. As the glow brightened and intensified, so did the dread that was spreading through him like thick black oil.

Jack ran toward the glow.

He knew where it was and what it was. He had seen it, briefly, a vivid splinter of recognition, hurled at him through The Fabric then smothered quickly by the red-darkness of the chaos which carried it.

Silvertown.

He ran until he was exhausted, then he walked, street after street, heading east. He was unfamiliar with this part of the town. Limehouse, it was called, a place of endless terrace dwellings, dense darkness pooled between the streetlamps, a tram trundling by, the muddy stink of the Thames, and something else. Smoke.

He pushed himself away from the wall and resumed his walk. The air was heavy with smoke now. There were people on the streets, many heading in the same direction as he. No one seemed to know what had happened. Jack was startled by a bell, a motor fire engine. Police appeared, shouting, blowing their whistles and trying to prevent people from getting any closer.

He slipped easily through the cordon and walked on. It rained. It was cold and he was worn out, but that didn't matter. He had to see what had happened. The need compelled him and would not let him go. He became part of a crowd, a wave of humanity drawn by the shifting pillar of flame and smoke that towered over the rooftops and coloured the clouds.

Another turn, Boxley Street, which took him in the direction of the fire. The houses here were damaged, their windows broken, tiles torn from their roofs. Jack saw other debris, scattered in the road. It looked like piles of tangled metal work, not part of the houses but alien fragments, hurled here by the force of the blast.

Further on the smoke became gritted with dust. The damage was much worse, roofs gone, a house on fire. People stood around as if helpless. Everyone seemed shocked. They stared blankly, eyes featureless vacancies. A child cried. Above it, Jack heard the harsh rustle of flames, the crash of falling masonry. The air was thickened by the heat of the fires.

Someone was screaming. Jack saw that it was a man, who struggled in the grip of several others. He fought and swore and strained toward the burning, eviscerated ruins of a house. "Phyllis!" he howled, "Please…somebody…Phyllis!"

Jack stopped and found himself staring at the burning wreck. Flame licked at the collapsed roof. Black and noxious smoke uncoiled from its wounds. People milled about him. They coughed. Their faces and clothes were smoke-smudged. The dark streaks, combined with the restless reflection of the dancing flames endowed them with the primitive. Some simply stood and stared, eyes as wide and vacant as the blown-out windows of their own homes. Others, like the struggling man sobbed in an agony of grief.

"Nuffink you can do for her, Will," said one of the struggling man's captors. "C'mon old mate, you're going to get yerself burned."

"I can't leave 'er," Will screamed back at him. "I can't...."

Jack moved his attention to the man's face and to the pain that was etched into it by the shifting cloudscapes of light and dark. He knew that pain. He knew loss and the grinding, twisting knife that it wound into the gut.

He ran into the house.

Jack went through the remains of a doorway and was immediately on his hands and knees. One side of the house had collapsed to form a tunnel. He forced himself into the smoke-laden darkness. The stink of it slid into his nostrils. Waves of heat scoured his face, scorched his hair, and pressed hot grit into his eyes. The roof of the tunnel groaned and snapped, a constantly shifting and settling weight that bore down on him and brought the panic of claustrophobia. He could see nothing. He could only feel the rough and jagged walls against which he slid, first on his hands and knees, then on his belly.

The smoke and heat intensified. The black was punctured by orange beams of light, forced through the tiny gaps in the tunnel walls by the flames. Jack tried to hold his breath, squinting against the heat and smoke as he burrowed further and further into the darkness. His heartbeat pounded through his head. His chest felt as if it too was on fire. He fought the need for a few seconds longer then collapsed onto his belly and dragged in a mouthful of foul, scorching air.

A sound.

Ahead.

Jack held his breath once more and tried to separate the noise from the crackle of flames and terrifying shuffles of the rubble and timber through which he crawled. Again. It sounded as if someone was whimpering. He remembered Ellen, Lizzy's daughter, crying in that alleyway as the Zeppelin growled overhead and its bombs whistled earthward.

"It's all right," Jack shouted and was immediately convulsed by a bout of coughing. "It's all right, I'm coming."

Jack pressed on. Something rumbled and he heard the snap of wood. He froze, waited, surprised by the feeling of resignation that imminent destruction brought with it. The noises faded. The house seemed to settle. Jack moved again, crawled through flame-punctured darkness for a few more seconds, then all-but fell into a larger chamber. He dragged himself onto his knees and relished the sense of space around him. It was like a dark, smoke-filled womb. There was light, shifting, hot and orange. Flame glowed through the latticework of broken timber and rubble from which he had emerged. The light revealed a wall, to which clung scraps of plaster and wallpaper. There was a fireplace and astonishingly the coals still glowed in its grate. A broken mirror was spread over the hearth. There was an armchair, dust-greyed, on its side. Lying beside it, huddled into a foetal curl, was a woman.

"Madam," Jack said. "Phyllis. We have to get out."

The women curled herself more tightly and made a mewling sound. Jack wondered if the shock of the explosion and being trapped in here had affected her mind. He reached out, slowly and gently, and touched her shoulder. She cried out and shrank away.

"Phyllis?"

She twisted her head round and looked up at him. The restless orange light revealed a delicate, heart-shaped face, made gaunt by the plays of shadow and light that swept over its landscapes. Her eyes were wide. She was filthy, her hair half-unpinned, dust thickened and wild. The other half was remarkably neat and pinned into the remnants of a bun.

"We have to go, now. The house is burning," Jack said. "And it may fall down onto us if we wait much longer."

"I...I can't, not down there."

She waved toward the entrance of the tunnel through which Jack had just emerged.

"There's no other way out. You go in front of me. I'll be right behind you. I'll look after you."

Something fell, a loud crash that drummed at the floor and sent a dense cloud of smoke and dust into the tiny space. The woman sobbed and grabbed at Jack. She wept into his shoulder, clawing at his filthy clothes. Begging him to save her.

"All right," Jack said gently. "Are you ready? Will is waiting for you outside. You want to see him again, don't you? He's crying because he thinks you've been killed."

"Will…?"

A moment, then she crawled over to the opening, looked back, then slid inside. Jack followed immediately and again all was dark.

"I'm right behind you," he said, over and over again. The sound of her breath and her frequent bouts of hacking coughs drifted back to him. He urged her on. She was struggling, near to panic. He felt the house weakening. He felt a change in the smoke-clogged air. The heat came in waves. Smoke was in every breath now.

Light, ahead, the doorway.

"Go on, nearly there, Phyllis."

Her reply was a determined yes. She crawled faster.

Closer, and the light became uncertain, cast by people with lanterns and torches, vehicles perhaps, and other fires. Then he heard shouts, urging Phyllis on. She was silhouetted in the light. There were hands, more calls of encouragement, then she slid away from him, dragged out by the people in the street. Jack pushed himself forward. He stretched a hand out of the tunnel mouth and into the doorway.

Felt the cold air.

The tunnel collapsed. A weight slammed onto his back with unspeakable violence. There was a white flash of agony that exploded through his mind and body. It crushed him against the floor and held him there. The weight of it seemed to force him deeper and deeper into the earth. He felt part of him break, felt his flesh torn open, the structures come apart. His head was held in place, his neck twisted so that his right cheek was pressed against the remains of the floor. He couldn't breathe, he couldn't move. More joints and bones snapped, each one with a flare of explosive pain. He could not survive this. He closed his eyes and bit down on the screaming need to move, to simply lift himself up. He tried to lose himself in the darkness, but the pain tore the darkness open.

He felt the barriers break down. He felt panic and madness swirl in to fill the spaces in his consciousness. He could move no part of himself. He was wreckage. He was ruin.

There were sounds, scrabbling and scraping noises. There were shouts that grew steadily louder. He was sure he saw light. He closed his eyes and waited. His neck, he realized, was broken. He wondered why he was still alive.

Light again, cold air.

The weight shifted then some of it was gone. He felt it rise from off his head and from across his upper back. He felt hands on him, heard people talking as he was dragged clear, but could not respond.

"'E's still alive!" someone shouted. "By Christ, how can he still be alive?" Light was shone in his eyes. Someone was trying to talk to him.

"It's all right friend. We'll have someone 'ere to 'elp in no time."

"'E needs a priest not a doctor." A woman's voice this time.

Jack lay on his belly, cheek against the pavement, which was wet and icy. He felt movement within his body. He felt sharp cracks of pain. He felt a little strength return to his neck and was able suddenly to lift his head a few inches from the pavement. He moved the fingers of his right hand. There was a jolt as something else snapped into place. He felt his skin ripple, waves of movement that crawled over him.

His body was repairing itself.

He rolled onto his back and saw that his right thigh was sliced open. There was no blood. And his flesh was not flesh at all....

He sat up. A woman screamed in shock. A man swore. He sensed people back away from him. He had to get to his feet and disappear into the confusion. He could not let them see this. He felt another shock in his leg. He fell back, exhausted by the brutal processes taking place within his body. Every so often he convulsed, twisted, and wrenched, uncontrollably, from side-to-side. Spittle flew from his mouth. Then, abruptly, he was frozen into place, his back lifted from the ground as great arcs of white-hot agony swept through him.

This was worse than death.

Time passed. It was a meaningless confusion of pain and weakness, of darkness broken by the smoke-fogged flicker of flame. Of voices and running feet, of shouted orders, calls for help, curses, and the high-pitched keening of the grief-stricken.

The pain eased. His breathing steadied.

Jack struggled to his knees. He saw a ring of people, shadowy figures silhouetted by the glow of fires. They had been watching him, transfixed by his distress and by the impossible changes that were taking place before their eyes. Slowly, carefully, he got to his feet. They moved back from him, as if driven away by some instinct that warned them that there was danger in the impossible.

Jack's body ached and he was exhausted, but he needed to find Lizzy. That was all that mattered. Lizzy.

Jack walked on and now everything was ruin. Houses torn open as if by the jaws of some monstrous beast. Police constables blew whistles and shouted at everyone to stay back. Another fire engine weaved its way carefully through the rubble and the knots of people. Its crew clung to the sides of the vehicle, their elaborate brass helmets glinting with reflected flame.

Jack slipped through, hidden by the confusion and the smoke. He reached the end of the street and saw Hell.

Fire painted the night orange, smoke boiled upward and rolled across the road. It stung Jack's eyes and prised its way down his throat. The TNT plant was now a vast open space, edged by the remains of adjacent warehouses and factory buildings. Giant conflagrations reared out of the wreckage. The road was piled with debris. Figures were gathered in ragged bunches. Some clutched blankets to themselves. Their clothes were torn and their faces blackened with soot. Jack moved among them, avoiding the constables who helped the walking wounded away from the fires.

"Lizzy?" Jack asked everyone he met. "Have you seen Lizzy?"

The question was cruel and fruitless. Most of the people he spoke to simply stared at him, uncomprehending.

Morning dawned, grey and cold. Soldiers had arrived and were now strung out across the devastated landscape, searching inch-by-inch for the survivors and the dead. Others were setting up roadblocks or acted as stretcher bearers. Seeing them, fogged by the smoke, greyed-out by the grim snow-laden air, Jack imagined that this was what the war must look like, the war these men were bound for, eventually.

Jack had joined a party who scrabbled desperately through the wreckage. They found nothing but tragedy; the remains of the dead, torn apart by the incalculable force of the blast. He had squeezed himself, more than once, into the tiny caves formed out of fallen walls and roofs. He had burnt and torn his clothes, and his flesh, but it healed. It always healed. He found no one alive, and precious little of those who were not.

As the morning lit up, the extent of the disaster became clear and what it revealed was terrible. The explosion had been titanic and had demolished not only the TNT plant, but all the nearby buildings and houses crowded in its shadow. Fires still raged. Twisted, scorched metal that had once been girders, pipes, and machinery was contorted into silent cries of agony. Any surviving walls, which reared above the sullen volunteers, were broken and jagged edged. Some leaned precariously. Every so often there was a shouted warning from somewhere in the fog of smoke and dust, followed by the rumble and clatter of falling masonry.

Panic drove Jack on. He wanted to know. He needed a sign. A scrap of Lizzy's clothing, anything.

He sat down, his back against a small section of wall that had, somehow, survived the blast. Its shockwaves still resonated through his nervous system. He couldn't hear Lizzy, though. His sensitivity was dulled. Her voice may have been there, but he couldn't find it. He stared across the newly carved wasteland and tried to find her. There was one hope, of course, the hope she had survived or, better still, that she had not been here, but on her way home from work when the place exploded. He had done all he could here, he needed to find out whether Lizzy was alive or dead.

The curtains were closed, a sign of mourning, or did it simply mean that Arnold had not yet woken up? Jack held onto that grain of hope as he rapped on the door. He felt his strength fail and rested his forehead on the rough, cracked paint.

Footsteps, then the door opened. He straightened and saw Arnold. The man was even paler and thinner than when he had last seen him.

"What do you want?" Arnold snapped and immediately dissolved into a convulsive, hacking cough. He held a blanket about himself.

"Is Lizzy here?"

"Why are you asking? You think she wants to see you?"

"Is she here?" Jack felt his anger rise. He wanted to grab Arnold and shake the man until he fell apart.

"Bugger off." Arnold made to shut the door.

Jack stopped him. "Answer me and I'll go away, even if she is here. I'll walk off and never come back. I just need to know."

"No," he said. "No, she didn't come home. I heard that a Zeppelin dropped a bomb on the TNT factory. She was at work...." His voice broke and he began to cry.

"Are you sure she didn't come back late when you were asleep? You're sure she's not in the bedroom?"

"I've been awake all night." Angry now.

"All right. You have to look after her daughter. I know how to find out for certain if Lizzy's alive. I'll come back when I know. I promise."

For a moment, Arnold looked stricken and Jack was sure he was about to reach out to grab his arm. But he grabbed the door instead and slammed it shut. Wearily, Jack turned away and set off down the street. He was cold and worn out, but there could be no rest until he knew the truth.

Down Street Underground Station.

Jack had not returned to this place since he had come to *be*.

The tunnel held a sense of home that took him by surprise. The sensation was intense enough to make him weep. He had never wept before, even when Lizzy asked him to leave. It was a satisfying sensation, a release, like rage and laughter.

There were few travellers today. There was an odd stillness everywhere, as if the vibrations from the explosion had spread outward to engulf the entire city.

Jack waited until a train entered, then left, the station. As it rattled and drummed out of sight, he clambered down over the platform edge. There was, he knew, little time so he needed to hurry. He moved carefully, avoiding the metal rails. He suspected that an electric shock would not kill him, that nothing short of complete disintegration in an explosion could do that, but the pain would be immense and it would cause him to lose precious moments while he healed.

Time was everything now.

He stumbled into the dark, which overwhelmed him for a moment, then slowly faded to grey, illuminated dimly by a web of blue-white threads that shimmered and crawled over the dank wall ahead of him. The light flared brighter with each step Jack took toward it, then as if it was agitated by his presence, crackled, hissed, and leaked white fire, fluid-like, onto the track below.

He reached out to touch the wall. The slimed, damp brickwork thrummed and grew warm. He felt the first contact with the light and murmured like a child. He pressed himself against the curved wall and laid his cheek against the liquid glow. It seeped into him, a series of electric shocks that shivered over his skin like a thousand needles. The shocks became heat as he felt the light flow through him.

His head was a sudden maelstrom of thought and images, sounds, smell, touch. Everything was wrenched from his memory, vivid and alive, the crackle of flame, the deep thud of a bomb, the drone of a Zeppelin's engines. He smelled sweat and perfume and the oily stench of the factory. He was dizzied by Lizzy's scent and, for a moment, she was in his arms, her skin smooth and soft and sweet tasting. It became intense, it became painful, a riot now, a clamour of voices and noise, a stink of melded odour, the sweet mingled with the rotten. His skin burned from a thousand touches, contacts with fellow humans, Lizzy's fingertips and lips, her gentle kisses were now magnified so that they scraped at his skin and danced fire on his nerve endings. And he saw every detail, every line and component of reality, every molecule and atom, slotted into its place within the flash and shimmer of The Fabric.

The womb withdrew and flowed away from him. It seeped back into the walls and was replaced by darkness.

There was a train coming, three minutes away. The air, the track and walls, The Fabric, all shook and hummed with its approach. There was no urgency. Jack was already walking back toward the platform. The magnetic field that surrounded the electrified tracks shimmered about him, green lines that danced like an aurora and stung him where they brushed over his body. He smelled sweat, tobacco, urine, and the bloody menstrual perfume of the people gathered in the station.

He hauled himself up onto the platform just as the light from the oncoming train slid out of the tunnel. He landed on his belly among the shoes and boots that shuffled back from him as if he was some unpleasant or even dangerous animal. He smelled eruptions of scent from the people round him. Each one denoted shock, repulsion, or sympathy. He heard their combined breath, he heard the rustle of their clothing, the beat of their hearts. Their voices were a babel of the deep and the shrill and stirred The Fabric until it was almost unbearable.

It *was* unbearable.

Jack struggled to his feet, unaided, and hurried through the crowd of waiting passengers which opened to let him pass. Out and onto the stairs, making for the exit where the city waited to pound him into submission with its noise and stink and swirl.

Beneath all this chaos was a song that was discordant to the point of madness. It was the sound of The Fabric, the hum and thrum of the universe, the thoughts and cries and confusion of the living and the echoed voices of the dead that manifested themselves as electronic waves and auras. It was the trembling of atoms and the careering and colliding of particles and waves. It was through this, the shimmering raging ocean from which reality was formed, that Jack needed to travel to find what he needed.

In and around Silvertown, the air was still heavy with smoke. A few fires still burned. Firemen, constables, soldiers, and other volunteers still scrabbled in the rubble.

Jack walked toward them, feeling every stone, every speck of dust under his feet. He walked to the centre, ignored by those determined to find what may be left of the unfound. He dropped to his knees and spread his palm over the rubble. It hurt. As did the voices and the tremors and relentless, urgent drum of energies in the air about the site. He didn't close his eyes but drank in everything. His mind spun and it was painful, but he drank it all.

And then he found her.

The thinnest thread of fear and pain and then peace, the slightest tremor he knew to be her. He reached out and there was a touch, brief and tiny. It was Lizzy. There, and then dissolving slowly into the singing thrum of the universe.

CHAPTER NINE (2016)

Two more mornings. These lonely. These bleak. No contact from Louise. No phone call, no email, no text or knock on the door of his flat. He could make some grand Hollywood gesture and rush to her door in the middle of a stormy night, but he understood that the door would not be opened.

He dragged himself from his bed and hauled himself to work. The air was again cold, grey, and dank. The farmhouse building site seemed like an outpost in some arctic wilderness.

There was the usual banter as the workers sat around for their early morning tea. Then it was off the far-flung corners of the house to get on with the job. Jack was back chopping plaster from the walls of yet another of the house's innumerable bedrooms.

It was hard to think this morning. He needed to pull himself together. Each beat of the hammer brought a dull pain. A throb in his temples. A beat synchronised with the rhythm of his heart.

It grew stronger. Until it was no longer a simple headache, but….

No, not now. Not here.

A pain was coming. He felt an insect-like crawl of static electricity over his skin, a tug at his mind then silence, absolute and impenetrable. The air seemed to scratch at him. There was a swirl of something in The Fabric and for the first time in many years, he was aware of it and of a disturbance within its weft and weave. He had been indifferent to The Fabric for a long time. It had been no loss. It was a distraction and sometimes overwhelming. He wondered if this wilful carelessness, the deliberate lack of maintenance of his heightened senses meant that he had abandoned all that he was intended to be....

The dust.

Jack stared at the motes, caught in the slanted sunbeams from the window at the end of the bedroom in which he was working. They didn't move, didn't dance or spiral through the light. Instead, they were frozen in place.

He realised then that there were no longer any voices or laughter. There was silence where there should have been the buzz and metallic howl of power tools. The cement mixer had been struck dumb.

Then from the bowels of the silence came a different sound, a deep thrum, like a heartbeat.

The pain came.

It was a thousand nails driven into his skull. It was hundreds of voices. They were here. They had come for him. This was it, the end. The finish.

Lie down, they said. Lie down and let us take you. Let us prise you open and scoop out the memories, then dissolve you and relieve you of a hundred years of pain and emotion and life.

He dropped slowly to his knees. The pain began to coalesce into a deep, throbbing pressure, something inside rather than an assault from without, something trying to burst out of him. It would be over soon. It would be done. All he had to do was lie down and wait.

He felt their approach, the increase in the sting of static, the intensification of the headache, the pressure now all but unbearable. He may have screamed, but he could hear nothing, not even his own voice.

No.

He had to fight.

He wanted to live.

He wanted Louise.

Fists clenched and eyes tightly shut against the agony, Jack forced himself back up onto his feet. He clawed for breath, struggling to drag in air that had become thick and syrup-like. He turned, his movements jerky. He took a series of small, awkward little steps. Each one drilled pain into his skull.

He faced the stairs now and saw the first of them coming up toward him. It was like the one he had encountered in the blues club. A human-shaped window into a star-dusted sky, where there should have been flesh and blood.

Jack, Jack, please come back.

The ridiculous rhyme was in his head, his own interpretation of what the thing was saying.

He shuffled to the top of the stairs.

"No," he said.

Please. It is time.

Jack felt it pluck at him. He felt it tug at his thoughts, and the pain was excruciating.

"No," he said again and set off down the stairs, toward it. His limbs were stiff, debilitated by the pounding hammers that smashed against the inside of his skull. The being blocked his path. Jack held out his hands to push it out of the way.

Nothing. No substance but the fierce jolt of an electric shock that erupted inside his head and blurred his vision. There was a moment of blackness and utter cold. Then he was half-running, half-falling down the last steps and into the gutted, skeleton of the hallway and lounge. He grabbed at a wooden upright to stop himself collapsing.

And saw the brickies, carpenters, and Jerry the plumber.

They stood in various frozen poses. A hammer raised, a saw caught in mid-slice, sawdust spouting from the wound like blood. Jerry's drill bit was halfway into a wall, misted by a cloud of displaced brick dust. Jack lurched toward the door. He was careful not to touch the frozen figures. Their proximity was a field of static that burned him.

His head felt as if it would crack from the pressure. He could barely see now. Something like a swarm of angry black bees boiled into the periphery of his vision.

More of the blank figures stepped out of the shadows in the corners of the room, each one identical to the others. They whispered kindnesses. They urged him to give up, sleep, and be done with it. Each syllable they uttered was a beat of pain. Jack turned himself around until he faced the front door. It was open. He glimpsed rain. Each drop was a frozen, glinting jewel. Freedom.

He tried to take a deep steadying breath, but the air was almost too dense to breathe. Desperate now, pummelled by their cajoling and urgent pleas for his surrender, he drove himself toward the door.

The electric shock of contact with the creatures threw him forward. His legs folded under him. His momentum propelled him through the sudden, icy blackness, where there was no air, no weight, and a glimpse of something vast and powerful and relentlessly, mercilessly white.

A word, hissed into his ear. A terrifying word. A promise and a threat.

Then he was outside. The rain fell. There was sound, dampness, movement, and life, the hammer, the saw, the drill. Someone laughed, someone whistled, tunelessly.

Jack struggled to his car and clambered into the driver's seat. He sat, breathless, letting the pain seep from his head, and the electric bee stings of contact with the beings dissolve. He had managed to beat them this time.

He remembered and was suddenly frightened.

There had been a word, at the end of their cajoling, just as he had broken free.

A threat.

Hound.

It had a name.

Lyle.

Jack sat in his car, several miles from the construction site. He was in a layby, which had been cut into the side of the lane as a parking space for those who wanted to walk in the woods which surrounded it. The woods looked at once to be a comforting womb of trees and shadow, and a place of loneliness and fear.

His creators had almost taken him this time. He closed his eyes and felt himself fall toward sleep.

No.

He had to stay awake and alert.

How was that going to work? He was too exhausted to make a decision now.

Air. That was what he needed. He opened the car door then climbed out. The snow had turned to sleet. The cold air snapped him awake. He looked up at the leaden, cloud-swirled sky.

He glanced into the woods. The hound, Lyle, was coming. He was out there in the shadowed corridors between the trees. He was hurtling along the road, eating the miles as he bore down on his quarry. There was no escape. He had seen it for himself all those years ago when Lyle had finally caught up with Josephine Anderson.

There was no time.

He slid back into the car and drew his notebook from the glove compartment. He was going to write a letter to Louise and explain who and what he was. Whether or not she believed this story was immaterial. At least he would have shown her the courtesy of telling the truth.

Coming. The hound was coming.

He wrote, striving to ignore the feeling. Imagination, reality, what did it matter?

Closer.

He looked up. The sleet was heavy now. It blurred the road ahead and darkened the woods even further. He caught a tremor in The Fabric. Worn and faded as his connection was, it was enough. He looked in the mirror. A figure strode along the road toward him. The wind blew his coat into wings. His face, though obscured by his old-fashioned fedora, was instantly recognizable.

Lyle.

The figure blurred as if smudged by the stroke of a charcoal pencil. Jack threw the notebook aside and yanked the ignition key. The engine coughed to life. He fumbled the gears, crashed them. The car lurched forward.

Don't stall… please don't stall.

Something slammed into the back of the vehicle, knocking it sideways. The tires spun on the slushy tarmac, then gripped and he was away. Another glance in the mirror. Lyle was still there, watching then walking again. Coming for him. Inexorable. Relentless.

This flight out onto the main road and back toward the town was pointless, a waste of energy. There was no escape.

"You'll have to run a bit faster than that Lyle," he murmured as he glanced in the mirror. The road behind was empty again.

For now.

CHAPTER TEN (1918)

Jack jumped from the back of the battered motor lorry and was immediately disorientated by the noise and confusion around him. There were soldiers everywhere. There was a babble of voices, shouted orders, curses, and cries of fear, pain, and anguish.

There was panic.

The chaos was punctuated by the irregular pulse of explosions, close enough to terrify, but not close enough to kill or maim.

A drifting pall of smoke obscured the heaving mass of men and equipment into frantic grey shadow. The smoke drew water from Jack's eyes, prised its way into his throat and lungs and made him cough. It was as if he had jumped from the cramped, diesel-stinking confines of the army lorry into a smoke-fogged version of Hell.

"Stretcher bearers! For God's sake, we have wounded out there!" It was an officer, unseen but making himself heard. He sounded frantic, on the verge of hysteria. The men in khaki who had travelled here in the lorry now danced purposefully around Jack and seemed to know exactly what to do. Jack was aware that he *should* too. God knew he had been trained for it, but, as he stood there, all of it seemed to slip from his grasp like sand through his fingers.

Slowly, he began to understand what was happening. The lorries were parked on a road that bordered the remains of a war-ruined French village. He glimpsed the broken spire of a church, a huge chunk bitten from the smooth leaded flanks as if by some gigantic beast.

Soldiers surged onto the road and between the lorries as they made for the village. Their filthy mud-spattered faces were blank, their eyes haunted. Some were wounded, blood mingled with the other filth daubed over their flesh and tattered uniforms.

They came in from a field that rolled away into the distance on the other side of the lane. There was a wood off to the left, its trees denuded and shattered. Another stand of injured trees guarded the field far to the right. The field curved up toward a distant, low hill.

The smoke issued from countless shell holes torn into the soil by a barrage that slammed down onto the fleeing Tommies. The nearest of the craters was perhaps a hundred yards from where Jack stood. It was recent and glowed and belched like the mouth of a furnace. There were many men were still out there, struggling through the mire toward the scant safety of the ruins.

Jack looked round. His new comrades, perhaps twenty of them, were either clambering into the backs of the motor lorries or standing behind them expectantly. All wore Red Cross arm bands, some, like his own, bright white and stark red. Others were faded, dirty, and tattered. He knew none of the men he had been thrown in with and sensed that it was the case with most of the others. A few hours ago, he had been a medical orderly in an advanced dressing station.

Stretchers were dragged out of the lorry. He moved closer, waiting his turn to help.

Jack saw his chance and grabbed the two carrying poles of a stretcher as it was shoved out of the lorry. Another man moved in to help him. He was tall and dignified, despite his well-worn, grubby tunic and puttees. He sported a neat moustache and looked as if he should have been an officer rather than a private. He nodded to Jack. "After you, old chap," he shouted. "I'll take the hindquarters." He grinned broadly. His accent heightened the feeling that this man was wearing the wrong uniform.

A sergeant appeared. His armband was in place and there was a white flag in his hand. "Follow me," he yelled in a voice that sounded as if he had swallowed a handful of gravel.

Keeping the sergeant in view, Jack set off at a jog, weaving through the oncoming waves of retreating soldiery. He and his new companion were flanked on either side by more stretcher bearers, all walking in a hunched, half-bent-over stance, as if a semi-bow would protect fragile flesh from bullets and shells. It was instinct, Jack supposed.

The ground was heavy-going. Duck boards had been placed in the mire and while they did provide a solid surface for walking, they were so slick with mud it was like walking on ice. The spring of 1918 had been a wet one so far.

It had also been disastrous for the British and French armies dug-in across Belgium and France. The Germans had launched a shockingly energetic offensive in March. The little that had been gained by the Allies in the previous four years was quickly lost. Within days, the British and French were in full retreat. The dressing station, to which Jack had been posted for much of his time here, had been moved back from the ever-changing battle front four times since the offensive began, with all the chaos and horror that entailed.

That morning, the sound of shelling had once more broken the still damp air. It was too far away to be an immediate danger, but it meant that the German offensive had reached their sector. The station was thrown into a fury of activity as they prepared for yet another move even further to the rear. The call had gone up for men to act as stretcher bearers. Without a second thought, Jack had run outside and clambered into the back of one of the waiting motor lorries.

Now this, Jack and the other volunteers, dumped in a nameless village, somewhere near Villers-Bretonneux, stumbling over slippery duck boards and hauling himself through the crater-pocked mud of the field, looking for anyone still alive amongst those who had fallen here.

Jack was startled by a bright flash and a sudden, deafening blast. He stumbled right and almost dropped the stretcher. He was spattered with mud, but, thankfully, nothing worse. He heard a snatch of laughter from behind. *Laughter, out here?* Another shell battered the earth and tore the air, then another. Memories of the Zeppelin raids in London broke surface.

Memories of Lizzy.

Jack knew that no one bullet, or shard of shrapnel would be fatal to him, but it would be agony and would cause the brutal process of healing to debilitate him for many minutes, if not hours. An explosion, however, would obliterate him. There would be no return from that.

He had joined The Royal Medical Corps three months after he finally walked away from the ruins of the Silvertown factory. The aftershocks of this unimaginable catastrophe continued to resound through The Fabric. Smoke and dust still misted the air. Fires still burned and people wandered aimlessly, like the undead, through the devastation. Their clothes were dirty and often torn, their faces smudged, eyes blank. Firemen and soldiers rested in the doorways of the less damaged houses. Police constables stood around, too weary to exert authority.

Jack walked for hours until the devastation was far behind him and found himself in the centre of the city. He walked across Trafalgar Square, heedless of the others who strolled or begged there. He was oblivious to his own filthy, battered condition. People shied from him, but he was used to that now.

The Fabric was alive with the aftermath of the disaster. He wanted it gone, but there was no shelter from the storm of emotion and violence it burned into his consciousness.

The city's buildings and roads were filthy. He saw every speck of dust, every particle of soot. He saw the swirl of bacteria that clouded the breath of anyone close to him. The air through which he walked was a soup of life and debris. It would fade, but not yet. He had to endure it. He had no choice.

At some point, he picked up a newspaper that lay discarded on a table in a cafe where he sought warmth and food. There was a short article about the courage of the Royal Army Medical Corps out at The Front. He knew, immediately, what he must do.

He could not save Lizzy.

Perhaps he could save others.

The logic was simple, the message so clear it was almost childlike. But it was true. Saving the woman from the burning house and then helping to search for the dead and injured at Silvertown had given the horror some meaning. It had done little to ease the pain of loss, but it had given him an energy he had not experienced before.

Perhaps by helping others, he could pay for Lizzy's death. It was not his fault that she had died and yet it felt as if it was.

Most of the humanity sprawled and broken in the muddy earth was obviously dead. Their bodies had been ripped open by shrapnel, blast, or bullets. Flesh was torn, vital organs exposed and dumped into the mud. Eyes were open in wide, sightless, yet accusing stares that seemed to follow Jack as he stumbled on through the smoke-fogged hell looking for any sign of life.

Jack's connection with The Fabric, though faded, was still intense enough for him to feel the last moments of these men. He strove to push it to the back of his awareness. He had quickly grown accustomed to the clamour of fear and pain unleashed by war, but this was different. This was immediate, raw, and starkly vivid. This was agony and terror and blood. At times it gathered itself into a maelstrom of noise and horror from which Jack could only cower until it dissolved once more into a dull pulse of darkness and light.

Someone moved.

Jack struggled over to the man and dropped the stretcher. The wounded soldier's face was grey and taut. He opened his mouth to speak but the only sound that emerged was a long, drawn-out groan. His left leg was a bloody, shattered wreck from the knee down. His right was startlingly intact. The contrast between them was strangely disturbing.

Jack's fellow stretcher bearer crouched and said, "Come on, old fellow, let's get you home." Then he looked up. "You grab his arms…uh, what's your name?"

"Jack."

"Jack. Right. I'm Alfred. You take that end and I'll see about getting his legs onto the stretcher. All right? Good. Ready? One…two…three."

They both lifted. The man was heavy and difficult to move, even though they were doing little more than raising him enough to slide him onto the stretcher. Jack worked his arms under those of the wounded man. Alfred scooped up the soldier's legs, obviously trying to keep the injured limb intact and prevent any of it falling away. The moment they took the strain, the wounded man unleashed a scream that sounded as if it was ripped from the deepest part of his psyche. Jack and Alfred were forced to ignore it. They had no choice. They had to either get him onto the stretcher or leave him here.

"All right, Jack, we've got him. I'll count to three again."

They lifted the stretcher. Jack was startled by how heavy their burden was. He wavered, lurched sideways, then steadied himself. The man cried out again when he was lifted but then lapsed into silence as they set off back toward the village. Jack's shoulders and arms burned from the effort. His hands felt as if they were crushed around the wood of the handle and would never open again. His back ached. His legs were leaden from his struggles through the muddy soil.

"Jack."

The world shrank to the three of them. Everything else, the bodies, the mud, the shouts and cries, the occasional bursts of machine gun fire and heavy beat of mortar shells were pushed back to the periphery of his awareness. The purpose of his life, his entire reason for being at that moment, was to reach the lorries parked on the edge of the village.

"Jack."

Jack knew that he was not human as these others were. At the same time, he had no idea what he was. He was not some man-shaped machine, he was certain of that. Beneath his strange, non-human skin there were organs that allowed him to eat, breathe, and process oxygen. He had bones, muscles. He was fallible and imperfect. He suffered as humans suffered, yet he had no idea what a surgeon would find were he to open his flesh with a scalpel.

"Jack."

Alfred's voice startled him out of his reverie. He looked back over his shoulder. "What?"

"He's gone."

"Gone?"

"Dead."

They lowered the stretcher back to the ground. The wounded soldier lay, motionless, eyes wide, lips parted as if to speak.

"We need to put him down and find a live one," Alfred said. "We're not a burial party."

Jack nodded, shocked, yet also bemused as to why he should be. He was surrounded by death. It stalked him. It fell from the sky. It was spat from machine gun barrels. Yet he was stricken by the sight of this one man. Once more Alfred grabbed the casualty's legs and Jack his arms. This time he was silent as they slid him off the canvas and into the mud. He lay there, seemingly at peace, staring sightlessly at the steadily clearing sky, an unspoken word frozen onto his lips. Jack and Alfred hefted the stretcher back up and set off in search of a *live one*.

After a few minutes they came upon a man sitting with his head in his hands. His helmet was long gone, hurled into the muddle of general detritus that littered the place. Blood ran from between the soldier's fingers to drip into the mud and over his filthy boots. He flopped onto the stretcher gratefully but made no sound. There was a brutal gash open across the left side of his scalp. The yellow-white smoothness of bone could be glimpsed at the bottom of the wound. He was young and looked lost and frightened, as if he had no idea where he was or why.

Jack and Alfred delivered him to a relay party who waited by the lorries to take the casualties to a Regimental Aid Post (RAP). After an hour of brutal slog into, and then out of, the killing grounds, the sergeant appeared and ordered duties to be swapped. The men on the relay set off into the field, while the men they had relieved, took on their former task. The sergeant even made this welcome order sound like a threat.

The RAP had been set up in the village school. Its roof was intact, as were most of its walls. It seemed to Jack, as he and Alfred delivered their first casualty, that every inch of space was taken by a wounded soldier. Some sat, smoked, and chatted, made cheerful despite whatever pain they were in, by the fact that it would certainly get them out of the fighting for a while. Others lay unconscious, or rigid with pain and shock. Some groaned, others wept, still others screamed. The place stank of sweat, excrement, and urine. A blue-grey miasma of tobacco smoke served to soften the edges of the stench but could not obliterate it completely.

When their hour was up, Jack and Alfred were once again sent out into the field. The Germans had finally stopped firing. The going might have been safer, but it was no easier. It was dark and raining by the time they brought in the last casualty of the day. There were, no doubt, others out there, but the sergeant, Merriweather by name but certainly not by nature, gathered up his rag-tag platoon of *passy-fists*, as he had christened them, and told them to eat and get some rest. Exhausted, the stretcher bearer platoon collapsed behind the lorries and drank black tea from battered tin mugs.

"Come on, Jack," Alfred said. He tipped the dregs from his cup then rammed a pipe between his teeth and proceeded to light it. "Some acquaintances of mine have found the perfect pied-a-terre here in this picturesque little hamlet. You're welcome to join us for a small-and-early."

"A small and what?"

Alfred laughed. "My God, man, have you never heard of a small-and-early? It's a party, a few selected guests, some dancing, and everyone home by half-past ten."

"Ah, so you were telling a joke when you said—"

"A joke? Certainly not, we have a string quartet and the loveliest young debs you'd ever want to meet, each one very soft and very, very willing. I hope you packed your dinner jacket. Can't have you letting our side down."

They made their way through the derelict streets. Alfred chuckled to himself then, stopped, turned, and jabbed his pipe at Jack's chest and said, "I like you. You're a breath of fresh air."

Smoke curled from a mobile army kitchen. The wind brought a meaty smell to Jack and reminded him that he was hungry. A few men sat around outside the ruins they had claimed as home, chatting, reading books, playing cards or, in one case, sprawled on what looked like a purloined and rather dusty kitchen chair, playing a mouth organ.

A sound like thunder rumbled in the background. Artillery, Jack realised. He had no idea if it was British or German. It was just part of some far-off battle that was of no concern to the men gathered in this place.

"This one." Alfred said and indicated a doorless entrance to what looked to have been a shop. Its shelves were empty and its plate glass window long reduced to shards of broken glass which salted the general grime and muck of the street and crunched beneath Jack's heel.

Alfred's companions were gathered in a storeroom at the back. There were three of them, camped out in wheel-spoke fashion, feet aimed at the room's centre. A paraffin lamp hung from one of the bare shelves and cast an uncertain glow over the dim interior.

"Hello, Alfie." It was a tall soldier, sitting cross-legged.

"Corporal," Alfred replied, then addressed the whole room. "Gentlemen. I'd like you to meet Jack, the newest member of our little family." Another of those rueful chuckles. "God, this is like bringing one's latest romantic conquest home to meet m'ma."

"Well, Jack, help yourself to the bridal suite." The corporal waved to vacant patch of packed earth. "I'm afraid the locals don't believe in floorboards. I'm George, by the way, but you can call me Corp."

"Pleased to meet you," Jack said as he stepped over a slight-built man who was laying on his side, reading a tatty-looking book.

"Bit long in the tooth, aren't you?" the reader said, without looking up from the yellowed page.

"I suppose I am," Jack answered as he laid his pack down and crouched beside it to unroll his blanket. "Just wanted to help out."

The reader looked up from his book and adopted a faux upper-class accent. "Well, I must say that's jolly decent of you."

A youngster on the far side of the room, who was sitting and smoking a badly rolled cigarette chuckled. "If you want to help, you can take my place on the sanitary gang, for a start."

"Show some respect to your elders and betters, boy, or I'll give you a clip round the ear." The reader closed his book, then held out his hand. He grinned broadly. "Walter, Wally to you. Welcome to paradise. And that uppity little bugger over there is Ezra, Ezzy to his friends, only he don't have none. Bloody stupid name if you ask me."

"I told you that it's from the Bible," Ezzy said. "Ezra was a prophet in the Old Testament."

"Well, maybe you can prophecy when this is going to be over."

"That's enough, Wally. Leave him be." George returned his attention to Jack. "Ezzy is a good lad. He's one of us. We look out for each other."

"We're a merry little band," Wally said. "Well, most of us."

Wally and George chuckled at what was obviously a private joke.

"And not a rifle in sight." Alfred waved toward the others with the stem of his pipe. "Conchies, Quakers, and other assorted dissenters, the lot of us, despised for not wanting to shoot anyone, but everyone's favourite when they're bleeding."

"Ezzy's a Methodist," Wally said. "But he can't help that."

"I am not a Methodist," Ezra said, with the exaggerated, gritted-teeth patience of the butt of a joke worn thin. "My family are Baptists, and pacifists, worst bloody luck. What are you, Grandad?"

"You know the rules," George said wearily. "Why we're here is none of anyone's bloody business, unless we want it to be."

"I don't mind," Jack said as he sat on the hard floor. "I want to save life rather than take it."

"Very noble of you," Wally said.

"But it isn't, really, is it," Ezzy said. "I mean to say, Jim...?"

"Jack."

"Jack right, yeah. We're not really saving lives are we, because some of the lads"—the term seemed incongruous when coming from someone so young—"we save are only going to go back and kill more Germans then get killed themselves."

"We don't know what anyone might do if they live on after being wounded," Jack said.

"Might even turn out to be the bloke who invents a cure for bloody chilblains," Wally said. "I'd buy him a pint, or two, if he did."

The flap opened again and a short, stocky character entered.

"Feeling better, Henry?" Wally said. "Left the best part of you in the latrine, did you?"

"Why does every bloody squad have to have a village idiot?" the man named as Henry grumbled as he sat himself down on his blanket. He looked across at Jack. "Who are you?"

"Jack Smith."

"Don't need a surname. You won't be around long enough for us to be friends."

"You really are a miserable bugger," Wally said to him.

"Wally's right," Alfred said. "You really need to cheer up, old man. Doesn't do to dwell on things."

Henry grunted, struck a match, and lit himself a Woodbine.

"Right Jack, seeing as you're the new…I can't call you boy, can I?" George chuckled to himself. "Anyway, you reckon you want to help, so you can fetch us some grub."

Jack got to his feet. "Yes, of course."

"There's some stew on the go out there," Wally said. "Just follow the smell. God knows what the meat is, but as long as they took off its collar and lead before it went into pot, I don't care. We've got water brewing for some tea when you come back. No milk though. Or sugar."

It was raining and the light was fading fast. Clutching a large tin pot Ezzy had given him, Jack retraced his earlier path to the kitchen. He felt an odd peace. It was a familiar sensation, something that he had experienced now and then since he had arrived in France. It was an ability to grab and hold moments of calm, to fully drink in good times when they came, however brief they might be. He had wondered, at first, how anyone could smile or joke in such a place. Even the wounded, in pain and suffering, would grin around their ever-present cigarettes and pipes and laugh and swap jokes and insults and, on occasion, sing some rowdy song that was never complimentary to those in charge or in praise of the war itself.

Now he understood. When Death dogged your steps and haunted your sleep, each beat of your heart, each breath taken, was precious and to be savoured.

Jack was glad of the welcome he had received from Alfred's squad. It was superficial, he understood that. The morose Henry was right. Friendships were brief out here, made then broken by the vagaries of army life, or by German shells and bullets.

The stew was good. Ezzy brewed tea on a small primus stove in the centre of the tent. He then set about mixing a dixie full of porridge for breakfast.

"All right, try to get a few minutes' sleep," George said as he drained the last of his tea. "Fucking Merriweather is going to have us digging trenches all night, so make the most of it now."

"If he can find us," Ezzy said, a voice in the dark now.

"He'll find us." Wally said.

"Bloody well shut up. I'm trying to sleep," Henry said.

It was difficult to lay comfortably. The ground was hard and damp.

"Here, you can make yourself a pillow with your boots and jacket," Wally said and showed Jack how to lay his boots on their sides and then place his uniform jacket over and between them. It worked. Jack lay down again, on his back, eyes open.

Despite the orders for everyone to sleep, the men talked. Their voices grew lower and Jack let them lull him toward the dark. Most of the conversation was about the current offensive. "Four bloody years of war," Henry grumbled. "And now we're running away."

A boot was thrown. Henry swore. The others laughed.

The next day dawned grey and damp. The collection of stretcher bearers, orderlies and a handful of medical officers were formed up and shuffled into a semblance of a parade just before the sun rose. Then they were sent back to the regimental dressing station for medical orderly duties while they waited for the inevitable German attack.

It didn't come. It began to rain. The day wore on. The rain grew heavier; the field across which the enemy would launch their assault was transformed from mud to quagmire. A brisk breeze blew up to lash the rain toward the German positions.

The tension in the village began to ease. No one in their right mind would try to attack in weather like this. The Germans didn't even send any shells over. Conserving their ammunition perhaps.

George's squad was sent to demolish a tumbledown building on the far edge of the village. The materials were to be used for yet more defences. They worked all morning then, after a lunch of tinned bully beef and bread, sat down for a long break. "Out of sight," George said.

"Out of mind." Cigarettes were lit. Alfred tamped and applied a match to his pipe. The lunch break stretched into the afternoon. Rain beat at the remains of the roof.

Alfred got up and stretched. "I'm fed up with being stuck in here. I'm going for a walk."

"I'll come with you," Jack said. He needed to get out.

The ground was once again muddy. The darkening sky, a ceiling of unbroken clouds. A light rain set in. Jack was glad of it. The soft shower was cleansing. The two men wandered along what had once been a street toward the church Jack had seen on his arrival.

"You married, Jack?" Alfred said.

"No. What about you?"

Alfred smiled around his ever-present pipe and shook his head. "No wife and, at the moment, no sweetheart."

"Are you lonely?"

Alfred stopped walking and regarded Jack carefully. "Are *you*?"

"Yes, I think I am."

"Best not to have any attachments while you're out here. No one to cry over you if you…. You know what I mean." He sighed as if looking for the right words. "I'm intrigued by you, Jack. You're an innocent. I don't mean you're like the religious types we get in the RAMC. No, you're different. Don't take offence, Jack, but it's childlike."

"I take no offence."

Alfred shivered, turned up his collar and drew his tunic jacket about himself. "I did have a wife," he said. "But I lost her."

"I'm sorry. Did she die?"

"No. She is very much alive, old chap. And happy, from what I gather, in the arms of a man who loves her."

"Didn't you love her?"

They reached the church and wandered into the graveyard. Alfred stopped again, this time to fiddle with his pipe and attempt to re-light it.

"I tried to love her," he said. "She deserved that, at least, but…." Alfred was suddenly serious. "I want to tell you something. I don't know why I feel as if I have to tell you, but…I married my wife because, well, I thought it might cure me and make me respectable again."

Jack waited. Alfred suddenly drew his arm over his eyes. He blinked.

"Do you have any idea what I am talking about?"

Jack shook his head. He did understand, however, that this was painful for Alfred.

"I don't love women, you see. I...I love...well, men, as it were." A pause. "Does that disgust you?"

"No. I'm curious."

"Curious?" Alfred laughed, but his mirth was somehow close to incredulity. "*Curious?*"

"Yes. It's my understanding that people are attracted to the opposite sex."

"And you are really not disgusted?"

"Why should I be? It's your choice, surely."

Alfred took an uncertain step back. His face was wrought with emotion. "God...My God, I have been waiting a lifetime for someone to say that." He looked suddenly fragile. "Jack, do...do you feel the same as me?"

Jack frowned, taking a moment to grasp what Alfred had asked. "No," he said and felt a sadness he had not expected. "No, I don't."

"Then count yourself lucky."

Jack was startled by the venom in Alfred's tone.

"Why am I lucky?"

"Do I sound like a private to you? Be honest now, haven't I got an officer's accent?"

"Yes, you have."

"My father is a consultant physician, an important and highly respected pillar of society. So, naturally, when I enlisted, I was given a commission and sent to Sandhurst. Jolly sort of place. Full of unspeakably awful young toffs and screaming RSMs. Thing is, I found out that not all those young toffs were awful. One of them was an extremely beautiful young man. We...we were found out. The young man in question was spirited away to a different camp for his training. He was the innocent you see, seduced by a vile old queer. I...I was thrown to the RSMs like a scrap of meat to a pack of wild dogs. I thought they were going to beat me to death."

"Beat you? Why?"

"Why?" Alfred sounded incredulous. "Because I'm a filthy sodomite, that's why. Do you have any idea…? No, you haven't, have you? It's as if I'm two people, divided down the middle. One part of me the smart officer cadet, the suave man about town, the dutiful son. The other half, seedy and shady, frequenting the lowest of dens of iniquity, nasty little clubs filled with the best and worst of my kind because there is nowhere else for us to go to be with our own." His face was red now, his words hissed through clenched teeth. "I was to be thrown out of the army, but I couldn't face that. My parents would have been devastated. So, I asked for a transfer to this lot. Gathered up with the conchies and Quakers and other assorted odds and ends who didn't want to carry a rifle." He calmed a little then sighed as if emptied of his rage. "Thank whoever calls Himself God that you don't feel the way I do, Jack."

Jack became aware that Alfred's hand was on his shoulder. "I'm sorry, old chap. I'm making a perfect fool of myself. I'll be all right in a minute or two. You can get yourself back if this is all a bit embarrassing for you."

"I'm not embarrassed. You're my friend."

"Am I? What a splendid thought. We've only known each other for a day, but yes, I suppose we are friends. Come on, we'd better get back or we'll be shot for desertion."

It had stopped raining by the time they returned to the barn. The others had resumed the demolition work, albeit with little enthusiasm.

"Where've you two been?" George called out. He shook his head. "You could have at least brought us a rabbit back for the pot."

The next morning dawned clear. The wind had lost its icy edge. Merriweather gathered his twenty-strong passy-fist platoon and was about to give out their day's duties when there was a sound like the tearing of cloth. A moment later the world was picked up and thrown around by a gigantic explosion. The muddy soil of the field beyond the lorries was torn loose and hurled skyward to fall like thick, slimy rain. As the platoon scattered for cover Jack glimpsed smoke billowing from a new crater only fifty yards or so from the road. Another shell broke into the echo of the first blast.

Merriweather ordered them back to the RDS. They ran against the tide of soldiers rushing to man their defensive positions. The platoon picked up as many empty stretchers as they could carry and dumped them and themselves outside the burnt out remains of a café. There they would wait out the assault.

The shelling grew in intensity. Smoke billowed over the shattered roof tops on the battlefield side of the village. A crescendo, then the explosive hammer falls eased, to be replaced by the rattle of machine-guns and small arms.

Although he couldn't see what was going on, Jack felt it. The Fabric flared bright as the cataclysmic struggle stretched and twisted the surface of reality and tore through to the raw flesh below. The terror and grief of the combatants flowed like blood through The Fabric's tremulous, writhing threads. Jack closed his eyes but there was no relief in the darkness.

"Stretcher bearers!"

The words were barely audible above the din, but Jack heard it well enough. He grabbed at the front handles of the stretcher he shared with Alfred and set off down the broken street toward the battle line at a jog. He saw Henry and Wally to his left, George and Ezzy to his right; Merriweather was at their head, crouched low, waving his white flag. His men now followed him, Red Cross armbands their only defence.

They passed through the parked lorries, many of which were now on fire, across the road and up to the nearest hastily dug defensive trench. Men were being hauled out. Merriweather ordered half the platoon to halt there and form a relay back to the RDS.

"Not you," he growled at Jack and Alfred. "You're coming with me."

Merriweather again led the way, this time onto the battlefield itself.

The land was churned and devoid of any feature other than craters, mud, and rolls of hastily installed but largely ineffective, barbed wire.

There was debris as far as Jack could see, discarded packs, mess tins, equipment.

And bodies, mostly grey-clad Germans slaughtered in what looked to have been a failed frontal assault.

A flash, a gout of flame and earth. The roar of the explosion bent Jack's ears inward. The shockwave drove a fist into his belly. The Germans had resumed their bombardment, a desultory and sporadic version this time, but lethal enough. The Fabric thrummed with the horror of it. Jack tried to shut it out, but the energies unleashed here were too strong.

The air was heavy with smoke, cordite-edged and throat-stinging. The world roared and shuddered. Each hit seemed heavy enough to crack open the world.

Then it stopped. The tension between the last explosion and the realisation that there would be no more, all but unbearable.

A figure emerged from the smoke-fog, an officer by the look of his uniform though what rank, Jack couldn't tell. He was mud-spattered, a shambolic filthy man who somehow managed to maintain his dignity and a sense of authority.

"Get the wounded out of here as quickly as you can. Look sharp, won't you? We haven't got all day."

He then went his own way, shouting orders, disappearing back into the smoke. There must have been a counterattack, as bloody and futile as the German assault had been.

Jack, his hearing mostly restored now, became aware that someone was screaming nearby, an endless plea for their mother.

It went on. Jack was exhausted. His arms and shoulders burned with pain. His back ached. He saw blood and human vitals spilled from torn-open bellies and into the mud. He saw the limbless. He saw the burned clutching their faces, blind, bleeding and screaming.

He saw the shock and terror in their eyes.

None of the stretcher bearers spoke now. The ones Jack and Alfred encountered as they trudged out into the battlefield then staggered back with their human burdens, looked as pale and shocked as the casualties they recovered. Jack needed a cigarette. He needed a drink. He needed water, a rest, a chance to stop.

Shells began to fall again. Another half-hearted barrage, but lethal enough.

A bad omen as well. The enemy would not give up today.

Then as he and Alfred once again stumbled through the mud looking for the hurt, Jack saw the German. He was sprawled on his back, his abdomen opened. His head was bare. His helmet lay beside him in the mud. The man's eyes were closed, but he was breathing, which meant that he was alive. He was simply one of countless injured and dead enemy soldiers that littered this place. Yet there was something about the man that snagged Jack's attention.

He towed the stretcher toward him.

"Leave him, he's a damned Hun," Alfred shouted from behind. "We're supposed to get our own first."

Jack ignored him.

Because the German was not bleeding.

Jack dropped the stretcher handles and crouched down to stare at the wound. It was splashed with mud, but clear enough. Jack had seen the inside of enough human abdomens in the past few months to know what should lie within. This man had none of it. The sides of the wound formed a deep cleft. The walls of the cleft were of a sponge-like material. Already a webbing, like the web of a spider had formed over the wound, which was healing itself.

Self-healing….

The man's eyes focused on his own. He must have recognised something there. He spoke. "Wir sind gleich…Wir…sind…"

Jack shook his head. "I don't understand. I'm sorry."

The man grabbed Jack's arm. "You…You und me…same…." He released his grip and slumped back. His face twisted into a rictus of pain.

Jack looked up at Alfred. "Help me get him onto the stretcher."

"No Jack. Orders are orders, Our chaps first—"

"Can you see any of ours?" Jack said. "This man, he's one of mine. He's like me. Don't you understand what this means, Alfred? I'm not alone."

"What the devil are you talking about? Jack? Are you all right?"

"Help me get him onto the stretcher."

"No."

"Fucking help me, Alfred."

Alfred seemed shocked by the ferocity of Jack's request. He swallowed hard, nodded then crouched down to take the German's ankles.

"Same…wir sind gleich," the man grunted as they manhandled him onto the canvas bed of the stretcher.

"Yes, you're the same as me," Jack said to him. "You're like me."

The German frowned then closed his eyes again. Consumed, once more, by the pain of self-healing.

"He's a bloody German," the corporal in charge of the relay between battlefield and RDS growled.

Jack made to explain. "We couldn't find—"

"*All* wounded," Alfred snapped at the corporal in his best officer's voice. "We pick up *all* wounded. We look after theirs, they look after ours. Do you understand corporal?"

The corporal grumbled but, conditioned to obey tone and accent and apparently blind to the lack of officer insignia on Alfred's tunic, he grabbed the stretcher handle and called for someone to help.

"Thank you," Jack said.

Alfred wiped his filthy brow and smiled that bemused smile of his. "No harm done. The poor bugger probably doesn't want to be here anymore than we do." He frowned. "What did you mean, you and he are the same and that you're not alone?"

Jack didn't answer but grabbed an empty stretcher and set off once more into the mire of the battlefield, dragging Alfred behind him.

Later, Alfred and Jack found Henry, and Wally slumped against the only remaining brick wall of what was once presumably a house. The four of them puffed on Woodbines and took swigs from their water canteens. "One of the sergeants told me that we're going to clear them out of their positions this evening." Henry scoffed. "I've heard that before."

"Defeatist talk," Wally said. "That's not like you."

"No, it isn't, is it?" Henry replied tartly. "I usually enjoy my days out here at The Front."

"You're still alive, Henry," Alfred said. "Surely that's something to be cheerful about."

"If grubbing about in an abattoir is being alive, then, yes, I suppose I'm still alive."

Jack only half-listened to the exchange. He was too restless to give the conversation his full attention. He wanted to get back to the RDS and find the German. He needed to talk to him. He had questions. How long since the man had come to *be*? Why was he out here, carrying a rifle on a battlefield? What did he know about their creators? Jack didn't care about orders not to fraternize with the enemy. What could they do to him? A firing squad would not harm him.

George appeared. "Merriweather says that there's a few wounded further up toward the hill. He told us to clear them out and then we can get some proper rest." He turned to Jack. His eyes were bright and sharp, like nails. "I daren't tell him you brought a fucking Hun back with you earlier. I hope for your sake, he never finds out. Don't ever do that again, do you understand me, Smith? Not while there's our lads out there. Let the bastards pick up their own."

"Yes, corporal."

"If you bring another one of them back, I'll bloody well shoot him in the head and turn you over to Merriweather."

"Yes, corporal."

"Good, now get back to work."

Getting back to work meant a return to that desolate wilderness of mud, smoke, litter, and dead and dying flesh. George, Wally, Ezzy, and Henry were on either side of him and Alfred, crouched over, eyes darting left and right. They crossed through the maze of coiled barbed wire. There were men draped over the viciously thorned steel. Heads thrown back. Mouths and eyes wide open. Blood runs were painted over their already filthy uniforms, both British khaki and German grey. Jack had noticed them the first time he had ventured into this place this morning, but this time he *saw* them. The horror of their deaths added a bitter poignancy to the sight.

The squad moved out into the vast, desolate ocean of mud and shell holes.

The number of bodies increased with each yard they walked. Many fresh, mingled with the decaying remains of those who fell during the retreat of three days ago. Uniforms no longer mattered. They were bundles of lifeless humanity, derelict, and broken. Empty. Sound filtered into Jack's consciousness now, breaking through the ringing of blood that sang through his head.

Alfred slipped and stumbled. Jack turned round to him and said, "Are you all right?"

Alfred nodded. His ever-present, wry smile was gone. He looked grim. He looked frightened.

"Keep your head down as much as you can, Jack" he said. "The Hun are still shooting and chucking mortar shells at us out of spite."

A casualty, on his back and breathing hard. His respiration made a wet sound. Blood and saliva bubbled from his mouth. He looked pleadingly at Jack.

"We'll take this one, corporal" Alfred called to Ezzy and George who were still close to them. Wally and Henry had veered off to the left, following a monotonous cry for help.

"Righto," George called back.

Jack and Alfred dropped the stretcher. Alfred moved in and grabbed the man's legs, Jack his armpits. The soldier cried out weakly as they lifted him onto the stretcher.

A burst of machine gun fire. Close, bullets cracked through the air. Jack threw himself down beside the casualty. He looked up to see a scrap of khaki and a lump of bloody flesh erupt from Ezzy's back. As the lad was thrown backward, Jack caught a glimpse of George as he doubled over then crumpled slowly into the mud.

Their sudden passing trembled through the dim threads of The Fabric. He heard the men's cries as they tumbled into its brightly glowing river of energy. Jack clawed at the mud and tried to cling to the dissolving shreds of their existence, but it was like trying to hold a handful of sand.

"Fuck." Alfred was on his feet. He tore his armband from his sleeve and waved it furiously. "Red Cross. Red Cross, you bastards. Red fucking Cross. Jesus Christ...." He sounded as if he was crying like a child. He sobbed and shouted and waved his armband until all his strength seemed to fade and he dropped to his knees, head bowed.

Now Jack got to his feet. He could see the Germans now. Grey and almost shapeless, peering up over the rim of a shell hole some twenty yards away. A forward position, he presumed. One of many, no doubt, established in the shell holes that stitched the ruined field. Exposed and vulnerable. Sacrificial offerings whose job it would be to hinder the inevitable British counterattack.

There was no more firing. Jack stood, tense, waiting for the bruising impact of a bullet. Nothing. Alfred turned to him, his face bleak, his eyes red-rimmed, and nodded. They bent down and picked up the stretcher and its burden who was still breathing.

"Oh God, oh hell." The casualty groaned as they lifted him, his voice wet with his own blood. "Oh...Oh...."

Jack looked back to where George and Ezzy had fallen. He didn't want to leave him there. He wanted to bring them back. But wasn't this how it was going to be, all through whatever time he had on this planet? If war and violence didn't kill those he came to love, disease and old age would.

They reached the trench. Exhausted and silent.

"Be careful, lads," one of the infantrymen in the shallow trench said to them as he helped manhandle the stretcher to the waiting relay party. "Some daft bugger's ordered patrols to probe the Hun's defences. That's what all the shooting's about. They want volunteers, but they can stick their fucking patrols up their arses as far as I'm concerned. It's giving the Germans the pip. They're shooting at anything that moves."

The German machine guns fired regularly now. The stretcher bearers were forced to crouch and weave and wave their armbands or anything that resembled a white flag as they sought out the remaining wounded. Alfred was silent. He seemed lost. He and Jack pressed on, closer and closer to the German lines. This was foolish. The Germans would surely rescue any causalities close to their own positions. Bullets kicked up the mud ten yards to the right.

Jack shouted, "Red Cross, Red Cross."

They saw a man, crawling toward them. He raised his hand and they hurried over. He turned out to be a captain. His head was bare, his hair, thought muddied, was fair. He was, Jack decided, both young and old. The officer climbed onto the stretcher without any help. His ankle, he said, was broken, nothing else. It hurt like the devil, but he counted himself lucky.

They set off back toward the trench. Jack was exhausted now. The pain in his arms and shoulders was excruciating. It would heal, but at this moment it was everything. He was tired. He wanted to sleep. Nothing more would satisfy him, only sleep.

A mortar round slammed into the mud somewhere behind them. The explosion was shockingly loud. Jack flinched and staggered. He heard Alfred let out an oath. Mud rained down, a brief, filthy shower. The captain swore as well. Jack heard the words "pigs" and "bastards," but little else.

A few minutes later, Jack felt the stretcher drop. He was yanked backward and released the handles instinctively as he tried to keep his balance. The officer cried out as he was dumped, unceremoniously onto the ground. Jack turned to see Alfred on one knee, fist plunged into the mud, like a sprinter at the starting block.

"I'm hit," he said through gritted teeth. "Bloody hell, Jack. It was that mortar."

Jack went to him. He put his arm about his shoulders and felt the wetness of blood between Alfred's shoulder blades.

No, this was too much to bear.

"I'll get you back," Jack said. He couldn't let Alfred go. He couldn't lose him. The wound wasn't bad. The officer could wait.

Alfred looked up at him and whispered, "Sorry, old chap. Don't think I'll last that long."

"It isn't far. Come on Alfie, please."

Jack tried to lift him. He strained and pulled, but Alfred was a dead weight, offering no help, simply kneeling.

"Can't…can't breathe, Jack…lungs, I think…Jack…Jack, stop." Then he coughed and blood ran from his mouth. He pitched forward. Jack tried to catch him, but he was heavy and slippery and in too many pieces for Jack to hold. Alfred lay in the blood-tainted mud, face down. He turned his head. His hand found Jack's and clutched it with surprising strength.

"Good man," he said. "Love you…Jack…I love…."

There was another word that seemed to emerge like a sigh and was too quiet for Jack to hear. He stared down at Alfred. He could see the shrapnel wounds, scattered over his back. Neat holes that had burned the material of his tunic and burrowed into his flesh.

Jack stood then, uncaring of German bullets, and walked slowly to the captain. "Come on, sir. We have to get back."

He helped the man up then put his arm about him. The Captain leaned on him and hopped as best he could on his good foot as they picked their way back toward the British line. It was hard and it was slow.

Jack saw another stretcher party, heading out, their stretcher folded and empty. Jack hailed them. The bearers were obviously glad of the nearness of the casualty to their own lines, thanked him and set off back to the village with Jack following close behind. He was angry. This was different from how he had felt when Lizzy had died. Then, there had been an emptiness, a vacancy in the world. This time there was rage that men were being forced to kill and die for no obvious reason. Three people he called friends had died before his eyes this afternoon. All of them trying to save the lives of others.

He was going to find the German. He would be in the RDS. He crossed the trench and strode onto the road that bordered the village.

"Jack."

Startled, he looked up to see an officer walking toward him. The man was big and broad, his uniform, unsettlingly clean. Somehow, he knew Jack's name. As he came closer, Jack recognised him.

Lyle.

His officer's cap cast a shadow over his face.

"Get out of my way." Jack made to step round him.

"No, Jack. Stop."

"I know who you are," Jack said. He felt uneasy speaking so informally to the man. Every instinct cried out for him to simply salute and snap out an obedient *Yes sir*.

"Can't you see the pips on my shoulder, Jack? You should salute me."

To hell with that.

Lyle's stare, though hidden, was hard. "Stay away from the German."

He took a step toward Jack, and it was all that Jack could do to stand his ground. There was something else at the heart of the man. His body, his form, was a lie. He was vaster and deeper than the confines of his flesh. The air was distorted around his outline. It shimmered as if he gave off intense heat. When he opened his mouth to speak again, Jack saw darkness.

Enraged at being blocked, Jack shoved at Lyle. His hands made contact with the coarse fabric of his uniform, then passed through into coldness. The man existed. He filled the void into which Jack had thrust his hands, yet he was a presence rather than a physical being. It was as if his body was a doorway to some other vast, empty place.

Jack felt himself falling toward the terrible blackness within the boundaries of Lyle's flesh. He wrenched his hands back and out. Off-balance, he dropped to one knee in the mud.

"Do not look for him," Lyle said, almost gentle now. He crouched and his hand came to rest on Jack's shoulder. "There will be no fraternising with the enemy. Do your duty, Jack. Do what you were sent to do."

"Jack!"

He started. Wally was calling to him. "Come on, wake up. Give us a hand, will you?"

Jack turned to see him and Henry, trying to manhandle a stretcher over the barbed wire. When Jack glanced back, Lyle was gone, yet, his presence lingered, dissolving slowly into the smoke and rain and stench of the place.

Jack set off to help with the stretcher. He would have to tell the surviving two men of the squad about the others.

Artillery rumbled in the distance. Crows circled the battlefield.

Jack grabbed one of the stretcher poles and did his duty.

CHAPTER ELEVEN (2016)

Jack drove without destination or plan. He knew only that he had to keep moving. Geography would make no difference when the time came, but he could not stand still and wait passively for the end. He headed north, the decision arbitrary. There was no rhyme or reason to this. He joined the stream of traffic on the A1 and found comfort in the illusion of safety in numbers. Jack Smith deluded himself that he was a needle in a fast moving, exhaust-spewing haystack.

His creators were powerful, god-like. They had made this world, yet they could be resisted, for a while. Josephine Anderson had told him that. Well, this was resistance.

Jack was afraid, yes, panicked, unable to think logically, yet beneath the irrational need for constant movement, he was wracked with sadness. When the end came, every feeling, adventure, impression, heartache, and joy would be taken from him and there would be nothing.

An impossible state to imagine. Oblivion. No sensation. No thought. No awareness. A darkness he would not experience. A sleep from which he would never wake.

Then there was Louise. He missed her. He felt as if his heart had been torn in half. It was a familiar feeling, but no easier to endure.

He wanted her.

This loneliness was as bad as the desolation left by the deaths of Lizzy and Marion. This loneliness was a heavy weight that exhausted him, that made him want to stop the car, give in, and embrace the end.

No.

He would not go quietly.

Lyle.

In the middle of the carriageway. Suddenly. Coat, hat, broad, solid, real. There.

There.

Jack slammed on the brakes. The car slowed. Horns blared from behind. Not real. Not bloody real. Jack grit his teeth and moved his right foot to the accelerator. The car surged forward. Toward Lyle. At Lyle. Who rushed closer, and closer. Jack pushed himself back in his seat, braced for impact, for the thud and the body thrown onto the bonnet and against the windscreen.

There was a sensation. An electric shock. A spear of pain that lanced into Jack's skull.

Then there were only the red taillights of the cars in front and the endless glare and fade of the approaching traffic. He drove on, trembling. Everything was out of control. He needed to stop and rest. He needed to find some services where he could drink coffee and calm down.

Lyle, again, in the carriageway exactly as before. Jack hurled the car forward.

Again.

And again.

Until Jack's arms ached from the strain of holding onto the wheel. His head pounded and his skin was seared by the repeated shocks as he killed, and yet, not killed, Lyle over and over again.

Jack. Jack don't leave us.

Alfred. It was Alfred, out there. Lost, dying.

Jack, where are you going? Come back. God…don't leave us here….

He had to turn the car round and go back for them. George, Ezzy, Alfred, they were hurt, bleeding. He couldn't leave them to die.

"I'll help you find them," said Lyle.

He was in the car, in the officer's uniform he had worn that time in France. He was there, in the passenger seat, big, bulky, heavy. He reached across and grabbed the steering wheel with his right hand.

No. No.

Jack fought him, held on, kept the car straight. He was weakening. He should let Lyle take over.

"That's right, Jack. Leave it to me."

Peace, the fight was over. He would give in. There were others in the car, each presence a darkness, a blank, an opening through which he could fall and be at rest.

No.

Peace shattered into the light-splintered urgency of the A1. He grabbed at the steering wheel and corrected the car's drift. He was alone. The car was empty. Lyle was gone.

Alfred cried out again. Jack heard the thud of mortar shells.

And around him now, figures, running, there, in the spaces between speeding vehicles. Shadowed, glimpsed, uniforms. Soldiers. No, his imagination. There was nothing out there except the Great North Road and its racing metal hordes. Explosions tore open the darkness.

Jack blinked. The road ahead was a blur of receding red lights and oncoming yellow. Like tracer. Were tracer. He was back there, in France. He was lost in the hell and chaos of battle.

No. No, no, no.

Ruin. Mud. He was running, alone, across No Man's Land. Out of breath, weeping, his friends dead in the mud behind him, three corpses among countless others. He had to find them. He had to turn the car round and bring them back—

A horn blared. He started and looked around wildly to see cars, vans, a lorry.

His head was filled with the clatter and roar of battle. The noise went on.

Services. A mile ahead.

Lyle. Again.

Exhausted. Badly shaken and feeling disconnected from the reality around him, Jack took a seat in a Little Chef and ordered tea. His need for that most British of drinks was almost comical, but it was also comfort and reassurance. There was a feeling of safety in this place, in the light, people, noise. Normal, human din began to clear the other sounds from his head. The flashback had been Lyle's doing. It was how The Hound worked. He reached out and dug into his quarry's vast trove of memories and reignited the worst of them.

Jack was hungry but his stomach rebelled against food. He chose a window table. It gave him a feeling of security. From here, he would see Lyle coming and have time to escape, even though the view was washed away by the reflection from inside the brightly lit cafe.

The tea arrived, a small metal pot and a cup. He poured. The tea was weak. He didn't care. It was hot and would do its job. His tension began to ease as he drank. Lyle couldn't hurt him, not yet. The connection needed to strengthen. Wasn't that what Josephine had said? He was safe for the time being. He had no idea for how long, but he needed a plan. He needed to face his situation head on and decide what he should do in the time he had left.

Louise.

She was damaged, and in mourning for an unresolved relationship. He could help her if she would let him. That was what he had to do. It was the only way to give meaning to his imminent demise.

CHAPTER TWELVE (1925)

There had been an invitation to the regiment's annual reunion every year since 1920, but Jack had never taken it up. He was fearful of meeting those with whom he had shared one of the most brutal yet exhilarating periods of his life so far. He was not sure why. Perhaps it was because he was afraid that the changes inevitably wrought by time in the lives and characters of the men would tarnish the good memories he had gathered and cherished. Or was it a dread that it would rekindle other, less welcome recollections?

In February 1925, as in the previous five Februarys, Jack arrived home from his day at Stannard and Long's—he was a machinist now—to find the familiar envelope on the doormat of his small, rented house in Wembley. As always, he hung up his coat then carried the unopened letter into the kitchen, where he set about making a pot of tea. Kettle on the gas ring, he sat at his small table and drew out the invitation. He would, at least, read it before dropping it into the wastepaper bin behind the curtain under the sink. Yes, here was the usual thick, brownish-yellow paper, a glimpse of the regimental crest as he unfolded it.

A second letter dropped out.

Puzzled, Jack picked it up from the floor. The writing was a loose, hasty scrawl. He read it with something akin to disbelief.

"Dear Jack," it said. "Are you coming to the reunion? I went last year, and it was great fun. I was hoping you'd be there, old chap, but sadly, no sign. Bit of a disappointment because I am keen to meet up with you again. I was pretty badly knocked about by that mortar shell and spent far too long in hospital. Missed the Armistice. Fighting fit now, though, and would love to reminisce over the jolly time we had at The Front. So, how about it, old chap? Time for another small and early. Yours affectionately, Alfred."

Alfred?

Alfred?

Jack sat at the kitchen table and stared at the letter. He had been sure that Alfred had died of his wounds. Yet here he was, back from the dead. The man's resurrection should have filled Jack with joy; instead, it made him uneasy. It was a shift in reality, hard to comprehend. The belief that Alfred had died was an integral part of the structure of his memories and emotions. He was happy, yes, but knocked off-balance. He examined his reaction as dispassionately as he was able. Then he began to laugh and cry at the same time. Euphoria again, but this time mingled with a deep sadness he could not fathom.

On the stove, the kettle whistled.

Wally and Henry had made it through.

The war ended with a suddenness that was almost as shocking as anything Jack had endured during the previous year-and-a-half. No one at the Ambulance Unit knew who had won. At the moment of its announcement, victory or defeat didn't matter.

Sergeant Merriweather brought the news. He stepped inside the tent and sat down, wrapped in his great coat against the November cold, his face red and pinched. He looked around at the five men lounging on their bedding, hands of cards forgotten, and growled in a voice that made it sound as if peace was a personal affront to an old warrior like himself.

"It's done."

The men looked at each other. Half of them virtual strangers to Jack; only Wally was left of the squad he had joined in April. Henry was still alive, but invalided home with a chunk of shrapnel in his thigh. Neither of them spoke, celebrated, or even smiled.

Jack tried to grasp the truth of what Merriweather had just told them. No more fighting and killing. Suddenly, everyone was friends. Suddenly, you could walk up to a German soldier and shake his hand, even though at breakfast time he would have gutted you with a bayonet.

There was cheering, from one of the tents. The sound grated against Jack's nerves. He wanted to stride over there and yell at them to shut up, but he didn't move. They were entitled to their celebrations.

Jack experienced a sense of loss. Alfred, Ezzy, George, and Robbie Wilcox, the lance corporal who had been among their replacements and proved himself a good companion. He was blown to bloody shreds by a German shell only a week previously.

While the war raged, those lost souls were still close. Now, he would have to leave them behind. He closed his eyes and lay down on his back, drowning under this new deluge of emotions.

But through it all, a light began to glow.

It was over.

He was going home.

To what?

To whom?

The reunion was held in a hotel just off Euston Road. The venue was not luxurious, but comfortable enough. Jack stood in the entrance to the hotel's ballroom while he summoned the courage to approach the noisy, smoke-wreathed crowd within, and make himself known. He recognised few of the men. He didn't expect to find many old friends there.

A hand was clapped onto his shoulder. Startled, he spun round to find himself face-to-face with the craggy features of Sergeant Merriweather.

"About time you reported for duty, Smith. You always were a slacker."

Jack resisted an impulse to stand to attention and shout, "Yes Sarge." Instead, he uttered an awkward; "Was I, sergeant?"

Merriweather laughed, something Jack had never seen before. "Come with me, Smith, that's an order. Can't have you standing around empty-handed, can we?" Without looking back to check that Jack was behind him, the ex-sergeant set off toward the bar. Jack followed. The knot of men crowded around it opened to allow them passage. Despite his civilian suit and thickening waistline, Merriweather remained an intimidating presence.

"Now then, I'm buying you a pint of whatever you fancy. You had guts, Smith, and you worked hard, you and that toff, Ellerton. He's here tonight, you know."

The sergeant sauntered over to some of his old buddies and was soon lost in the general melee. Jack found himself the owner of a pint of mild. He took a sip then turned to study the room. The air was hot and thickly fogged with cigarette smoke, reducing the crowd to an amorphous mass. Medals adorned many jackets. Conversation and laughter were loud. There was a hint of desperation in that mirth.

Jack noticed that some of the men looked pale and drawn. Some sat silently at the fringes. Others were missing limbs, or terribly scarred. A few trembled visibly.

Hunting for a familiar face, Jack moved into the press. He collected snatches of conversation as he weaved his way through to the other side. It was peppered with army slang and stories being told and, no doubt, retold; comedy, tragedy, and the melding of the two as horror was transformed into humorous anecdote and bittersweet reminiscence.

Jack was about to give up. The meal would begin soon.

Then he saw him.

Alfred.

He was chatting and laughing with a corpulent, balding character who leaned heavily on a walking stick. It took a few moments for Jack to recognise the man as Henry. Jack carved a path toward them, making apologies for spilled beer and trodden toes as he went. Alfred glanced at him, frowned then grinned broadly. Henry's eyes widened.

"Jack Smith, as I live and breathe." Henry was the first to extend a hand for Jack to shake. He was beaming, energetic, not at all the sour, world-weary character with whom Jack had spent those last long months of the war.

"I'm glad to see you, Henry. You're looking well."

Henry nodded and patted his expanding belly. "Marriage does a man the world of good."

"Congratulations."

Then Alfred stepped forward. His eyes shone and for a moment Jack thought the man was going to cry, but he smiled broadly and they shook hands. Alfred looked sleek and well-dressed; indeed, he was one of the smartest men in the room.

"Jack." He stepped back and shook his head. "Still the same yesterday, today and forever. How is that? We've all aged terribly, and you look no different to the last day I saw you."

"I don't think you're looking closely enough," Jack answered. "I'm glad to see you, Alfred."

"The feeling's mutual. What do you think of our friend Henry then? I didn't recognise him with that stupid grin on his miserable old face."

"The war's over and done with," Henry said. "What could be better than that?" He nodded at the near-empty beer mug in Jack's fist. "What'll it be?"

"Mild, please."

"Pint of bitter for me," Alfred said. His glass was still half-full. "I'll have this dealt with by the time you get back, old chap."

In that moment Jack caught a glimpse of the old Henry as a sour expression flitted across his face. He obviously hadn't intended to buy a whole round.

A loud voice announced dinner. Merriweather of course. "Once a sergeant, always a sergeant." Alfred said. "Stick with me, it's a bit of a free-for-all when it comes to who sits with whom. We'll try to save a spot for dear old Henry as well."

Alfred was quick and deft and moved in fast to secure three seats. Alfred sat down beside Jack; Henry, when he returned with three, precariously balanced pints, sat opposite. There was a brief welcoming speech from the colonel, greeted by a deafening cheer and a tattoo of fists on the table and shoes on the floor. Grace was said by the padre, who, Jack noticed, looked pale and worn and suffered a tremor in his left hand. After that, the men got to their feet to roar out a rousing version of "God Save the King" then food arrived. It was simple fare, roast beef, mashed potatoes, cabbages, carrots, and gravy. There was a lot of it, and it was tasty enough. Then there was apple pie and thick custard. Followed by cheese and port.

Most of the meal was taken up with conversation about what the three of them were doing now. Henry was an assistant bank manager. Alfred had not followed the medical career his father had wanted him to pursue but found employment in a gentleman's outfitters on Regent Street.

"A little dreary, but it's an honest living," Alfred said when he had a moment to talk to Jack on his own. "The thing is, I have made some wonderful friends and I would love you to meet them. I know that they're pretty keen to meet you. We get together every Sunday evening."

"I'm flattered that you even mentioned them to me."

"How long did we know each other, Jack?"

"Two or three days."

"Less than a week and yet, I feel as if it was years. I mean, time didn't seem to work out there the way it does here. You made friends quickly. Had to. Never knew how long you'd got. But you…." Alfred was suddenly serious. "You made an impression on me, old chap. I can't explain it and it certainly wasn't because I…well, it was nothing to do with the thing I told you about, that day, you know…." Alfred seemed close to tears. "God, I'm glad to see you, Jack."

"You too, Alfred. So, what happened to you?"

"Bloody mortar shell. I remember the bang then it all went black until I woke up in a German army hospital. They must have hauled me out of the mud after they drove you lot away. Decent chaps really. I got off lightly by all accounts. Broken ribs, lots of bruises, burns, cuts, and a bit of concussion. It hurt, but it wasn't going to kill me. I never made it to a prisoner of war camp because the place was overrun by the

Americans. I finished up in one of their hospitals, no idea where, and stayed there until it ended. I rather liked the Yanks. A bit loud and brash, but generous to a fault."

After that, the reunion became too noisy for conversation. There was singing. Not good to begin with, it grew progressively worse as the evening wore on toward its inebriated conclusion.

When the party finally broke up, the men surged about the cloak room, staggered through the hotel reception, and spilled out onto the street, Alfred took Jack aside and said, "Remember, Sunday evening, at about six o' clock." He handed Jack a card "At this address."

"A small and early?"

Alfred laughed. "Hardly. Small, yes, but certainly not early. Look, it's not formal or anything. The host is a chum of mine, Antonia Palgrave. You'll adore her. We have a drink or two, engage in lively chatter, enjoy a bit of music. You will come, won't you?"

"If I can."

"Splendid old chap. See you there."

Jack took up the invitation on the following Sunday, which was seasonally wet and cold and not conducive to leaving a warm hearth for an evening out. Antonia Palgrave lived in Onslow Square, which abutted Brompton Road.

Antonia herself was slender, willowy, her dark hair cut into a fashionable bob, a cigarette holder gripped between the first two fingers of her left hand. She moved with an exaggerated, cat-like grace and trailed silk and perfume in her wake. Jack estimated her to be in her late forties, although she dressed and styled herself as a much younger woman. He silently applauded her rebellion against the conventions of age.

"You must be Jack. So, pleased to meet you." Antonia's voice was deep and languid, as if she hovered on the borderlands of boredom.

"Pleased to meet you and thank you for the invitation."

"Alfie has spoken highly, and often, of you. How could we not want to meet Jack Smith?"

She put her arm through Jack's and led him into the drawing room where half a dozen other guests were gathered. At the lower end of their age range was a thin, pale-looking man in his mid-twenties, currently improvising something classical-sounding on the piano. At the upper end was an imposing elderly gentleman in a pin-stripe suit, who was engaged in a furious debate with a young woman seated in an opposing armchair. As far as Jack could establish, their argument concerned the merits, or otherwise, of the revolution in Russia.

The woman, who looked to be in her mid-twenties, was blonde and reminded Jack of the stars of the silent films, which had become an immensely popular form of entertainment over the last year or so. At that moment, her eyes flashed with righteous indignation as she leaned forward to count off the benefits of the uprising on the fingers of her left hand.

"...The workers, ordinary people, can control what happens to them. The disgustingly rich Tzar and his cronies have gone. Their wealth can be shared by those who need it most—"

"Oh, come now, Marion, do you really believe that Lenin and *his* cronies are sharing all that loot with a bunch of peasants? You really are quite naïve."

Marion's counting finger became a pointer. "You would say that, wouldn't you? Look at you, Harry, content and fat and scared out of your wits by the thought that there could be a revolution here."

"Not at all. Because there never will be. The British worker knows his place—"

"My God, you really are an arrogant snob—"

"And there we must leave it, Marion darling." Alfred, oozing charm, was suddenly beside Jack. "Before sleeves are rolled-up and noses broken." He took Jack's arm. "Let me introduce you to Marion Fisher."

Her scowl became a smile as Jack shook her hand. "Don't mind us," she said. "Harry and I have been at war ever since we first met. He's rather sweet really."

"Sweet? Are you mellowing in your dotage, Marion?" Harry was on his feet. "The Honourable Harry Edmunds MP, Junior Secretary in the Home Office and all round, arrogant snob." Edmunds chuckled and took Jack's hand. "How do you do?"

"Pleased to meet you, sir."

"Oh, call me Harry, please. No one stands on ceremony here. The lovely Antonia won't allow it, will you darling?"

"Certainly not. Everyone must be exactly who they are when they enter my house. Even a disreputable queer like my Alfie must *be* a disreputable queer at Antonia's."

"So," Marion said, looking up at Jack from her armchair. "Who are *you*?"

"I'm not sure," Jack answered before he had time to think. "I mean...."

"Don't spoil it," Harry said. "We love an enigma."

"Jack, a mystery even to himself. How exciting." Antonia said. "Are you a spy, Jack, or a member of the Special Branch?"

"Hardly, I work in an engineering factory, as a machinist."

"So *you* would have us believe," Marion said and chuckled. Jack found that he liked her laugh, and her voice.

"A worthy profession," Harry said and raised his whisky tumbler in salute. "Good for you."

"What can you tell us about Jack, Alfie?" Antonia said. "He's your friend after all."

"What I know is that he's a courageous fellow. He's kind too, and rather innocent."

"Oh dear." This was another of Antonia's guests, a broad, heroic-looking man with a square-jaw and savagely slicked dark hair. He stood by the fireplace, brandy globe in hand. "You won't keep your innocence for long if you spend an evening here."

"I beg to differ," Alfred said. "This man, Jack Smith, is different from anyone I've met before."

"That sounds like the beginning of a love affair, Alfie," Marion said.

Alfred reddened a little. Jack, discomforted by the sharp-edged and somewhat acerbic repartee, could find no response.

"Certainly not," Alfred said. "Jack and I are pals. We won a war together."

"Something of an exaggeration, Alfred."

"Disappointingly, however, he is rather fond of ladies."

"Then I am *very* pleased to meet you, Mr. Smith" Marion said. She stared at him for a moment too long. This was something he had not experienced since he had walked a battered and bruised Lizzy home from that police station ten years ago. The night they had first kissed.

"I was interested in your conversation," Jack said, as much to break the intensity as to discuss the Russian revolution.

"Were you?" Marion was mildly challenging now. "And what side do you come down on?"

"I have to say that, as much as I support the idea of the workers having a fair share, and some say in the way their country is governed, I can't see how it could work in practice, human nature being what it is, so I tend to agree with Mr. Edmunds, I'm afraid."

"So, you think I'm naïve, do you?"

"Not exactly."

"Because that's what Mr. Edmunds thinks of me. You used that very word, didn't you, Harry?"

"I did and I stand by it, Marion, my dear. I'm pleased that our new friend has the good sense to see it too."

"Good sense?"

"I'm sorry." Jack felt hot and clumsy. "I didn't mean to insult you. I was merely giving an opinion and I certainly don't think that you're naïve, Miss Fisher. I'm afraid I—" Why was it that every sentence he uttered made things worse?

"It's Marion. Not Miss Fisher. No one is allowed to be formal here, Jack," Antonia called out. She had moved across to talk with the heroic type by the fireplace.

"Marion, yes...."

Marion adopted a conspiratorial air. "You are wrong, you know." She smiled and her smile seemed dazzling to Jack. "Come along, we need to get you a drink. You look a little flustered." Marion slid her arm though Jack's and led him across to the drink cabinet. "Scotch?"

"Yes, please. Do you really believe that a revolution is coming?"

Marion finished pouring and handed a tumbler to Jack. "Not in the way it's happened in Russia or is happening in Germany, although I don't hold out much hope for that one. But something *is* building. You must feel it. People are struggling to make a living. Wages are atrocious and too many families live in appalling conditions. All the men like you, Alfred, and Charles over there—" She waved her glass toward the square-jawed man who was talking to Antonia. "—who fought for their country, you're expected to come back and put up with everything being exactly as it was before. It's shameful."

Sleek, healthy, and well-fed, Charles didn't look as though he was having to put up with anything. Jack understood Marion's point, however.

"Are you a communist?"

Marion's glass stopped halfway to her lips. Her eyes widened.

"I'm sorry, that was rude of me."

"Not at all, Jack. It's refreshing. It's why I like being part of Antonia's set. People here are honest, disarmingly so at times, but there's no pretence. No good manners, thank God. But, no, I would not consider myself to be a communist. I am a member of the Labour Party. I want to see things changed in this country of ours."

"Well, we agree on that."

They clinked glasses.

"Where do you work?" Jack said.

"For the BBC, at Marconi House in The Strand. You can always tell which building it is. There are wireless towers growing out of the roof. I've been with them since they were called 2LO. Nothing glamourous, I'm afraid. I type up the scripts they use. I'd love to be an announcer, but it's very hard for women to get that sort of job. It was hard enough getting the job I have, come to that. They were surprised I'm not married and seemed to think that no sooner had they settled me in, I would go off and wed the first chap that asked me and that would be that."

"Can't you carry on working after you get married?"

Marion stared at him, obviously shocked. "You really are an innocent. No self-respecting man would want his wife to work."

"Why ever not?"

"It's a slur on his manhood. He would be ashamed that he couldn't provide for her on his own."

"Seems ludicrous to me."

"Really?"

"Of course it does."

"A last, an intelligent man. I was beginning to think there was no such thing. I should marry you, shouldn't I?"

Yes, Jack answered silently. *You should.*

"Let's meet everyone, shall we?" Marion said and put her arm through his once more and led him to the piano where the rest of the set had gathered.

Charles was, in fact, Charles Morton-Ryder, the second, and spare, son of a Lord. He had no particular profession but was, as he described it, helping to run his father's affairs in London. The vagueness of the statement suggested to Jack that he was engaged in very little at all.

"I was a captain in the Yorkshire Yeomanry, you?"

"Ambulance Unit," Alfred said before Jack could answer. "Stretcher bearer like me, cleaning up the mess you warrior types left behind."

"Ah, it took a brave man to venture out into no man's land without a rifle. Well done." Charles raised his glass to Jack. "But how on earth did you put up with this idiot?"

"Alfred was my friend."

"Is that so? Well, I hope you didn't lend him any money."

Laughter. Charles placed a hand on Alfred's shoulder and the two locked eyes for a moment. Jack saw it then. There was more than simple friendship there.

The final members of the set present that evening were Nicholas Read, a Professor of History at Cambridge University and Samuel Levinson, the pianist. Nicholas looked the part of academic; bald, a little dishevelled, tweed jacket, spectacles, and a somewhat distracted air. Samuel was a gaunt, quiet character who chain-smoked, seldom spoke, and seemed content to play in the background.

"We're bored, Samuel," Antonia announced. "Sing us some of your ditties to lift us from our ennui."

Samuel entertained them with a handful of witty little songs he claimed to have written himself. Then Antonia forced Professor Read onto his feet for a waltz. Samuel was an accomplished musician and switched effortlessly from eccentric ditty to Johann Strauss. To Jack's chagrin, Marion chose Harry Edmunds as her partner. Jack found himself partnered with Antonia. Disappointed as he was, Jack was startled by the erotic charge her nearness gave him.

"Are you enjoying our little soiree?" Antonia asked him.

"Yes, thank you." Not as much as he would enjoy it if he could dance with Marion. She had hardly paid him any attention since bringing him over to the others and he wondered if it had been a way of politely relieving herself of his presence. The thought dampened his mood. He was, he realized, utterly bewitched by her.

"…any time you like."

"I'm sorry?"

"I said, you're welcome to come here any time you like. The more the merrier, that's what I say."

The drink flowed. The conversation grew more acerbic and the laughter louder. Jack felt like an outsider, not a party to the jokes and teasing that were obviously well-established here. He had drunk too much and was light-headed. He became aware at one point that Harry and Antonia had gone. When they reappeared sometime later, both looked a little flushed and dishevelled. No comment was made. Marion was on the opposite side of the circle, seated between Nicholas and Charles. Jack tried not to stare at her but couldn't help himself and was disarmed when she caught him doing so and looked back at him.

"One last dance before we all fall asleep," Antonia announced suddenly. There was laughter. Samuel was back at the piano in a moment.

Marion grabbed Jack's hand and whisked him into a quick step. Although he was no stranger to dancing, being this close to Marion made him once more clumsy and awkward. She was hot and fragrant in his arms.

Half an hour later, as he walked briskly toward South Kensington Underground Station, hurrying to catch the last of the night's trains, he felt happily inebriated and energised. Antonia's set were loud and deliciously disreputable. A group of people who behaved as adults in the world, yet, in private, refused to grow up and conform to the rigid strictures imposed by the society in which they lived. He felt sexual energy and glimpsed free liaisons. He sensed a desperate desire to live life fast and as wildly as possible. They had welcomed him in. He had not particularly shone tonight, but he had talked freely and joined in when needed. He was, they all agreed, that most important thing of all, a sport.

He looked forward to next Sunday evening.

He looked forward to seeing Marion again.

So, Jack became a member of Antonia's set. He grew used to the acerbic wit and challenges to the opinions he held. He was comfortable among these people. No one wanted to know who you were or where you came from unless you felt like telling them. The only proviso was that you joined in as enthusiastically as you could. He learned that it was a place where he could speak his mind and despite the fierce debates that often broke out and sometimes resulted with swift angry exits and slammed doors, an argument never broke any friendship or earned a dishonourable discharge from the set.

Then there was Marion.

She fascinated and infuriated him. One moment she would sit with him and talk and flirt for hours and give him the impression that she wanted more from him than mere friendship. Then she would suddenly break away and give her full attention to someone else as if the time she had spent with Jack meant nothing. On other Sunday evenings she would ignore him completely, perhaps granting him the occasional boon of a smile or exchange of opinions during a drunken discussion over some political or artistic matter.

Some evenings Jack would wend his way home, his heart full. On others he would feel empty and miserable. He knew he was being foolish. There were almost twenty years between them if his apparent age was counted as his actual one. He was a good-looking man, apparently. But it meant nothing, because he was too tightly tangled in the threads of this obsession with Marion, to care how others saw him. She robbed him of sleep. She invaded his concentration when he worked. He wanted it to stop, but also for it to grow and lead to some sort of resolution. This was worse than the emotion and confusion he had experienced with Lizzy. That had been longing tinged with melancholy. This was madness.

Always, no matter how thrilling the Sunday evening adventure, there would be the silent vacancy of his own house. Worse, the reality of who and what he was. No matter how the set drew him to itself, he was aware that he was an outsider. He was different in ways they could not begin to comprehend.

One night, deep into March, there was to be an extra soiree on a Saturday evening. All guests were advised to bring an overnight bag because they would be staying. An hour or so after they all arrived, Antonia gathered the set around the piano and announced that Samuel had brought a treat for everyone and, no, it was not a new song. There was a murmur of expectation as Samuel carefully unfurled a cloth roll on the gleaming lid of the piano to reveal several vials of clear liquid and a handful of glass syringes.

"What's that?" Jack asked.

"The best dream you ever had," Antonia said.

"I don't understand."

"Opium, old chap," Alfred said. "We like to have a little taste now and then. Makes a change from whisky."

"We only indulge occasionally," Antonia said. "You can get to like it too much and then it's got you hooked like a fish on a line."

Jack glanced about the room and saw hunger in the eyes of some of the guests. The usual half dozen was present, including Marion, who looked at the syringes and vials nervously. She did not seem to be looking forward to the experience but was, nonetheless, pushing up the sleeve of her dress to expose the veins of her left arm. Nicholas, on the other hand, seemed transfixed by the liquid as Samuel skilfully filled the first of the syringes then lifted it to eye level and depressed the plunger a little to rid it of any trapped air.

"Who's first?" he said. His voice was surprisingly deep for so fragile looking a man.

"Ladies first, of course," Harry said. "Come on Marion, for the revolution, eh?"

"You really are a horrible man, Harry." She sighed then nodded. "All right, do your worst, Samuel."

He produced a leather strap and wrapped it about Marion's upper arm. He asked her to hold it tight with her free hand. The veins bulged under her pale skin. Samuel pushed the needle in and emptied about a quarter of the contents into her bloodstream. He then unwrapped the tourniquet. Marion pressed a handkerchief against the tiny bubble of blood that seeped from the puncture then lay back against the rear of the sofa and closed her eyes. Her hand went limp and the handkerchief fell onto her lap.

Samuel wiped the needle with a ball of cotton wool soaked in a dark chemical that smelled like iodine. "Jack?" he said.

"Yes, all right."

"Make yourself comfortable and roll up your sleeve."

The tourniquet was painfully tight. Samuel frowned.

"Can't seem to find any veins," he muttered. "You really are rather odd, Jack."

"Allow me," Jack said and took the hypodermic from Samuel's hand. He was unnerved. The man was right, he was rather odd. Odder than any of them could possibly know.

He gritted his teeth then plunged the needled into his arm. As he withdrew it, he noticed Samuel frown at the absence of blood, but made no comment. The opium would be absorbed by his flesh and the correct response would be triggered by the nerves and sensor nodes that networked the tissue.

How did he know that?

Jack lay back in his armchair, wondering what was supposed to happen. He was still wondering when he fell into the drug's warm, soft embrace. There was peace, acceptance, and an odd oblivion. He drifted in and out of awareness and found himself lying on the deeply carpeted floor of Antonia's drawing room next to the sofa, his hand closed about Marion's, their fingers entwined. That point of contact seemed to melt and run until it was hard for him to tell at which point his own flesh ended and hers began.

Then The Fabric exploded into view. Its energies flowed like a sparkling, multi-coloured river that bore Jack in its currents. Cliffs, formed from the entwined threads that were the stuff of all-things, reared sheer and dizzyingly high on either side. There were presences here, snatches and glimpses. No face, no body, but the essence, the spark of life, the soul, the id. All interweaved with the stuff of The Fabric, their voices joined with the overwhelming song of the universe. The song was the cry of its stars, its nebulae, its atoms and molecules, and its teeming, uncountable life.

The river of energy swirled and raced downward. The cliffs grew even higher, their summits lost in a swirl of lightning-streaked clouds. There were stars in that cloud, diffused by the gases of their womb and which they now gathered about themselves.

The decline sharpened and the river currents accelerated, until it surged over the lip of a sheer drop and plummeted toward a vast whirlpool of energy and matter. The whirlpool was titanic, incomprehensible. Its borders were hemmed in by the distant, but vast cliffs formed of threads.

Jack fell. He knew no fear as he tumbled down toward the great spiral of fire and sound.

That was where the creators dwelled, down there in that impossible expanse, creatures whose dimensions stretched across universes, who could not be contained in one space. He felt them and now he knew terror.

No.

The word was howled out toward him by a voice that was not a voice.

He should not be here. He should not see. He shouldn't know.

No.

The force of the word slammed into him and hurled him back upward cartwheeling dizzyingly toward the nebulae-misted sky.

Lizzy. He caught a hint of her, a touch, a cry. He felt her joy, the ecstasy of being part of the weft and weave of everything.

Then his back was slammed against a wall of solidity, and he was shocked awake...

...to find himself on the floor, his hand still entwined in Marion's and surrounded by the unconscious opium dreamers that were Antonia Palgrave's set.

Daylight was perfumed with the scent of coffee.

Breakfast was provided then Antonia announced that she was going to church and would be back later. Anyone was welcome to join her. Alfred said that he would and the two of them left. Her guests were, as usual, free to stay and enjoy her home and garden. They would, she said, have an outing in the afternoon. Perhaps a walk by the Thames or a stroll through one of the parks.

"You know," Jack said as he drank a last coffee. "I'd like a walk now. It's a beautiful morning and I think I need some fresh air." He turned to Marion who sat beside him. His mouth was suddenly dry. He tried to analyse the reason for his nervousness but found only a ridiculous desperation. "Would you like to come with me?"

"Yes," Marion said. "I would, rather."

The sun was bright, the air bitterly cold. They strolled along Brompton Road, past the regal frontage of The Royal Marsden Hospital, not touching, but close. Neither spoke for a long time. Then, Jack asked Marion if she had taken opium before. The question felt clumsy. He was, however, genuinely curious.

"Yes, three or four times." She seemed to ponder the fact then said, "I don't like it very much. I like the sensation it gives me well enough, who wouldn't? It's like floating on a cloud. All your troubles seem to dissolve, but I'm frightened of it as well. It's the needle and the way I'm putting something into my blood that shouldn't be there. That's a rather horrid feeling. You can come to rely on it, you know."

"Yes, Antonia mentioned that."

"Samuel takes it all the time. He looks ill though, doesn't he?"

"I suppose he does. Do you have many troubles?"

"I'm sorry?"

"You said that opium makes your troubles dissolve."

"Oh," Marion chuckled then slid her arm through Jack's. It was a good feeling, companionable and yet electric. "No more than anyone else."

They strolled on. Jack was oblivious to the distance they covered. He wanted the walk to never end. He wanted there to be no reason for Marion to leave his side.

"Look" she said. "There's a café open. I would love a cup of tea."

They sat at a window table. Marion smiled at him often and seemed as happy and contented as Jack felt. He asked her about her job at the BBC.

"I suppose it is pretty exciting. It's all rather new, isn't it? The words I type are heard all over the country. It's a bit like magic."

"Yes, you're right. I'm going to buy a crystal set tomorrow, so I can hear those words and imagine you typing away and putting them onto paper."

"You are silly," Marion said. "But rather sweet as well."

"No one has called me sweet before."

"Oh, someone has. Alfie is very taken with you, Jack. He talked about you all the time and he would often call you sweet."

"I would rather it was you who talked about me all the time."

"Now, now, don't spoil it by getting all romantic. It's eleven o' clock on a Sunday morning, hardly the time for declarations of love and all that rot."

Stung, even though he could tell that Marion was teasing him, Jack said, "Do you really think that being in love is rot?"

"I don't want to talk about love." She seemed uncomfortable. The mood shifted.

"I'm sorry. I won't say another word about it."

"Thank you." She suddenly reached across the table and took his hand. "I did like what you said, though. It's just too much for me at the moment, all right?"

"Of course. So, come on, tell me more about the BBC."

"Well, our boss is a Mr. John Reith. I've never met him, but everyone is afraid of him because he is supposed to be a bit of a tartar...."

Once back at Onslow Square, Marion merged into the general conversation and social ebb and flow of the set and Jack felt that he had lost the closeness he had enjoyed with her that morning. As evening approached, coffee and tea were replaced by whisky and brandy. Alfred had left after lunch but returned at about nine o' clock with a male companion whom he introduced as Bernard. Bernard was a handsome, athletic type, given to an easy charm and conversation. Jack found him likeable and was happy that Alfred was obviously enamoured of the man. All-in-all it was relaxed and subdued.

And disappointing for Jack because Marion spent most of the evening deep in conversation with Charles. They were still together when he finally left, and he was sure he saw her reach out to touch his face.

Late March. The sky bluer, the air warming a little, the set began to meet on Sunday afternoons and venture outside for their entertainment. Harry, Antonia, and Charles all owned motor cars, and there would be a scramble to ensure a seat with whomever one was pursuing on that day.

There were trips to the seaside, Brighton usually, where there would be deckchairs, a chill breeze, a picnic hamper and paddling in a sea still icy from the winter.

Bernard was now a regular presence. He took much of Alfred's attention, although out here in public, even on a near-deserted beach, they were more circumspect in their affections.

At one of these seaside outings, Antonia brought a gramophone and the set members partnered up to waltz in the surf, feet bare and quickly numb. The men's trouser legs were rolled up, but unavoidably drenched by the bitterly cold spray and occasional rogue wave. Jack made for Marion but Charles snatched her up, with a glance in his direction that made Jack wonder if this had become a game to him. Jack found himself in Antonia's arms. Not an unpleasant experience, but he wanted to share this mad, happy moment with Marion.

Later, back in Onslow Square, Antonia took Jack's hand and led him up to her bed. By then he was too drunk to remember how he had come to be there. Somewhere deep in that alcoholic fog and confusion there was anger. It was a clenched fist. It was a red-glowing hot coal. Charles was making a fool of him. The man didn't want Marion, he merely enjoyed keeping her from Jack. He was sure of that now. Well, this time he would take something for himself, and that was Antonia.

She was a skilful lover, but even here, that disconnection was evident. She never spoke a word. Like the waltz they had shared, however, it was far from unpleasant. She kissed him hotly and with something akin to passion. She let him explore every part of her and demanded his invasion of her. He clung to the brief comfort and fulfilment it offered, knowing that once it had passed, Antonia would simply rise from her bed, dress, and return to her guests.

When she did so, Jack stayed where he was and lay, motionless in the dark. Now he felt regret. Marion would have seen them leave the room together. She would have known what was to happen. Was she jealous, angry, hurt? Or, worse, did she not care at all?

Easter Saturday fell on April 3rd and because the weather was mild, the set celebrated the holiday with a picnic in Epping Forest. Antonia had promised a special Easter treat for them all that evening and once again, overnight bags had been packed.

The three-motorcar convoy reached the forest in the middle of the afternoon. The set made its camp in a clearing at the end of a short woodland path and the hamper was opened. Conversation turned quickly to the threat of a General Strike.

"It would be illegal, sedition in fact," Harry Edmunds said. "Simple as that." He poured himself another glass of champagne and leaned back against the tree he had made his own.

"Nonsense, as usual, Harry," Marion said. "The Trades Union General Council are considering a sympathy call-out in support of the miners. That's all. No one is interested in a revolution."

"I thought you loved revolutions. I seem to remember your telling me that Lenin was a hero of yours."

"I admire what he did, but it isn't going to happen here."

"Really? What about the Communist Party of Great Britain?" Harry all-but spat the words out. "They even have their own MP, what's his name, that coloured chap, Shapurji Saklatava?"

"He's a Labour MP," Marion countered.

"He's a communist troublemaker, who's hiding behind Ramsey MacDonald's coat tails. He's spouting all sorts of red rubbish, whipping up the masses."

"You're wrong, Harry."

"Oh, am I my dear? What do I know? I mean I'm only a member of parliament. I'm only a junior secretary in the Foreign Office. A young woman in a typing room would obviously know much more about it than I would."

Harry's barbed remark looked to have stung Marion badly. She was red-faced and for once, struggling to respond.

"That isn't fair, and you know it," Jack said.

"Isn't it?" Harry said. "I don't remember seeing you wandering the corridors of Westminster either. But you're obviously better informed than me, like your pretty little chum here. So, come along, tell me more."

"Please, darlings, that's enough," Antonia was on her feet. There was an edge to her voice which brooked no disobedience.

The gramophone was cranked into life. Nicholas jumped to his feet and proceeded to make an ass of himself trying to dance the Charleston with Antonia. His face was red, and he was obviously out of breath, but he was laughing and enjoying himself immensely.

"Shall we dance?" Jack said. His voice was dry and thick, but here was an opportunity and he had to take it. He got to his feet and held out his hand to Marion. She looked up at him, quizzical for a moment, then she smiled, and in a moment, was in his arms.

Soon the clearing was filled with brash jazz and the out-of-breath laughter of the set at full pelt. After the record had scratched its way to its end for the fifth time, Alfred replaced it with a waltz. He took Bernard in his arms. Jack admired their courage. The clearing appeared to be secluded and there were few others in the forest today, but there was still a chance of discovery.

Jack realised that Marion was close to him. He took her hand and she folded herself against him and they danced. He held her tightly and she didn't resist. It became more caress than waltz.

When the record crackled to its conclusion, Marion broke away and ran off into the forest. Without a pause, Jack followed. He heard someone in the clearing impersonate a hunting horn and there was a burst of cheering. Jack was aware that he was behaving like a love-sick fool. He didn't care. At that moment, Marion was all that mattered.

When he caught up with her, she was leaning, coquettishly against a tree. She stared at him from beneath heavy eyelids. He went to her and kissed her. The heat of it was a delight. She clung to him and pressed her body against him and he consumed her.

It was dark when the party returned to Onslow Square. The lights and the warmth and the immediate resumption of music and drinking was, Jack decided, the most exciting moment of his life so far. He belonged to these people. He was part of them. He was made dizzy by the way Marion clung to his arm as they had walked back to the clearing after their kiss and insisted he sit with her in the back of Harry's motorcar. Now she sat on the arm of his chair in Antonia's drawing room.

Everyone was drunk. Harry asleep, Nicholas heavy-eyed and no longer part of the party. Samuel took his usual place at the piano. In the corner of the room, Alfred kissed Bernard shamelessly.

Jack rose to replenish his and Marion's drinks. Alfred met him at the cabinet.

"Seems like we're both happy men, eh, Jack?" Alfred said.

"Yes, so it seems."

Alfred looked across at Bernard who was now deep in conversation with Antonia. "He's a thoroughly decent type, you know. He reminds me of you in some ways."

"You're pretty decent yourself, Alfred."

"Seems like another world now, doesn't it?"

"What does?"

"The Front, France, the bloody war."

"I suppose it does."

"All that killing and fighting, bloody waste of time if you ask me. So, I for one, do not intend to waste another moment and nor," Alfred pushed one of the drinks he had poured gently against Jack's chest, "should you, old bean."

The party grew noisy. Jack was uncomfortable. Charles had brought some of his friends along for the evening. This new crowd was much younger than the others and were getting out of hand. Antonia, however, looked on and smiled her inscrutable, benign smile.

"Jack," Marion whispered and drained her glass quickly. "Come with me."

She stood. Jack laid his own scotch down and followed her out of the drawing room and up the stairs to one of the many spare bedrooms. His heart pumped heavily. He trembled a little. He was excited, yes, but also afraid. He was not sure why that should be, but he could not deny the emotion. He closed the door. The lights were out, but the curtains open to let in the glow of the street. Marion stood at the foot of the bed. She reached behind her neck to unclip something then allowed her dress to fall to the floor.

She was naked. She wore no undergarments. Nothing. She stood, unashamed, blatant, and waiting for him. Dry-mouthed, uncertain, Jack approached the bed. He could see her face in the dim light. She looked afraid. He saw her swallow then she said in a half-whisper, her voice dry; "It's your turn, Jack."

"My...My turn?" He stepped back. "I thought you...."

"Don't you like me?" Her voice was light and teasing, but there was an undertone of hurt.

"Yes, but this is so…blatant. I don't know—"

"Come on Jack, this how we are. None of us belong to each other here." Her tone was forthright now, slightly mocking even, but that hurt was still present. "We made a pact that we would live as free people and that no one would own anyone else in the set."

"You mean that you and the others have—?"

"Yes, of course." Her voice broke a little "But that doesn't mean…I'm not a whore, Jack, if that's what you think. We all…."

"I thought…I thought you…."

"What? That I loved you? Is that what you thought? You ridiculous man. I love everyone in the set. We all love each other."

She didn't mean it. Surely that couldn't be true.

Angrily, she grabbed her dress from the floor and held it against herself as if for protection. "Get out," she said. "Go away, Jack. Please. Now."

He swung round and clattered downstairs toward the inferno of voices and laughter. He wanted to leave but couldn't. Samuel was still playing. The cloth roll he sometimes brought with him lay on the piano, which meant that the treat Antonia promised would not be long in coming. Jack needed it. He craved the hazy borderlines between wakefulness, dreams, and oblivion it allowed him to travel. He had no use for reality tonight.

Two, perhaps three weeks passed. Jack didn't go back to the set, because seeing Marion would be too painful. The decision to abandon Antonia and her clan, however, left him bleak and lonely, a state he knew well enough. Loneliness built walls about him and blocked out the world. It stranded him on an island of his own thought and emotion and suffocated him with the realities of his *difference*. It picked at the ever-open wound of his aloneness and shrieked the truth in his ears until it drove him to the nearest bottle and away into an alcoholic netherland where there was no pain.

He functioned. He worked, ate, washed, shaved, and slept. He remembered, too, when alone in his cramped terrace dwelling. He relived every moment he had spent with Marion, every glance and smile, moment of hope and moment of disappointment. Then came the shattering moment of his coming to *be*, the meeting with Lyle in that bombed-out house, Lizzy, oh Lizzy, the screaming crew of that burning Zeppelin, Silvertown, the horror of war.... It was a brightly coloured dance of sound, scent, and touch, growing ever faster and wilder until he would shout for it to stop, cover his ears, gasp for breath, then stumble to the little cupboard in his minute kitchen and draw out whatever liquid comfort he could find. When there was no bottle, he would pull on his jacket and hurry out to the nearest pub.

But, in the end, no matter how jolly the company, loud the music and vicious the fights, it would always end in that oh-so-familiar stagger homeward where solitude waited like a mangy, softly growling dog.

This was such a Saturday night. The dazzling glare of Antonia's set seemed like a dream now, something remembered but that never happened. Jack worked hard to keep his gait steady and his course straight. He navigated the streets between the Prince William and his house by instinct. There were sudden flares of light, brief glimpses of The Fabric, common when he was drunk. It was as if some part of his mind, his being, had been opened by the alcohol, a door unlocked, a view given. In those moments he walked a road of fiery threads in the company of a million, million souls, who glowed soft white and sang with joy. He would smile then. He would feel his heart mend. He would ache to stay and join them, here in the weft and weave of the universe. Then, just as suddenly it was dark and cold, puddles splashed under his feet, and the air was tainted with the perfume of coal fires.

Almost home.

And what of it? What awaited him there other than his bed?

A figure lurched into the road in front of him and blocked his path, a few yards from his front door. A fellow drunk, no doubt.

Resigned to trouble, Jack called to him, "Who's there? What do you want?"

"Jack. It's me." Clipped accent, breathless. Familiar.

It took a moment or two for Jack to recognise the voice.

"Alfred?"

"Bernard's dead, Jack. They killed him."

"Dead? Who…?"

Alfred staggered a few more steps to fall into Jack's arms. He wept. He sobbed like a child. He shuddered and choked as Jack struggled to hold him upright. He smelled drink on him.

"Come on, let's go indoors."

Jack half-carried the broken, inebriated Alfred into the hall of his house. When he switched on the electric light, he saw that Alfred was injured. His left eye was puffed almost shut. His cheek was bruised and grazed. Blood seeped from a cut bottom lip; more was dried under his swollen nose. Alfred grunted as he slumped into one of Jack's armchairs in front of the fireplace. Sobered by his shock, Jack put the kettle on the gas ring then dampened a towel and returned to Alfred to clean his face a little.

"What on earth happened?"

Alfred's voice sounded thick and strangled. There was pain in his voice. "We went to The Caravan, it's a private club for those who feel as we do. There were men, waiting outside."

"What men?"

"I didn't see them. It was too dark. But they set upon us. They called us fucking sodomites and filth. I managed to fight them, but they had Bernard on the ground. They…they kicked him and hit him with billiard cues. When they finished, they ran off. I thought Bernard was alive. His eyes were open, but he wouldn't speak or move. I couldn't find a heartbeat, and I realised that…I've seen it before. We both have, Jack. That stare. All that blood. He was gone. Those fucking cowards beat him to death. I let him down. I couldn't save him."

"Alfred, I know you would have done your best. You're badly injured as it is. They might have killed you. Did you call the police?"

A rueful, humourless chuckle. "The police? They would have finished what those bastards had started if they caught me. No, I ran. I didn't have a choice. That's how it is for us." He rubbed at his eyes with his sleeve. "I need a drink. A proper drink."

"No, I'm sorry. I don't have anything tonight." Why else would he have ventured out to the Prince William? "What about a cup of tea?"

"No, thank you."

Jack wished there was somewhere he could find a bottle but knew that would be impossible at this time of night.

"I love him, Jack. I love him with all my heart." He collapsed into helpless crying again. This time there seemed to be no consolation. Jack sat on the floor beside him and held his hand until the tears dried and Alfred finally fell asleep. Jack found a blanket and covered him, then settled himself into the other armchair with a blanket of his own.

An hour or so later, Alfred lifted his head and said, "I think I need that tea now, old chap."

Jack fumbled and struggled through the job of making a pot of tea. Alfred's sudden appearance and news had sobered him a little, but his hands still shook and took their time obeying the commands his brain gave them.

"He's gone." Alfred clasped his cup tightly in both hands and rocked steadily back and forth. "I've lost him."

"I know—"

"No, you don't. I've *lost* him. I can't go to his funeral. I can't go and see his body. I can't...I can't mourn for him."

"Surely, you can go to the church."

Alfred shook his head and drained his cup. Jack poured him another.

"There's nothing to stop me, of course, but do you think I want to skulk in the back pew while the man I love is mourned over and buried by others who think they have a claim to him? We belonged together and now he's been taken away from me." He sounded angry. "That club, The Caravan Club, is a foul place, Jack. They all are. They attract the worst as well as the best, but where else can we go? And all the time we're there, we're wondering if the police will burst in and crack our heads and then drag us all out for everyone to see our shame."

"That isn't right. It's cruel."

"Yes. It is." Alfred drew the back of his left hand across his eyes and sniffed loudly. "To think I went to war for this." He raised his glass in a scornful toast. "Fuck the King and fuck the country."

The night wore on. Alfred slept fitfully waking to sob out his heart over and over again.

Jack covered himself with a blanket and finally fell asleep in the armchair. He left the electric light switched on. His last moment of awareness was of Alfred staring across the room, his eyes blank and devoid of any life.

When Jack woke in the morning, Alfred was gone.

Worried and fearful for his friend, Jack found a neighbour who owned a telephone and called Antonia to ask if she knew Alfred's address.

"Jack Smith? This is a surprise." Not a pleasant one by her cold, disinterested tone. "I thought you'd abandoned us. Are we that boring? Why on earth are you calling me at such an ungodly hour? Are you gracing us with your presence tonight or snubbing us yet again?"

"I'm not...." Why the hell was he explaining himself? "I need to know where Alfred lives."

"Whatever for?"

Jack fought his own irritation, which was veering rapidly toward anger. "His friend...lover, Bernard was attacked and killed last night. Alfred was here and in an awful state. I think he's gone home, but I'm worried for his safety."

"Oh God, poor Alfred. Just a moment." Her tone belied her expression of concern. She sounded bored by the whole thing. A pause, then she was back with an address. A flat in Tottenham.

It was past eleven by the time Jack arrived. He was tired and hungry but determined not to rest until he found Alfred. The Sunday-quiet street was workaday, scruffy, and well-worn. Entrance to the flat looked to be via a door next to the shop. Jack hammered at the knocker. No reply. He tried again, harder and for longer. There was still nothing, but the plain, paint-peeling facade of the door. He stepped back and called up to the window of the flat.

"Alfred! Alfred!"

No reply. He returned to the door and pounded it with his fist. He had to get in. He had to know that Alfred was alright.

"Are you having trouble, sir?"

Jack started and turned to see a police constable standing a few feet away. A light drizzle had begun and the constable wore his cape against it. He was a beefy looking character but seemed friendly enough. At the moment, anyway.

"I'm concerned for my friend. Alfred Ellerton. He lives here. In that flat."

"Doesn't seem as if he is in."

"Hopefully."

"I'm sorry?"

"What I mean is, I'm afraid that if he is in there, he may have hurt himself in some way."

Now the constable looked concerned. "Are you sure?"

"The last time I saw him, he was distraught over a bereavement. Please, I need to get in to see him."

The constable appeared to consider this for a moment then nodded.

"You wait here," he said, then went to the entrance of the grocer's shop. Closed. "All right, desperate measures are called for. You'd best look away. You didn't see this." The constable produced a small fabric roll from his pocket "There's times when we can't wait for anyone else to help and we have to take matters into our own hands." The roll contained wires and hooks. The lock picker's tool kit.

The moment the door was opened, Jack surged ahead of the constable who called for him to be careful. There was a steep narrow staircase that led to a small landing and the door to Alfred's flat. Praying that it would be unlocked, Jack turned the doorknob. The door gave. He rushed inside.

He knew.

He knew before he stepped into the bedroom and saw Alfred.

Who lay on the counterpane.

A bottle of whisky was overturned on the bedside cabinet, its contents long soaked into the rug by the bed. For a moment, Jack believed him drunk and felt a wash of relief. Then he saw the syringe and vial on the table, beside the bottle. Both were empty. He recognised them as the same as the ones brought to the set's special evenings by Samuel Levinson. Alfred's left shirtsleeve was rolled above the elbow. A belt, presumably used as a tourniquet, was loose about his bicep.

Alfred's bruised and battered face was ashen, his lips blue, his mouth open and slack. His eyes were closed. When Jack grabbed his hand, it was limp, lifeless, and horribly cold.

He became aware of the constable's presence behind him.

"I think he's gone, sir."

"I was in the war with him."

"Were you, sir?"

"We were stretcher bearers."

"You have my deepest respect, sir. I was carried off the field by the likes of you and him. Under fire it was, but they got me back safe and sound."

Alfred looked oddly angry. Jack had seen his share of ruined human bodies, but this one broke him in a way none of the anonymous soldiers scattered over the battlefield ever could. He felt his strength give and he collapsed to his knees and sobbed like a child.

Dear, kind, funny, brave, and heartbroken Alfred.

It was raining much harder by the time Jack arrived at Onslow Square. Antonia, who greeted him at door, was, as always, expensively dressed, perfumed and utterly self-contained.

"He's dead. He killed himself."

Antonia was ashen, but there was no change to her demeanour. Jack still felt the erotic charge, tightening the atmosphere, as if their shared sorrow had ignited their lust. It was wrong and horrible, but he couldn't shake the feeling away.

"This is dreadful news," Antonia said, her voice still the same languorous drawl as it always was. "You must come in and sit down, Jack. You need a drink. Perhaps I could telephone Samuel to bring you—"

"No, thank you."

"Of course. Thank you for coming to tell me. I shall pass a message on to everyone. We will hold a wake in Alfie's honour next Sunday night. I do hope you can come, Jack."

"Yes," he said before he had time to think about his answer. "I'll be there."

Everything went on much as usual on that following Sunday night. people were out enjoying the balmy May evening. Picture houses and theatres were open, the muddle of motor cars and horse-drawn transport clogged the capital's streets as always. The fashionable cloche hat and scandalously short skirts were much in evidence as were the dinner jacket and slicked and shiny, sharply parted hair.

Marion was among the members of the set gathered at Antonia's. Jack saw her the moment he walked into the drawing room. Everyone was there, including a handful of occasional members Jack had not come to know well. Rather than an air of mourning, the room seemed to be gripped by an odd excitement. The atmosphere was taut with anticipation. Most of the conversation was not about Alfred, but the forthcoming General Strike. In this room, however, there was little doubt as to whose side the majority were on.

"I've already volunteered to act as a Special Constable," Charles was saying. "Break a few of those communist buggers' heads, that's what I say. That'll soon put a stop to this nonsense."

"Here, here," Harry said from his armchair. He raised his scotch in a toast.

"I hear they are going to need people to run trains and buses," Nicholas said. "That's the job for me. Always fancied myself as something of an engine driver."

Laughter.

"Have you signed up with the OMS yet, Jack?" Nicholas said.

"No, not yet. I'll be working as normal. Engineers are not being called out."

"Not going to be able to do much, though, are you?" Charles said. "So, you need to think about how you're going to do your bit for the country."

Marion, Jack noted was quiet. He didn't blame her. Any dissent from the popular view in the room would be crushed tonight. She sat apart, by the piano, sipping a cocktail of some sort. She glanced up at him then back at her drink. She held a wall about herself, which made her unapproachable.

Antonia rose and tapped a spoon against the side of her glass for attention. She then checked that each of the member's glass was charged. The room was silent. She raised her tumbler of whisky.

"To Alfie. Our friend."

"To Alfie," the set chorused. "Our friend."

Jack was deeply moved by the simple toast. At last, it seemed as if the set were showing some respect for their fallen member.

"Now," Antonia said. "Each of us must relate some memory of Alfie. Tell us what he meant to you. I will go first. Alfie could always be relied on to turn up and join in."

Others followed.

Marion: "He was the first person to befriend me when I joined the set."

Harry: "Great fun, always cheerful and sunny."

Nicholas: "You could talk to Alfie about anything."

Charles: "Delightful company. A dear chap."

Samuel: "He could be sad sometimes, but he never wanted to make anyone else feel that way."

Jack: "I didn't know him for long and yet he was my friend." A shallow tribute, but what else could he say that would truly express what he felt? There was too much, and most of it not to be thrown to this group for them to snuffle over.

There were other words from the irregular members. Another toast, then Samuel played ragtime and one or two of the younger irregulars began dancing. There was an air of relief, as if the hard part was done and they could move on to more uplifting distractions.

The set drank heavily. Samuel produced a small packet of white powder. Using two tiny spoons, the guests began to sniff it into their noses. He also had the syringes and vials. The wake transformed into a party. People danced frantically to the gramophone. All Jack could see were their red faces, their sweat, and their desperation to lose themselves and forget their loss. He knew that Alfred was part of this. He knew that Alfred loved the wild times, but he was gone and surely there should be some restraint here.

Jack sat in a corner and watched. Marion was in Harry's arms as he led her through some ugly excuse for a dance. Jack felt nauseous. It was as if the room spun about him. He caught Marion's eye and she looked unhappy. Jack got to his feet and took a step toward her. He was dizzy and angry. The younger guests, friends of Charles, were noisy and made clumsy by drink. A vase of flowers was knocked over. Glass shattered; water splashed across the carpet. Antonia ignored it. Nicholas made a fool of himself by trying to join in with their mad dancing. He tripped and fell, much to their amusement. The party threatened to spin out of control.

The doorbell rang loudly through the din.

Antonia took the gramophone needle off the record. There were moans of protest. She clapped for attention. She had, she announced, arranged something special for the remainder of the evening. The set declared it "delicious" and "jolly exciting." Antonia smiled her enigmatic smile and said no more as she swept out of the room. When she returned, she trailed a tall, serious looking woman in her wake. The woman wore a luxurious, and obviously expensive fur coat. When she removed it, an equally expensive dress was revealed.

"Ladies and gentlemen," Antonia announced. "May I introduce Mrs. Josephine Anderson. Josephine is a medium…" a highly successful one by the look of those clothes, Jack mused "…and tonight she will be holding a séance, here in my drawing room. So, people, let's gather around the table and commune with the spirit world and perhaps enjoy a reunion with our beloved Alfie."

"I will do my utmost to call upon your dear friend," Josephine said. She smiled a sad smile that seemed excruciatingly insincere to Jack. He was intrigued, nonetheless.

She was affectedly elegant, but hawk-faced, her eyes hard and devoid of expression. She took her seat at the gleaming round table in

Antonia's dining room and the regular members of the set arranged themselves about her. The half dozen or so others sat and lounged around the room, settling down for the fun. One of them, an obviously tipsy young woman giggled helplessly. Josephine silenced her with a sharp command.

"This," she declared solemnly, "is not some frivolous entertainment. We are to approach the dead. We are to commune with those we have lost. If you cannot treat this with respect, then I would ask you to leave."

A pause. No one moved.

"Very well. Those of us around this table must join hands. Once joined, no one must break the circle. Do you understand?"

Everyone nodded and murmured an assent.

Jack found himself next to Harry Edmunds on one side and Charles on the other. Harry's grip was soft, slightly damp. Charles' strong and firm. He glanced across at Marion, who sat on Antonia's left. She looked uncomfortable. Jack wanted to hold her hand and tell her that it was all nonsense and that there was nothing to be afraid of, but he couldn't. Some ridiculous, fearful part of his fake humanity stopped him.

It was past ten. The curtains were closed against the night. The lights in the drawing room were all turned off but for one standard lamp, which cast a soft orange-red glow over Josephine Anderson.

"If anyone wishes to leave the circle, please do so now."

A moment. Exchanged glances. Did anyone dare? Was anyone such a rotten sport as to walk away from this marvellous game? No one was.

Josephine took a long, deep breath. "We have lost many. The war has taken those we love. Many of us here, if not all, have someone who has passed through the gates during those times. I sense that one of you has lost too many. A soldier perhaps?"

"Yes," Charles said.

"And you have all suffered a great sadness of late. A tragedy. There will be comfort for everyone tonight."

Jack pushed back on a wave of anger. These people had hardly mourned for Alfred. They did not seem in need of comfort.

"Then there will be many who wish to speak to us. We will not have time for all of them, but at least we will hear from some of those to whom we have bid farewell. Now, I must have complete silence. I must clear my mind so that I may become a vessel."

Jack was unimpressed by her showmanship.

The silence was now complete, but for the ticking of a clock on the mantelpiece. A few sounds filtered in from the city outside, but were oddly distant, like the murmurings of another reality far away from the small, intense world Josephine had created in this room. She sat upright. Her eyes closed, lips parted. Her breathing deepened and grew faster until she panted, as if out of breath.

A sound emerged from her mouth. A groan.

The Fabric flared, bright and vivid in Jack's mind.

He was startled. He had not visited Down Street station since Lizzy's death. His connection to The Fabric had dimmed, apart from his recent drunken glimpses and that opium-fuelled journey into its heart, an experience that may or not have been real. Now, suddenly, he could see it in his mind's eye as clearly as when he had first come to *be*. He felt its thrum and shudder. He saw the plaits of its infinite thread. He heard the voices and felt the energies of a million, million beings both living and dead. Those fed by, and those that had become part of, this nerve system of the universe.

The medium's trance had loosened the constraint put on her by consciousness and flesh. He saw her life energies boil into The Fabric like a glowing tentacle that reached for the glittering fragments of those who had died. He saw it drag a delicate form from the swirling fiery currents and it lift it clear.

"Charles," she said in a deep, male voice. "Old fellow. Charles, how are you?"

"Watson?" Charles breathed. "Is that really you?"

Jack saw the dusty, sparkling shards that were all that remained of Watson. They spilled from the tentacle's grip like glistening grains of sand. Jack felt Watson's pain and grief at being plucked from his rest, set against his desperation to speak with the living he had lost.

"I'm all right," Watson said through Josephine's unmoving lips. "Don't worry about me, old fellow…I miss you…." He dissolved then and fell softly back into the gentle embrace of The Fabric. There was a brief flare of energy and connection.

Then Jack knew. He understood who and what Josephine Anderson was. He tried to reach her. He tried to force himself through The Fabric and connect with her. But it wasn't possible. The energy flows were too dense. The swirl of the dead as they coalesced about her was blinding. He saw and felt pain. This hurt them. She dragged them from their peace to parade them before her audience like circus freaks. The dead were being yanked to life again for their amusement and comfort. What remained of their consciousness flared bright. The pain was too much to bear. Many of them simply broke apart again and settled in the glowing threads of The Fabric.

Which glowed brighter and brighter as his own connections to it blazed into life. Jack *felt* the world around him and it was unbearable; the stench of human flesh, the storm of dust that swirled through the air around him and scraped at his skin. He felt the grief, anger, fear, and bewilderment of the people here. He felt their breath and was bombarded by their heartbeats. His flesh felt as if it was peeling from his body. His eardrums bent under the onslaught of sound.

He wanted it to stop.

Josephine was speaking again. The voice that issued from her frozen mouth was Alfred's. Jack felt him, heard him.

"I'm all right. I'm happy here. Sorry, I can't stay and chat but...." There was pain behind the words. He wanted to be released. His essence flapped in the prison of Josephine's grip like a butterfly, frantic in a glass killing jar. He slipped through her fingers and melted back into the comforting embrace of the fabric.

"Jack?" A woman's voice now spilled from Josephine's frozen lips. "Jack, I'm here."

Lizzy.

Jack saw her re-formed. She reached toward him. He felt her unutterable grief as the moment of her final agony returned to her. She was a puppet, dancing to Josephine's ugly tune.

"*Stop this.*"

Jack lurched to his feet, breaking hands with the others as he did so. His chair tipped over onto the floor behind him. Josephine screamed and grabbed at her head. The room erupted into shouting and crying. Someone demanded that the lights go on.

Jack's rage was the most intense he had ever felt. Tears coursed down his cheeks. "Leave them alone," he yelled, unable to control his voice, unable to control anything. It felt as if some seal had broken inside him to release an unstoppable hurricane of emotion. "Leave them where they are."

The shouting ceased and the tumult stilled. He was aware that everyone's attention was on him, even Josephine. She trembled violently. Her face was ashen.

"You're hurting them."

Josephine shook her head. She began to cry. "No, I'm not. I'm reuniting them with their loved ones."

"You're like me," Jack yelled at her. "You're the same as me."

"I don't know what you're talking about." She sounded frightened now. "Please, go away."

"You're an observer, a collector—"

"That's enough." Harry shoved himself between Jack and the table and shoved him back. Charles grabbed Jack's arm and snarled into his ear. "Get out."

"You don't understand. I have to talk to her. She's...we're the same...she's...."

"Please make him go away," Josephine sobbed. "Please."

"Jack," Antonia said. Her arm was about Josephine's shoulder. Her face was stony, her voice cold. "Leave this house, immediately. Go. Now."

Distressed, humiliated, confused, Jack needed a drink.

He found a pub that was still open despite the lateness of the hour. The landlord poured him a pint and a whisky chaser. "You look a bit pale, old chum." The landlord slid the drinks toward him. "This'll cheer you up,"

Jack paid and set to work. He turned round, elbows on the bar. The place was empty, but for a few characters who looked as if they were regulars. Everyone was quiet and huddled into themselves. There was another figure, over in a corner, a big man in a heavy coat, his trilby firmly in place and hiding his eyes, despite being indoors. Jack shivered. The man was watching him. Jack didn't look away. He was suddenly in the mood for an argument.

The man reached for his own glass. It looked like a gin and tonic, but Jack couldn't be sure. There was an air of threat about him. He drained the glass, got to his feet, and made for the bar. Jack tensed. He was sure he had met this man before.

"Another," the man said and there was authority in his voice. He glanced at Jack. "Good evening."

He extended a big, strong-looking hand. Only then did Jack recognize him and experienced a moment of cold dread.

"Lyle," Jack said. "What do you want with me this time?"

"Jack Smith. It's been a long time." There was a hint of something in Lyle's voice that Jack didn't like. Was it scorn? Amusement?

"It has, thank God."

Lyle chuckled to himself as he paid for his drink. "You look as if you've had a bad night."

"What do you want?" Jack asked. His drink was only half finished and he was having trouble forcing it down. He didn't want to talk to Lyle. He didn't want to be anywhere near him. He wanted to go home. He wanted to hide.

"It took a while to find you," Lyle said. "Contrary to popular belief, we are not omniscient."

"We? I still don't know who you are, Lyle."

"I told you, on our first meeting. I represent the creators of this wretched little world."

"So, you're an angel. Is that it?"

"If you want to think of me in that way, then, yes, I'm an angel." He shrugged. "Although, the name suggests the divine, which is wholly inaccurate. The creators are builders. A planet is no more than a brick in the wall of reality. If the brick is flawed, the wall is weakened. We assess every one, discard the broken, and replace it with something better." Lyle moved closer. Jack stayed where he was. Defiant. "You're troubled, Jack, and it is because you are filled with your own sense of existence and obsessed with your needs. Remember, you are no more than a tool, a gauge, employed to measure the worth of this place."

Lyle's off-hand contempt was more painful than it should be.

"Then why make me like them. Why give me all these feelings and emotions? A slide rule doesn't need a heart."

"A good and fair question. Landlord? Another, for me and my friend." Lyle considered his answer for a moment. Then he said, "A gauge needs to measure. It needs to be calibrated and suitable for the task. An automaton would merely gather dry facts and figures from the surface. You and your kind need to absorb, and to *be* what the inhabitants are. When you are recovered and examined, the creators will be able to understand motives and reasons."

"Recovered?"

"Not yet. Not for a long while. You collectors are expensive to build, so you are made durable, almost unbreakable. The first collector was placed here two thousand years ago. It was not a success, but I'm sure you're familiar with that story by now. We've learned a lot over those two millennia. The most important lesson was that you collectors must be hidden and as innocuous and human-like as possible, so as not to arouse suspicion, superstition, and hostility." The mood changed; the intensity eased. "Now, to the real reason I've dropped in to meet you tonight. I understand that there has been an incident."

"I presume you are talking about Josephine Anderson."

"Yes." Lyle leaned forward. "You two should not have met, but, as I said, we are not omnipotent and cannot control everything."

"I need to talk to her. I need others of my kind."

"I'm here to warn you, as I did in France, a friendly warning mind, to stay away from Josephine, because she has been here for much longer than you, and her end is drawing near."

"Her *end*?"

"I'm called The Hound. Did you know that? I hunt and I enforce. Josephine is fighting the inevitable. When the creators call you back, it's always easier and less painful to go willingly. Most of you do, others fight back, or run. I always win, Jack. Always."

"Don't hurt her," Jack said.

"What happens to Josephine is none of your concern."

"You bastard—"

Lyle moved close again and this time Jack saw his eyes. He saw darkness. He saw infinity. He saw cracks in Lyle's skin, hairbreadth seams that bled light, as if the man was stitched together from sheets of flesh, a hastily constructed sac in which the real Lyle was concealed.

Lyle sighed, the sound oddly sad. "I'm going to be lenient this time Jack, but, please, stay out of trouble."

Jack wanted to get out. He struggled to breathe because the air in the room was suddenly viscous and hot. It clogged his throat and congealed in his lungs. It tasted foul. Lyle held out his hand. Jack shook it, unable to resist. Lyle's grip was hard and tight.

"Goodnight, Jack."

And Lyle was gone, replaced by patterns of light and shadow, by a loud burst of laughter from one of the elderly patrons, by the smell of beer, by the clink of glasses, by the loud beat of Jack's own heart.

He had to warn her.

He returned to Onslow Square, convinced that he was too late, and that Josephine had already left. More than two hours had passed since he had been asked to leave. It was almost midnight, meaningless to the set. The lights were still on, which meant that they would still be dancing and drinking or falling into an opium dream, behaving as if the night was eternal and the real world was an illusion. At that moment, Jack hated them.

Jack waited in the shadows on the opposite side of the road and stared at the light. His hatred quickly dissipated into regret. He wanted to be in there, as lost in pleasure as they were, riding The Fabric as Samuel Levy's chemical delight surged through his body. He could forget his otherness when he was with the set because they embraced otherness.

The Fabric....

There was a brief flare, as if the molecules that made up the street, the house, the air he breathed had been prised apart to reveal the threads that bound them together. Those threads pulsed and flickered. He felt....

Her.

Josephine Anderson.

Close. In the house.

There was something else, feeling its way along those threads. Something dark and malevolent.

Lyle. The Hound.

Jack ran across the road and all-but threw himself at Antonia's door. He stabbed at the bell, again, again. He pounded its surface with his fist. He shouted to be let in. The door remained firmly closed. He was panicked. He was dizzy, hot. It was hard to breathe. He had to get in. He had to warn Josephine—

The door opened. Jack made to rush through but slammed into a body who pushed back. Someone grabbed his left arm. Charles and some other, younger, man who was obviously fit and strong.

"No, you don't." The words were hissed through Charles' gritted teeth.

"How dare you." Antonia, standing behind her guards. "Go away. Leave us alone."

"I need to speak to Josephine Anderson."

"Absolutely not. She is very upset; in fact you have made her quite unwell."

Jack made a renewed attempt at breaking through, but the two men wrestled him back into the doorway.

"You heard her. Fuck off, Smith." Charles again. He was panting with effort, his face slick with sweat. He stank of anger and spite.

"Josephine. Josephine, it's me, Jack Smith. The collector."

Someone else stepped into the hallway. Marion, her face pale. She held back, as if frightened of him. At the same time, she seemed on the verge of tears. Jack made to speak to her.

Jack was suddenly driven over the threshold. He stumbled, then lost his balance and fell onto his back. The violent impact jarred through him and he lay for a moment, struggling to breathe, unable to move.

"Wait. Wait, I'll talk to him."

Josephine?

Jack struggled into a sitting position as Josephine Anderson emerged from the brightly lit house. Jack heard protest from within, Antonia, Charles, who urged her to go back inside. She raised a hand, an indication that it was all right.

"Lyle." Winded from his fall, Jack could barely form the word. "The…The Hound…He's coming."

Josephine crouched beside him. "I know."

"You have to run. You have to get away from here. I'll help you."

She placed a hand on his shoulder. The touch was electric. He experienced a storm of thoughts and impressions; a dark cold alleyway, lost, confused, frightened, a girl, kind yet hard, who led the way to a house full of women. Visitors, men, wealthy men, money, sex, pain, and pleasure. Chains, ropes, canes. Wounds that heal in minutes before being inflicted again and again. A grubby, crowded, dim-lit theatre, a show in which the dead spoke through the lips of the performers on its stage. A revelation, flight from the house of pain and pleasure, a new art…a maelstrom of sensations and moments brief yet vivid enough to tell a story. He realized, with a start, that they were Josephine's memories.

"You're very young," she said. "And kind." She shook her head. "You're too human, Jack. You have to step back. You have to detach yourself or you will suffer."

"You need to go, now. He's close."

"I know and I don't care. I've been here too long. I'm tired. I thought I could outrun them, but none of us can when the time com — ah." Josephine grabbed at her head, palms pressed against her temples, eyes screwed shut.

Jack held her and wanted to hold her like this forever. He never wanted to let go. He was lost in the contact. Her body shifted and changed, and he felt his own distort slightly, his flesh was drawn into her geometries and hers into his. It was the way flowers are drawn toward the sun, the way their blooms are turned to feed on the light.

He wanted to merge with her, to somehow crawl into her skin and find the core of her. Threads of light wound themselves about the two of them, as if the Fabric had reached out to reclaim them.

Josephine drew away. "I'm all right now. Please, I'm all right."

Jack noticed then that Charles, his fellow bodyguard, and Antonia all stood in the doorway. There was something wrong about the scene. They were motionless. The air seemed dense. It was hard to breathe. The light from the gas lamps that lit the street was oddly stable. There was no sound.

As if the world had frozen in that moment.

"You were never one to do as you were told, were you?" Lyle stepped out of the nearest spill of streetlight. Jack was unsurprised to see him.

The edges of the hound's body seemed unsteady, as if he was a projection rather than a physical presence.

"Josephine," Lyle said again. "Come with me."

"No." More croak than word, a primal groan torn from some deep, raw part of him.

Josephine pulled her hand away from his, suddenly. The break was painful, like an electric shock that ripped through his nerves and muscles.

"Go home, Jack," she said. "Leave us."

"You can't give in."

"I have to."

"Do as she says," Lyle said.

"No, I want to stay here, with you, even if this is the end. I have to—"

Something broke. Something welled up, desperation, anger at Lyle, a need to save the woman, a need to push back. It was a storm of unfocused emotion and it drove Jack to his feet then across the intervening space to collide violently with the hound, who seemed to crumple under the impact. He grunted, a human sound, staggered back and for a moment it seemed as if he would go down.

"This is why we keep you apart," Lyle said as he recovered. He sounded weary, saddened by the foolishness of those he was sent to instruct, guard, and collect. "Now, go away, Jack."

Then there was light, blinding white, that burst from the fault lines in his flesh and clothes. Jack was jolted by spears of icy cold. His skin burned. He was paralysed, frozen in place.

And from the core of the cold came scorching heat....

Flame licked at him and blistered and tore his skin from his bone. A voice howled out from the inferno. A woman. Screaming and screaming as she was consumed.

Lizzy. It was Lizzy.

Jack rushed into the inferno, deeper into the remains of the factory where metal was red hot and molten, where the air was hot enough to scorch lungs. He had only moments to find Lizzy in the glare of the fire, in the fog of toxic smoke. He tried to call her name, but his throat was burned and no sound came.

Jack's own agonies had become an impossible all-consuming cloak. They drove into him and shattered his mind. They tore him into a million white hot shards. He had no strength, his will dissolved.

He had to get out.

He had to find Lizzy.

A few more feet.

He fell back, regained his balance, and fought for breath.

Then the world was torn apart by the explosion. He felt every moment, every instant of pain as his skin and bone was shattered to ash. He screamed long after he had no flesh, no throat or mouth. And he saw Lizzy's destruction. He saw her char and blister and break and dissolve. He saw it and knew it and was aware of the fragment of time in which she felt her own agonies.

There was darkness.

As it cleared, he saw Antonia's house, the three frozen figures in its entrance, the unnaturally steady glow from the streetlamp.

He was on his feet.

Uninjured.

Lyle was human once more. A coat-muffled figure, hat low over his eyes. Broad, bulky, solid, yet there was something of the coiled snake about him. Something that could strike very quickly if necessary. "Go home," he said.

"Josephine, no...."

"I'm ready. It has to be this way."

Jack felt his strength drain. "Lyle?"

"What do you want?"

"Don't hurt her."

"Hurt?" Lyle sounded as if he didn't understand.

Everything was light. Jack heard Josephine's cry.

Then there was nothing but the street. Gas lamps flickered, the sound of nearby motor cars and horses broke the silence as Jack walked away.

He was sure he heard Marion call his name but did not look back.

CHAPTER THIRTEEN (2016)

"All right," Jack yelled. "I'll answer all your questions, just open the door!"

He stood in the road outside Louise's cottage. The snow had dissolved into sleet, which had dissolved into rain. A light burned in the downstairs window Jack knew to be Louise's sitting room.

He took a breath and shouted again.

"I'm not going away. I'll stand out here all night." He balked at the desperation in his voice. He must look and sound like a madman.

A moment, then the door finally opened. Louise stood, silhouetted against the hallway light, barring entrance, A familiar tableau. He wondered how many doors had been barred to him throughout his life.

"Go away, Jack. Please go away."

"Not until you listen to what I have to tell you."

Louise shook her head. A gust of icy wind drove through the layers of Jack's coat and work-dusty overalls. He shivered.

"Louise. I'll walk away if you want me to, but please, let me talk to you first. I need to help you."

"Help me? With what? Why do I need your help?"

"Richard."

"Richard is none of your business. You don't know anything about him. Please go away." Louise made to shut Jack out.

"I might be able to find him."

Louise paused, door half closed.

"Don't you dare make promises like that," she said. "Don't you dare."

"Hear me out. I'll stand out here and talk if you like. But please hear me out."

She was crying now. "Why can't you leave me alone? Why are you doing this to me?"

Jack said nothing. He waited, soaked and cold.

Another moment then Louise disappeared back into the cottage. She left the door open. Jack went inside and found her in the lounge, sprawled on the sofa. It was then that Jack saw a half-empty bottle of red and a glass on the floor by her feet.

"All right, sit down and talk to me." Louise jabbed her finger toward the armchair by the fireplace. It was unlit. The central heating had warmed the air, but the empty grate gave an illusion of coldness.

Jack sat down. Louise refilled her wine glass.

"So?" She sounded scornful. "Tell me how you're going to miraculously find my husband."

"It isn't a miracle."

"Magic then. Or do you have superpowers?" Alcohol had sharpened the edge of her voice. This acerbic version of Louise didn't sit right with what Jack knew about her.

There was no easy way to do this, Jack realized, so he took a moment then said, "I'm not what I seem. I've been on this Earth for a long time."

"You and me both."

"No, I'm serious. I've been here for a century. I wasn't born, I...came to be, at this age." He stopped, already floundering. He could see Louise's scepticism change into scorn.

"So, Mr. Lyle is your doctor. Is that it?"

"Lyle is my enemy."

Louise got to her feet, unsteady but maintaining her balance. "Go home, Jack. I can't deal with your crap anymore."

Jack struggled to find a response. Time was running out. He knew what he should do but was reluctant. Magical tricks seemed sordid at that moment, but what else did he have to get Louise's attention?

"Okay. I'll go, but I want to show you something first. Will you let me do that?"

Louise shrugged. "Whatever." He hated seeing her in this state. The wine had dissolved the kindness and the strength of her personality into bitterness, anger, and weakness.

"Stay there."

Jack got up and went into the kitchen.

Louise slumped back onto an armchair and covered her face with her hands. The beginnings of a hangover were already making themselves known. She felt muzzy but under the mush, horribly sober. Whatever Jack wanted to show her, was all right by her. She was too tired and dazed to argue. She laid her head back on the top of the chair and closed her eyes then opened them again when she heard Jack return. She was startled to see her sharpest kitchen knife in his hand.

He looked at her, took a deep breath then said. "I have to do this before I can answer your questions honestly. Okay?"

Louise heard herself answer in the affirmative, but she was suddenly frightened. How well did she know Jack? And here he was with a knife. She must have shown her fear because he raised his hands in a calming motion. "I'm not going to hurt you, I promise. Louise, I would never hurt you."

She nodded. Still unsure. Still tense and ready to fight or run.

Jack laid his left hand on the arm of the sofa and in a swift, sudden movement, sliced the blade of the knife across his wrist.

Christ. He had cut his wrist, here, in her house.

Louise cried out in shock and shrank back. She flinched from the expected fountain of blood. The cut was deep. Jack groaned in obvious pain and dropped the knife. He grabbed his injured arm with his right hand and wrenched his left hand back to expose the wound. Another groan of agony.

Louise shot to her feet. What the hell was he doing? Was this some melodramatic suicidal declaration of love? "Stop it. God, Jack, stop it."

But there was no blood.

None, not one speck.

Jack's face was drenched in sweat, his breath hard and ragged, but he didn't take his eyes off Louise. She forced herself to move closer and stare into the wound. The cut was down to what looked like the bone, which was a deep red in colour and unnaturally smooth. Jack's flesh was also wrong. It was sponge-like and honeycombed with holes that looked to be conduits for the countless, tiny filaments that had been severed and now writhed about themselves as if in pain.

"Keep watching," Jack said through gritted teeth. "Louise! Keep watching, for God's sake, please."

Nauseous, repulsed, she forced herself to look.

The wound was healing.

More filaments emerged from their organic tunnels to probe the opposite walls of the cut then burrowed into the tissue and drew the two faces of sponge-like flesh toward one another.

Suddenly, Louise was staggering for the stairs and the bathroom.

She was still on her knees by the toilet bowl when Jack found her. She felt his hand on her shoulder and surprised herself that she didn't flinch away. Jack wasn't human, at least, not as she understood humans, unless the arm was some sort of artificial limb. That was it, the thing had to be a revolutionary prosthetic....

No, it wasn't. It was *his* arm. He was different. He was *other*.

Despite this, despite the impossibility of him, his touch was welcome, comforting, and human, because she felt that he was not going to hurt her.

"Who are you?" she croaked, still on her knees.

"Jack Smith," he answered. "That *is* who I am."

A few minutes later, Louise was back downstairs. She wore her dressing gown and gripped a mug of black coffee in both her hands. Jack was perched on one of the armchairs, holding his wrist, which still appeared to be giving him pain even though there was now little sign of any injury at all.

"I was born," he said. "No, not born, I came to *be*, aged forty-five years old and just as I am now, in a London Underground tunnel near Down Street in 1916...."

Louise remained silent throughout. When Jack finished, she sat very still for a long time, her gaze directed at the empty fireplace. It was deep into the night. Wind-driven rain beat at the windows.

"So," Louise spoke quietly. Her voice was unnervingly level and matter-of-fact for someone who had just heard what amounted to a plot for a science fiction story. Was it a sign that she believed him, or was it because she was humouring or testing him in some way? "You claim that you were able to find out what happened to Lizzy. You said that you *felt* her after that explosion."

"I did."

"And that's how you think you can find Richard?"

"Only if we knew where he was when…."

"You would need to go back to the tunnel first, is that right?"

Jack nodded.

Another pause. "I should throw you out. I should scream at you to go away. I should call the police and have you sectioned."

"I would understand if you did."

"Perhaps I'm the one who needs to be taken away."

"No."

"Your arm, did I really see that? I mean, look at it. It's almost healed. There's barely a scar. And then there's Lyle. He knew me. He knew my name. He whispered and I heard him. and he terrified me. It was like a weird dream. God, I really am going crazy." Her voice broke. "And now I'm going to lose you. Fuck, they're going to sweep you into the sky or kill you or whatever and I'll be alone again and…. No, no, I can't believe this. I don't care what I think I've seen. It was an illusion, hallucination, I don't know…."

Jack reached across and took her hand. She let him.

After a while, Louise quietened and appeared to have fallen asleep. Jack lit a fire in the grate. Time was short, but if he could get Louise to agree to his plan, they would need to rest before they made a start.

A baby cried.

Louise started awake.

Esther?

She sat up too quickly and was punished by a wave of dizziness and nausea. She clutched at the arm of the sofa as she waited for it to settle into the throbbing beat of a hangover. She was disoriented. This wasn't her bed or bedroom. She wasn't alone. She felt heat on her face and saw the glow of a dying fire in the grate. The sitting room then, yes. There was Jack, asleep in the armchair. He must have lit the fire.

A baby was crying.

Esther. It was Esther. Louise scrambled from the sofa and half fell onto the floor. She clambered to her feet and lurched, still half-asleep, out into the hall and onto the stairs.

The cries became urgent.

"I'm coming," Louise called out. "Sweetheart, I'm coming."

She hauled herself up the narrow stairs and onto the landing. Esther's cries were loud here, too loud for a baby. The sound pressed against Louise's eardrums. It sliced into her already aching skull. Too bloody loud.

Come to me, Mummy, it said. *Please hurry.*

Which room? There were two bedrooms up here, but the sound wasn't coming from behind either of those two doors. The bathroom, then. She was in the bathroom. Confused, afraid, desperate, Louise threw herself at the door and crashed inside. She wrenched at the cord of the pull switch. The light was sudden, cold yellow-white, yet misted by steam.

Steam? Why steam?

Esther's cries were so loud she couldn't think. They were rock band loud, ear-bleeding, head-splitting loud. It was humid and hot in here. The water, it was boiling.

The crying stopped. Suddenly. Now there was silence. God, how she hated silence. *That* silence.

Esther? Where are you?

She knew. Of course she did. Oh God, she knew.

Louise dropped to her knees, grabbed the edge of the bath, and slowly leaned over to peer into the bubbling, steaming inferno it contained.

There, lying motionless on the bottom of the bath, a dark shape distorted by refraction. Esther. Screaming now, Louise plunged her arms into the water. The pain was immediate. Her flesh blistered, seared by the unspeakable heat. She felt the child. Grabbed at her. Grabbed at—

Nothing.

Frantic now, Louise stared into the empty bath, groping for her baby, sobbing her name over and over again.

"Louise."

She didn't look up. She felt Jack's hand on her shoulder.

"She was here. Esther was here…."

"No, no she wasn't. She was never here."

Louise wept, her forehead pressed against the hard plastic of the bath's edge. Jack was right. Of course he was right. It could not have been her daughter. Esther was gone. She was dead.

"Lyle did this," Jack said, his voice gentle. "Which means that he's close. We have to leave now if I'm to help you find Richard. London first."

"The Underground station?"

"Yes. Down Street."

Louise let Jack help her to her feet.

"Louise, come on."

She nodded, which hurt her aching head. When she finally turned away from the bath, she saw that Jack did not look much better than she felt. He was pale and had the fingertips of his left hand splayed across his forehead and pressed against his temples.

"Okay?" he said.

"Okay," she answered.

"Lyle will hurt you," Jack told her a few minutes later. They were dressed, ready to go out into the cold. "Not physically, but he will find what hurts you the most and rip it open. He did it to me, many years ago."

"He's already found what hurts me most," Louise said.

CHAPTER FOURTEEN (1938)

Christmas 1938. The twilight of a tumultuous decade that had seen the mighty fall and monsters in the ascendant. Remarkably, Stannard and Long not only survived the effects of the Wall Street Crash and subsequent worldwide economic depression but had prospered. Parts were still needed for farm machinery and, for a while, airships, although the tragic crash of the R101 at the beginning of the decade had abruptly closed that line of business. The machineries of the land were, in the end, the machineries of the company's success.

To celebrate their survival and the recent upturn in their fortunes, the company threw a yuletide party for its staff. The venue was the Regent Palace Hotel, off Piccadilly Circus. Entertainment was provided by the Stanley Whitman Jazz Orchestra. The ballroom was decked out with festive decorations and dominated by a huge Christmas tree. Drink flowed. The music and the laughter were loud, and all was misted by a comforting veil of tobacco smoke.

Having danced with a couple of ladies from the office, Jack was now content to stand by the bar and watch the festivities. He smoked steadily, another habit he had developed over the years. It relaxed him. It helped him concentrate. Dresses rustled and shoes squeaked on the polished wood of the dance floor. The music pulsed through him and seemed to match the rhythms of his body.

He was lonely, as always, but, otherwise, had learned to be at peace with himself.

Until, suddenly, there was Marion.

There, on the dance floor. Marion. He was sure of it.

It had been twelve years since Jack had last seen her, which meant that she was now in her thirties. The passage of time had brought a deeper beauty and grace to her, an elegance that had been there before, but was now stronger.

Marion's partner was a sleek, well-dressed character on the borders of middle-age. He exuded money, and self-assurance. Jack took an instant dislike to him, but then he would, wouldn't he? His feelings toward the man were infected with jealousy.

Marion seemed to have melted into his arms as he swept her through circuit after circuit of the room. She wore an expensive-looking black dress. The sight of her ignited hurt and desire in equal measure. It was a potent cocktail. Jack could not take his eyes off her. He wanted her. The intensity of that need was a physical agony.

She had not seen him. Her whole attention was on her partner.

She wore no ring.

Jack hurried for the French doors that gave onto a balcony. He needed air. He needed to be away from here. He could not bear to see her, happy and, no doubt, in love. This pain was as brutal as the pain he had endured when Lizzy asked him to leave her house. It was a ridiculous pain that weakened and confused him.

Outside, Jack leaned on the ornate balcony railings that gave a view onto Sherwood Street, a narrow, busy artery that led into Soho. He drew in deep lungfuls of icy air, closed his eyes, and tried to calm himself. He was being foolish. He was acting the way he had seen children act. It was done with. A brief encounter that was over. Marion had found what she wanted and needed. What could he, Jack Smith, offer her? He was not even human. He was comfortable but far from wealthy. His future was…what? More of this? Year upon year of the same? He had to let her go. Hands trembling, he lit a cigarette and drew in a long deep draught of nicotine smoke.

"Jack? Jack Smith?"

He started and turned to see her. She clutched a fur wrap about her shoulders. Her eyes shone and there was that familiar smile on her lips.

"Dear God, it really *is* you." Marion took his hands in her own. He felt their familiar smallness under the soft fabric of her gloves. "Jack."

"It's wonderful to see you again."

Was it? It had hurt, but now he had her to himself, just for a moment.

"How strange, such a coincidence...."

"How are you?" Jack asked. "Are you still at the BBC?"

"Yes, I am. I am in charge of the typing office now, although that isn't as grand as it sounds, I'm afraid."

"So, you're not out there fighting the Black Shirts."

"I'd like to. Thugs, the lot of them." That old fire was back. "But look at me. I'm positively middle-aged. I'm far too respectable to brawl on the streets." She paused and held Jack's stare. "Are you well, Jack? Are you happy?"

"Yes," he said and wondered immediately if that were true. "Life is quiet and steady. I've got a job, which is more than a lot of people have."

"You know, you haven't changed one bit," Marion said. "You're not a day older than when I last saw you. Not one grey hair or wrinkle. It's almost frightening."

What an innocuous little phrase that was, *when I last saw you*. So blithe and breezy, no hint of the pain, anger, and grief of that evening.

"Clean living," Jack said. "But thank you. And you're even more beautiful—" He stopped himself, appalled at such a forward statement. "I...I'm sorry. You're with someone. I...."

"Don't be silly, Jack. It was a lovely thing to say, and I appreciate it." She looked away to gaze out over the street. "I really am glad you're here. I...I've often wondered what became of you."

"I've missed you a great deal," Jack said and knew he shouldn't be saying this, but he couldn't stop himself. "I wish...."

Wished what? He wanted to kiss her.

"Marion?" Her beau was in the doorway. "You've been gone for an age. I was beginning to wonder if you'd stood me up."

"Sorry." She seemed flustered but recovered quickly. "I needed some air."

The man's attention moved to Jack, who extended his hand and introduced himself. "Jack Smith."

"Geoffrey Brize-Hampton. Pleased to meet you." He didn't sound as if he was. He stared at Jack for a moment longer. Then held out his arm for Marion. "Come along, you'll catch your death out here."

Jack didn't watch them return to the dance floor. He leaned once more on the balcony and lit another cigarette. He would go home and try to forget this.

The song was ending. A sudden urge drove Jack back inside. He threw down his cigarette and ground it with his heel then moved to the edge of the dance floor. The song finished with the band's usual flourish. Jack hurried in Marion's direction. She was being led toward a group of tuxedo-wearing guests,

"Excuse me," Jack called out. "Excuse me, Marion."

She stopped and turned. Geoffrey too. He looked bemused then suspicious.

Jack came to a halt. He kept his attention on Marion and managed a breathless, "May I have the honour of the next dance?"

"I'm sorry, but no," Geoffrey said. There was brusqueness beneath his friendly tone. "There are people I'd like you to meet, Marion—"

"Yes," Marion said. "I would like to dance with you, Mr. Smith."

"No, you can't," Geoffrey said. "You really have to meet them."

A slow waltz had started.

"All in good time," Marion said, her smile as fixed as Geoffrey's. Then before her partner could protest further, she took a step toward Jack and took his hand. "Come along Mr. Smith."

Jack held her formally, her gloved right hand clasped in his left, his arm about her waist. She trembled a little. Neither spoke. He had committed a gross faux pas here. He had snatched an obviously important man's lady from him and insulted him by dancing with her.

"...Jack. Are you listening to me, Jack?"

He started and looked down at Marion.

"I said, take me home. Now."

He stopped dancing. This was a moment when he could lose or keep her. Whichever decision he made, would be costly.

"What about Geoffrey?"

"I don't care for or about him. It's not as if we're married or anything. Please take me home."

"All right," Jack said and led her quickly through the other dancers toward the exit.

Geoffrey stepped into their path.

"Where the devil are you going?" His face was tight with fury, his hands clenched into white-knuckled fists.

"Home," Marion said.

"With *him*?"

"Yes," Jack said. "With me."

"You stay out of this," Geoffrey said. "Marion, come with me. You will not cause a scene. We will discuss this matter later." He held out his hand.

"No," Marion said. "I'm sorry."

"Don't be such a stupid little fool. Come with me. Now."

"You have no rights over her," Jack said.

"You mind your bloody business, or I'll give you what you deserve."

Jack said no more. His whole concentration was on the enraged man in front of him. Jack felt the heat from the man's body. He sensed his tension, indicating a readiness to strike out.

Other figures appeared at Geoffrey's shoulders.

"What's happening?" one of them said, voice clipped, like an army officer. "Geoffrey? Are you all right?"

Geoffrey nodded and unclenched his fists. "Come on, old chap," he said to his friend. "She isn't worth it." He brought his lips close to Marion's ear as he passed by. "Once a slut, always a slut."

Jack felt that odd, exhilaration surge through him. It boiled up like a storm. It cancelled logical thought. It came in on a tidal wave of emotion. It was primal and all-consuming. It drove his fist into Geoffrey Brize-Hampton's face.

He felt the impact of his knuckles against the man's chin. It was a satisfying jolt. Geoffrey was thrown sideways. His friend caught him and staggered under the sudden weight but managed to keep them both on their feet.

Geoffrey recovered and stood, a little unsteadily, and glared at Jack. He held his jaw with his hand. Behind him, the party continued, apparently unaware of what had just occurred.

"I'd watch yourself if I was you, Smith," he growled. "Roger Stannard is a good friend of mine. You're going to be looking for a job."

Then he was gone, back into the bright-lit fury of the ballroom. Jack breathed slowly and let the tension drain from him. He looked at his hand. The knuckles were split, but already healing. He pushed his hand into his jacket pocket. Marion, who once more held her fur wrap tightly about herself, looked pale and frightened.

"I'm sorry…"

"Take me home," she said.

The taxi came to a halt outside a house in St. John's Wood.

"Shall I see you to your door?" Jack asked.

Marion hesitated. The taxi's engine ticked over. Then she moved close enough to whisper, "I want you to come in."

Neither spoke as she unlocked the front door and they ascended the stairs to her flat. It had electric light. The wallpaper on the landing and stairs was tasteful and Marion's flat was large and given an extra feeling of space by its high, Edwardian ceiling. An enormous bay window looked out over trees. The glinting lights of London were visible through their skeletal winter branches.

Marion switched on only two of the standard lamps then stood in the middle of her sitting room and stared at Jack. She was strong, almost defiant, yet, at the same time she seemed frail and vulnerable.

"How is your hand?"

"Perfectly all right."

"I've never had anyone fight over me before. I thought it would be degrading, but I rather enjoyed it." Marion's smile faded. She hesitated, looked away then said, "Do *you* think I'm a slut?"

Jack took her into his arms. "I think you are lovely."

They kissed. It was beautiful in its familiarity. It was as if the boundaries of time were broken. It was as if they had never parted.

After a moment, Marion drew back, took Jack's hand, and led him to her bedroom.

"It really is your turn now, Jack," she whispered.

Later, Marion rolled over in the bed, switched on the small bedside lamp, fumbled for her cigarettes. She offered one to Jack. They sat, leaning against the headboard and smoking together.

"So, *now* am I a slut?" Marion asked.

"You never have been and never will be."

A rueful chuckle. "How on earth do you know? Have you been spying on me since…since we parted ways?"

"I just know."

"I am the villain, you know."

"The villain?"

She tapped ash from her cigarette into the ashtray she had placed on the counterpane between them.

"Of a scandal. I was married before I joined Antonia's set, but I walked out on my husband. And no, I wasn't a beaten, cowed, or betrayed woman. I left my husband because I never loved him and couldn't stand being with him anymore, so one day, I packed my bags and walked out."

"That was brave."

"Brave?" Another of those chuckles. "You must be the only person in the world to ever call me brave for that. I have a daughter. I left her too. She was three at the time. Am I still brave?"

"Is she being looked after?"

"Yes, she is, as a matter of fact. My ex-husband married again quite quickly, to a wonderful lady, note, *lady*, not *woman*. She dotes on Olive. She can't have children of her own, you see. No, my daughter is well cared for. Better than I could manage. She was sent to Rodean, given the best of everything. She is eighteen now. I still meet with her now and then and we get along all right, but she loves her stepmother more than me, and who can blame her?" Marion had adopted an offhand persona, but there was a catch in her voice. "So, what do you think of me now?" she said.

"You had a reason for leaving your husband."

"My darling, Jack, always straight to the point, simple and childlike. No, according to the whole world, I had *no* good reason. The fact that I didn't love him was seen by my family and friends and everyone else I encountered as quite trivial, certainly no justification for leaving. It doesn't matter how miserable you are, how hateful your life, you're supposed to stick with it and not damn well complain. It drove me to drink. It was the only way I could endure the dullness, the deadness. This was my one and only life, Jack, and I was already a corpse. That's what it felt like, anyway."

"I don't see it as trivial."

"Of course you don't. Alfie was right about you. He said that he told you about his…his preferences, because he knew you would accept him and understand. He said that he had only just met you when he confessed, but he just *knew*." Marion stubbed the cigarette out then sat up, arms about her knees. "How can it be that the rest of the population tells me that I am an appalling woman, a slut, and yet a man from my distant past, who has stumbled back into my life, tells me that I'm not?"

"Love is important. I don't understand why anyone would want to stay with someone they don't love."

Marion smiled at him. "You are such a dear, Jack. I think I'm falling in love with you all over again."

"You've fallen in love with me before?"

"Of course I was in love with you, you idiot. That's why I was so difficult. I was afraid of my feelings. I didn't want to end up in the mess I'd been in before." She lit up once more and took a deep drag that seemed to steady her nerves.

"I don't judge people. That isn't why I'm here."

"What do you mean?"

"You did what you needed to do."

"I don't think you will have your job for much longer. Your boss is good friends with Geoffrey."

"So he said."

"I don't like him that much. He's terribly jealous and possessive. I'm losing all my friends because he doesn't want me to spend too much of my time with them. The thing is that, like me, he's no youngster, so I think he was a little desperate to get me to the altar, and I've been a little desperate myself. I left Antonia's set during the general Strike. I took the wrong side, and afterwards, was no longer welcome. Geoffrey was a cure for loneliness, I suppose."

"Engineering workers were not called out, but I helped out in the evenings with distributing the *British Worker* newspaper."

"I never took you for a socialist firebrand, Jack." Marion paused. Then said; "God, how I've wanted to see you again, Jack, and here we are...." She sounded as if she was crying. "I'm sorry. I'm being such a fool. I'm talking rot and I've ruined it. Jack, please, I'm sorry."

"No, you haven't. I've never stopped wanting *you*, Marion."

They married three months later. A quiet affair in a Registry Office. Jack found a new job as a mechanic in a bus repair workshop and they moved into a small terrace house in North West London. 1938 faded into 1939. The sky was endlessly blue that summer and Jack was lost in a happiness he didn't know was possible. He and Marion were content, at peace. It was if they had both found a refuge at last. But there was a shadow that passed over the sunlight of their love every now and then, when Marion said that there was a locked door inside him, and it hurt her that he would not tell her what it concealed.

He blamed the war, a terrible childhood, vague excuses, and fabrications. A past he could never talk about.

He could see that she did not believe a word of it.

So, what would happen when she began to age and he didn't, when she found the first grey hairs, and lines on her face, while his own hair remained dark and his skin smooth?

It would happen, but not yet. Right now, they were in love and life was mostly joyous.

There were other shadows.

Jack felt the storm build. It thrummed at the threads of The Fabric. Dulled as his connection might be, Jack sensed the monster's approach. A huge and terrible joke was about to be perpetrated upon him just as he had found peace.

The tempest arrived on a clear, sunny Sunday lunchtime. It was announced on countless British wirelesses by the kindly voice of Prime Minister Neville Chamberlain.

Another bloody war, and against the same opponent as last time.

Jack stood outside on the street. Marion joined him. Children played, lawnmowers whirred, kettles whistled and willow smacked leather as people went about their quiet, lazy Sunday business. The announcement had been a ripple in the stillness and that made it a strange horror. Jack remembered the quiet of the churchyard in which he had walked with Alfred twenty-one years before. That odd silence, broken only by bird song and the gentle agitation of the trees by the breeze. This was that same quiet. That same false calm. He looked up and saw that the sky was clear blue. The next day was the same, and the day after that....

The war finally arrived for Jack and Marion, on a quiet evening early in October 1940. Until that night, the Luftwaffe's London raids seemed a distant terror. As the heart of the capital burned, Jack and Marion were comforted by the belief that the Germans would be interested only in the docks and centres of government. There was nothing for them here in the quiet suburb of Pinner where they now lived.

On that October night, a Monday, the sirens wailed as usual, and Jack led the way outside and down into the Anderson Shelter he and his neighbour, Bennie Goldsmith, had built in the garden.

Once inside, Jack lit a hurricane lamp and he and Marion climbed into the two small beds Jack had made for them. It was hot and clammy. The air was damp. Marion didn't like the shelter and adopted a busy efficient air whenever she was down there to hide her claustrophobia. They were, after all, cowering in a hole in the ground, lined and roofed with an arch of dank, corrugated steel. Jack read to her once they were settled. It calmed her nerves, she said. Tonight, it was *Great Expectations*. Jack loved the language of Dickens, the names of the characters and their idiosyncrasies, the arch, and not so arch, humour. Marion moved close to him.

"This isn't so bad is it, darling?" he said.

"Not at all," Marion answered. "Quite cozy really."

Aircraft could be heard now. German bombers, recognizable by the rise-and-fall tone of their engines. Bombs stamped into the earth. They sounded louder than usual. Jack was suddenly back in that street, all those years ago, trying to find Lizzy's daughter. Trying to save the child as one bomb after another pummelled the city and brought destruction closer and closer.

There was a series of deafening crashes. Each one more violent than the last. Marion cried out and clawed at him. He held her tight. The hurricane lamp flared then went out as all other sounds were hurled together into the abrupt roar of an explosion. The earth shuddered and seemed to break apart. The air was sucked from the shelter. It felt as though the sky had fallen onto them.

Ears ringing, gasping for breath, Jack lay motionless. It was dark. He became aware that he was on the floor. Marion was on top of him. She trembled violently, her breath a series of quiet moans. Jack gently extricated himself from beneath her and helped her to her feet. He grabbed at the handle of the shelter door and felt heat. The rush and crackle of fire broke through his momentary deafness. He took a breath. The air was hot and smoky.

He opened the door.

The night was painted a restless orange. Jack scrambled up the makeshift wooden steps that led out of the shelter and tried to comprehend what he saw.

Their house seemed intact, its dark bulk unchanged. The buildings to the left and right of it were also standing, but the house beyond the latter was ablaze. As he watched, a section of its roof fell inward with a loud splintering sound. Gouts of flame roared upward from the new wound. The air was smoke-clogged and dense. Every lungful was hot and unpleasant.

There were more explosions, a little further away. The smoke thickened and cast a softening, misty pall over the flames. Jack heard Marion's cough, turned, took her arm, and led her indoors. At least they would be out of the smoke.

Their house had not escaped intact. All the windows were broken, the blackout curtains torn, and the floors littered with glass. Crockery had been blown from its shelves in the modest kitchen and the cutlery drawer had been wrenched open. The damage was messy but superficial. Jack flicked switches in each room, but none of the lights worked.

Marion lit a candle, which seemed feeble against the light shed by the burning houses nearby. Jack now saw two more of them on the opposite side of the street. There was little relief from the smoke in here. The air was misted and sour, the peace broken by the din outside. A fire engine arrived. The incessant clang of its bell tore through the chaos.

Marion sat on the edge of the settee, arms tight about herself. "Do you think there is anyone in those houses?"

Jack stood at the shattered window. Firemen were unreeling the hose on the rear of the engine. People stood on the street, watching, heedless of the raid, which was still in progress. Bombs could be heard, no longer in the direct vicinity, but close enough. Jack knew what he should do. He didn't want to, but he knew he had little choice. "I don't know," he said. "I should find out and try to help."

"No, Jack. It's too dangerous outside. We should go back into the shelter."

"You go," he said. "I'll join you in a few minutes."

"Jack—"

He was already in the hall and at the front door. He sensed Marion following him but didn't look round. Outside, the onlookers had been driven back by a police constable and Air Raid Warden in a three-piece suit and steel helmet. The firemen played water over the flames, but it looked to be a losing battle. Four buildings were burning; the butcher's shop and its flat two doors down from where Jack and Marion lived and three houses on the opposite side of the street. The road was littered with debris and glistened with water from the hosepipes.

People were gathered in the road, many in pyjamas and dressing gowns or wrapped in blankets and coats. They stood helpless and shocked as the familiar was devoured by flame and their neighbours died.

A ripple in The Fabric snatched Jack's attention. It was a small, brief reconnection, an itch. A cry. Jack did not hesitate but rushed through the torn-open doorway that led to the flat above the butcher's shop. He heard Marion cry out his name then scream at him to stop, but he couldn't.

Flame engulfed him as he rushed through the opening and then scrambled onto the stairs. The pain was excruciating as his clothes burned and his flesh blistered. A baby howled out from the inferno above. Jack's strength was failing. Miraculously, the stairs were intact, but Jack knew they wouldn't be for much longer. Weakened by the pain, choking on smoke, he dropped to his hands and knees and hauled himself up to the landing. He felt his flesh trying to knit and then burning again. There was nothing but pain and the relentless shriek of the baby. He glimpsed a door, closed. He drew himself to his feet and turned the knob.

And stepped into a surreal nightmare. There was little left of the back of the building. It had been dissolved into an avalanche of rubble, shrouded with smoke and dust. A cot stood to his left on a six-foot ledge of floorboard and shattered joists. As Jack moved cautiously toward it, the joists shifted and the surviving floorboards bowed under his feet. He stretched and snagged at the corner of the cot. The flesh of his burned hands erupted into agony at the contact. He yelled out his pain and dragged the cot slowly to himself. The pain was now a scorching white wall in his mind. He reached down to extract the baby.

He heard voices. There were people in the back yard, clambering up the rubble. Jack shuffled carefully toward the edge of the floor fragment. He saw a fireman below, balanced on the rubble as far as he could climb. He reached upward. Jack paused then threw the baby toward him. The fireman caught it then scrambled down the rubble and out of sight.

There were more shouts, encouragement to jump. Jack felt heat at his back as the flames boiled through the open door and bit into the ledge of surviving floor. It was beginning to crumble. All strength gone, he allowed himself to fall. He slammed into the rubble, but the impact seemed a remote thing, a dull ache from somewhere outside himself.

Smoke billowed around him. He lay on the ragged surface of the rubble and waited for this burned, broken body to heal.

Then he sensed that he was not alone. He opened his eyes, blinked against the shifting light of the fire and the sting of the smoke, and saw Marion. She kneeled on the broken bricks and splintered wood, heedless of injury. She laid Jack's head on her knees and keened out her grief. He felt her tears on his face. He couldn't speak. He wanted her to stay, but also to go. He did not want her to see his body heal.

But she did. She saw it.

She said nothing, but she saw all of it.

Later, deep in that sleepless, fire-stained night, once more huddled in the grave-like safety of their Anderson shelter, Jack unlocked the door to the truth.

Marion listened and, once more, said nothing. Jack couldn't tell whether she believed him or not. It was as if she took his story and buried it deep inside herself, because she never spoke of it for the rest of her life.

CHAPTER FIFTEEN (2016)

It was dark outside. The torch Louise had hunted down at Jack's request did little to alleviate the blackness. A sharp wind had sprung up. Louise was forcing herself to believe in this quest. Madness this may be, but it was hope, a tiny, dim-lit ray of hope.

Rain stung Louise's face. The hood of her parka restricted her view. Icy wind battered her. She was surprised to see that Jack stood beside her car rather than his own.

"I'm sorry, you'll have to drive," he said. "My headaches are getting worse."

Louise drew the keys from her coat pocket and hurried round to the off-side door.

There was movement in the back of the car.

Then a cry.

Louise heard the baby-howl through the glass, above the relentless blast of the wind and the patter of rain on the hood of her coat. She heard Esther. She grabbed at the door handle and wrenched at it. It was still locked. What the hell was she doing? She fumbled at the key fob, trying to remember which button opened the door. She couldn't get in. She had to get in. Her baby was crying and needed her mother.

Then there was silence.

No, no not again.

Louise peered in through the window. There was only darkness.

Then Richard spoke. "Louise, I'm here."

She spun round to confront him but there was only the rain and the night-black bulk of the cottage. And Lyle, unseen, a presence.

"Louise! Hurry up!" Jack this time, on the opposite side of the car.

Shaken, Louise finally managed to unlock the doors and slid into the front passenger seat.

"Get us out of here," Jack said. "Now! Get us out!"

The car was warm, dry, and dark. It was a hiding place where she could be safe and invisible in the darkness.

They were being followed. Or watched.

The thought, the *feeling* crept in as they joined the A1M. It was three-in the morning. Traffic was light. The road dark and lonely. It was, no doubt, her imagination. Louise was tense. The edifice that was her self-control teetered on the edge of collapse.

Nevertheless, she was glad when the London glow lit up the horizon and began to resolve itself into the street-lighting, houses, office blocks, and glossy car dealerships lining the road that pierced the capital's north-western skin.

"Where do you suggest we head for once I'm finished here?" Jack said as he drove. "Think carefully. We only have one chance."

"The Garden of Eden," Louise replied.

"The Garden...Ah, the little town by the river where you honeymooned."

"Woodbridge, that's right, by the slipway. Richard said that when we died, our ghosts would haunt that place."

Jack followed the A1 deep into the city. He didn't speak and Louise was glad of it. She had no conversation at the moment. She quickly lost any sense of where they were now. Until they reached Archway and she saw the glittering jewels of the city skyline, jagged with lit-up science fiction constructions that would not look out of place in some futuristic artist's impression of the city.

They parked on a side road off Piccadilly. Despite the lateness of the hour there was traffic and people, which was good. Louise still felt the presence of Lyle. She took Jack's arm and stayed close to him. She pulled the fur-edged hood of her coat over her head. It closed her in and she was comforted by the childish delusion that if you were unable to see the bogeyman, it couldn't see you.

On a lesser, uncomfortably quiet street, Jack stopped at a door set into the wall of a hulking, almost featureless brick building. It was painted a maroon version of red and looked as if it was sealed shut. So, what was this? A lock-up? The place Jack brought his victims?

Where did that thought come from?

It frightened her, nonetheless.

"How do we get in?" Louise asked. "Have you got a key?"

"I don't think I need one. It knows I'm here." There was an odd, emotional catch to Jack's voice.

"What does?"

"The nearest thing I have to a mother."

Seemingly unsure about what he was doing, Jack closed his hand about the ancient-looking lock. Louise saw a brief flare of light, around Jack's fingers. For a moment, the merest instant of time, it spread outward over the surface of the door. A webbing of blue-white fibres. The light came from the door itself, rather than from Jack's hand. It was as if whatever lay on the other side had reached out to let him in. Then it was gone. Jack pulled the lock from its hasp. The door swung open.

"How did you do that?"

He shook his head, shrugged. "*I* didn't do anything. Like I said, it knows I'm here."

Inside.

Where it was dark of course, that smothering, gritty dark that always came with abandoned buildings. It was a darkness full of worrying sounds, most of them made by their own passage through it. Jack flicked on the torch. Its beam danced uncertainly for a moment then began to pick out details. They were in a large hall of some sort. There were the remains of a set of gates in front of them. As they passed through, crunching on decades of dust and debris, Louise was astonished to realise that this was an abandoned Underground Station.

Down Street, where Jack had been born.

It was a place of ghosts. Outside the cone of torchlight, the dark was complete. The black walls pressed in, alive with threat.

"I don't know about this, Jack…."

He stopped and turned toward her. "Please, don't be frightened," he said. "There's nothing here that can hurt you, like I said before, if you want to go back, if you want to go home, that's okay by me."

Something in that offer strengthened her resolve. "No, I'm okay."

"Sure?"

"Sure."

They resumed their slow, careful journey, coming at last to a long-frozen escalator.

"Going down," Jack said. The corny joke eased Louise's tension and even made her chuckle.

"The Elgin Marbles were stored here during the Blitz," Jack said. "There was also a civil defence command post here."

"Have you ever thought of getting a job as a tour guide?"

"I'll need a job when this is over. I don't, think I'll be welcomed back into the building trade."

The stairway plunged into unyielding blackness. The torch gave Louise glimpses of the dusty-white metal treads of the escalator, and the walls, to which most of the tiles still clung. What had leaked through the gaps did not bear close scrutiny.

They reached the bottom and walked along a short passageway, through an opening and onto a platform.

Louise shivered, suddenly overwhelmed by the sense that the thousands who had passed through Down Street Station had left some part of themselves, some fragment of their souls, here in this place.

Jack, a thing of silhouette and torch-glow moved quickly to the edge of the platform and then he was gone. The torch beam flicked about, as if momentarily out of control, then swept round to illuminate the platform again.

"Come on, it's safe, the tracks were taken up years ago."

"Really? I thought I'd just wait here and catch the next train home."

"Louise, hurry up."

Stepping off a platform went against every instinct, every iota of conditioning she had accumulated in a lifetime of visiting London and travelling the tube. You kept away from the edge. You never jumped down onto the tracks. Louise got down onto her hands and knees then reversed herself off the platform. There was a brief drop then the hard surface of the track bed. There were smells down here, the damp, the musk of animals. Noises startled her, scuttling sounds. Rats.

Another walk, into the tunnel mouth to the left of the platform. Louise hurried to catch up, all the time trying to reassure herself that a train was not about to explode out of the blackness in a fury of light and noise and solid, bone pulverising steel. If Jack was leading her to her death, then she was going willingly. He stopped. The torch played over the dank, mouldering brick curve of the tunnel. How many bricks had gone into making these places? Millions?

"Here, take this." Jack held out the torch to Louise. "Switch it off and save the battery."

She did as he asked. The torch beam went off and was replaced not by soul-crushing darkness, but by a glow, dim, like the pulsing sheen of coals on a dying fire. It illuminated the seams between the bricks. Louise raised her hand toward it. There was no heat and no threat.

"This is my womb," Jack said. "This is where I came to *be*. Right here."

"You came from that?"

"Yes." There was that catch again.

"How? I don't understand."

Jack didn't answer, instead he reached toward the burning bricks and the light flared bright. It seemed to boil and spread. Louise jumped back. She stumbled; the ground was uneven, its materials loose. She recovered and watched as Jack pressed his splayed fingers against the light.

Which ran down his arm, liquid yet absorbed into his clothes and, no doubt, his skin.

Jack breathed fast. He groaned, as if in pain. The glow spread through him and lit up his flesh from within. X-ray-like, it shone through his overalls and coat and revealed his body in silhouette. He began to speak. Louise didn't recognise the language. It sounded like a song. It grew louder and more anguished, until he unleashed a long, child-like howl. The sound erupted from his open mouth in a burst of light.

Louise wanted it to stop. She wanted him to let go, to release himself, but it went on and on. The light was now a mass of white snakes that spiraled about his arm then spread over his face and chest like the fibrous roots of a vast, burning tree. His eyes were black featureless holes; his body trembled and convulsed. The light flowed through the brickwork, streaming through the joints like a blazing stream and poured itself into Jack. Its child.

Then winked out and the darkness returned.

Louise switched on the torch in time to see Jack stagger back. He doubled-up, his breathing ragged. He trembled violently. Louise went to him and put her arm about his shoulders and held him tightly.

"Jack? Jack, are you okay?"

He straightened, suddenly, almost violently and pushed Louise away. "It hurts…."

Jack stared up at the place on the curved wall where he had touched and drank in the light. There was no trace of it left.

"It's gone," he said, unnecessarily. It took a moment for Louise to comprehend the depth of that statement. The light, the thing that created him, given birth to him, was gone and for a moment, a brief moment, she felt his loneliness.

Then he seemed to snap himself out of his mood and turned to her. The torchlight picked out the pain etched into his face in stark relief. "I'm sorry…I pushed you away. This is unbearable. It doesn't last, but while it does, every speck of dust that lands on my skin is like a white-hot spark, every sound is deafening. Everything is pain." He paused, as if hearing something. "We have to go. Now."

Louise took the lead, aiming the torch at the uneven ground.

There was a sound now. A rumble and hum, almost as if a train *was* coming. They stumbled out of the tunnel mouth and grabbed at the platform, which was suddenly a cliff face and almost unclimbable. Louise felt as if she had no strength left to her, but she had to get off the track. Something was happening; something was coming and they had to run.

Jack scrambled up with startling agility and speed. The rumble and hum were louder now. She felt the ground tremble. She glanced round and saw a glow in the tunnel. This glow was cold, angry, remorseless, and relentless.

She shone the torch up onto the platform and saw that Jack was reaching down for her. She grabbed his hand and driven on by panic, by a raw fear she had never experienced before in her life, the terror of the prey in the presence of the predator, she scrabbled at the platform wall with her feet and clawed herself onto the filth and grit of the platform itself.

The rumbling became something like an earthquake. The rumble was a voice now, rising in volume. It was a cry, a scream.

"Christ," Jack said. He took Louise's hand and they ran. Light erupted into the tunnel, white and fierce. They plunged through the exit into the passageways beyond and headed for the escalators.

Louise glanced over her shoulder and saw something huge and powerful erupt out of the platform area. For a moment, she thought it was a train, a train, here in this abandoned station. The she was sure she saw a face, like those on a child's train, but not a face any child would want to see.

She screamed then ran. The torch was of no use now. The halls and the escalator were bathed in light. Up the steps, up, exhausted, struggling for breath. She looked down and saw the light split into glowing fingers that surged through the station and up the stairs behind her.

It was coming, and it was terrifying. She felt the air shiver. Her skin prickled. Electric shocks shivered through her, jolted her, but she didn't slow down. The light flared and for a moment all she could see was dazzling, cold white. From its heart she heard voices, Richard, a baby's cry. The sounds weakened her and she felt the need to turn and rush back into the glare.

She fought the urge. Her resistance roared out of her as a scream of guilt and grief and rage.

Then it was gone.

But for the flame-red after-burn that coloured the abruptly restored darkness.

CHAPTER SIXTEEN (2016)

Outside now. Jack found it hard to breathe. The air was thick and filthy, a soup of bacteria and viruses. It was laden with dust and noxious gases.

There was little safety here, the odd, lonely pedestrian or cyclist, sporadic bursts of traffic, the occasional lorry or bus. Jack could hear every word spoken, every breath taken. It was hellish enough in the relative small hours calm; it would be unendurable when the city finally woke. He smelled the sweat that bled from the pores of those they met, felt the soft thudding of their heartbeats. It hurt. His skin was raw and sore. The air he breathed rasped against his throat and burned its way into his lungs. He could taste the carbon monoxide and ammonia that hung undispersed in the polluted air. Louise's hand, tightly gripped in his own, was slick with secretion; perspiration, city grime, moisture from the air, and the oils from whatever cream she smeared onto it to protect her skin.

These images, however, the accompanying sounds and smells, were no more than a surface veneer. The very atoms of this place vibrated madly, the air was a thrumming vibrant, storm of thought, sensation, and emotion. Streamers of human spirit swirled from every building and from the pavement under their feet.

And crawling through the deafening tangle of energy and dark matter, came the hound. Here, in the weft and weave of reality, the entity was formless yet arachnid. It was a sac of nightmares. Its sting, which reared over its back like a scorpion, was the hypodermic through which terrors could be fed into its victim's mind. Familiar terrors, the worst kind. It would pick up the trail within minutes.

Louise's face was almost hidden by the hood of her parka, but Jack could see enough to know that she was ashen, wide-eyed, and confused by what she had seen and heard. Despite this, she was still in a better state to drive than he. And he had to fend off those who demanded his return. He had to fend them off and stay free for a while longer.

Jack was impressed by Louise's driving skills. Her reactions were quick and precise and seemed unaffected by what she had been through in the last few hours. She committed no traffic misdemeanour and drove like someone who had the near-mythical taxi-driver knowledge. She avoided the main thoroughfares but cut nimbly through side-streets and alleyways. Not the most picturesque route Jack had ever followed, but an intriguing one, nonetheless. Not that he was in the mood for sightseeing. Every part of him hurt. Every part of him was on fire.

And he knew fire.

"Are you okay?" Louise's voice rose from the car's drone. A drone which, to Jack, was made up of a hundred different individual sounds, the crack of spark plugs, the sloshing of pumped fuel, the muffled whumps of exploding petrol vapor, the scrape of piston against tube.

"Yes. Just."

They reached the north-eastern edge of the capital, now on the A12 which would take them almost all the way. A few miles further on, now settled into the monotony of highway driving, Louise asked a question. "Have we passed the test?"

"What do you mean?" He didn't want to talk but couldn't deny Louise the comfort of conversation.

"Your creators, whatever they are, do you think they'll let us carry on?" There was an odd mix of gentle mockery and fear in her voice.

"I don't know. I believe that there's hope for you."

Not for me, but for you.

"That's encouraging."

"No, I really do believe that." Jack sighed. Talking was an effort, the vibrations painful in his throat. The thought processes involved in choosing and forming words were exhausting. "I came to *be* during the First World War. London was being bombed by Zeppelins, everyone was afraid and most of the men were in the armed forces, fighting and dying. There were thousands of orphans and widows. There were thousands of wounded men and the world was tearing itself to pieces. But despite all that, there was still some kindness and nobility to be found."

"That's what I believe. We're flawed but good, deep down." Louise's hand was on Jack's knee. It was heavy and the pressure of it scraped painfully over his skin beneath his jeans. He didn't protest, however. It was a sign of her affection. It was a tiny act of love.

"It's your leaders who drive you down into hell," Jack continued. "Not the ordinary man and woman, and not even all of those are bad. Many of them start out with the best intentions."

"What is your world like?"

Jack shook his head. "I don't know. I've never been there. I'm not even sure the creators have a world of their own. They exist in The Fabric."

"That's sad."

"What do you mean?"

"That you've never seen your home."

You have no home….

"I'm human. *This* is my world."

Her grip on his thigh momentarily tightened. Another gesture of love, but one which sent a shaft of agony through his leg.

The car droned through its endless mechanical cycles. Dawn broke, clear at first, but soon the sky greyed as clouds closed in.

Then Louise asked; "Why do you want to help me so badly?"

Now there was a question.

"Because…." Jack struggled for the word. "Because of how I feel about you."

"And how is that?" She didn't look at him when she asked the question.

"I love you, Louise."

He saw her tense, felt her confusion and delight, and pain as well.

"There was someone else," he continued. "A long time ago. I fell deeply in love with a woman. There was an accident so catastrophic that she simply disappeared. I needed to find her. I needed to *know*. So, I went to the place where she died. She was gone but I felt her, for one brief moment. It wasn't enough, but it was all I would ever have of her, and I gained some peace from that. That's what I want for you. I want you to know what happened to Richard."

"He's dead."

"You can't be sure."

"No, you're right, I can't be sure. I've never been sure. Sometimes, it's a hell that can't be described or imagined. I experience panic attacks. I don't know what to think or feel, whether to sit down or stand up. And the guilt…." Louise shook her head and turned her full attention to driving for a few minutes then spoke again. "Did you see Lizzy? Is that how it works, could you speak to her?"

"I'm not a medium. It's an echo. It's a trace they leave behind, although, years later, I found out, from another of my kind, that I could seek out the dead if I wanted to."

"Why didn't you?"

"The dead no longer belong to us."

Talking had exhausted Jack. He leaned his head back and closed his eyes. It did little to shut out the barrage of sensory input, noise, smells, sensation. His clothes scraped at his skin, the dust in the air was abrasive. He could also see The Fabric, its brightness now marred by a dark stain that was spreading along its threads and webbing. It was Lyle, reaching out and searching for them. Jack felt the first gentle brush of its fingers over his nerves.

It was a race and it was going to be close.

Louise had done with crying and now there was fear, breathless, heart-pounding fear. There were reasons to be afraid. They were being pursued. She did not fully understand what was chasing them, but it terrified her, nonetheless. She felt it bearing down on them.

There was also the fear of what Jack would find and how it would make her feel. Would it free her from the past or tighten the chains? The sense of finality was like a storm gathering on the horizon, an emotional whirlwind that threatened to tear apart her careful but fragile defences.

She had to stay calm. There was nothing she could do now. She needed to concentrate on driving and not getting them both killed. Hands on the wheel, gears, accelerator, lorries, cars, vans. Rain had arrived. It spotted the windscreen, a curtain of water, the whine of the wipers. The road was endless. Grey, everything was grey. Breathe steady. In, hold, out. Blank the mind, think white. The road, the rain, the mechanics of driving.

The night had given way to a dreary grey dawn by the time they reached Ipswich. She followed the dual carriageway round the southern edge of the town, which was a rain-misted, amorphous mass to her left. Louise's anxiety was back, grief-edged this time. She wanted to cry, she wanted to stop the car and sob herself into exhaustion.

She had to keep going.

The road curved east and there was the graceful arch of the Orwell Bridge. A glimpse of the river below was immediately shut off by the bridge walls. Closer now.

Louise?

He was in the car.

Behind her.

Richard was in the back of the car. She wanted to look round, she wanted to glance in the mirror. She resisted. He wasn't there. He wasn't in the car. Yet she smelled his aftershave, felt his breath on the back of her neck. His hand was on her shoulder. She reached round, instinctively, and grasped nothing but her own coat material. There was no hand and no Richard.

Woodbridge was a small town that seemed at once self-conscious and characterful, but Jack saw the cracks in the façade. He saw the dirt and grime and the particles of grit around which each glistening raindrop was formed. He felt the presence of the river and the dark weight of its water.

A railway station appeared to the right. Louise swung into its car park and found a slot. Engine off, its rhythm and hammer replaced with the drumming of rain on the roof. Neither Jack nor Louise moved or spoke. Then, without a word, Louise opened the door and climbed out. Jack gathered himself and followed suit. The rain was a grey, greasy curtain of icy dampness.

Louise led the way toward an ancient-looking metal footbridge that crossed the railway line on the northern edge of the station. There was a cinema ahead, a café to their right. The cold ate into Jack. The sound of his footsteps was thunderous, and the impact of his feet on the tarmac jarred through him. The air was laden with moisture, the wind a painful burn on his face.

The bridge clanged as they mounted the steps. Jack was already exhausted and distracted by the endless madness of The Fabric. Lyle was close and moving quickly. He brought flame, heartbreak, and a yearning for the lost. He brought the reality of Jack's loneliness in his wings and was already forcing an emotional barrage outward toward him, like a fighter plane beginning its strafing run.

A train snaked its way into the station as Jack and Louise crossed the bridge. It was a three-carriage affair, a local station hopper. Its dirty black roof slid under the two of them, further darkened by the relentless rain. The engine rattled and clanked, the sound a deep, penetrating vibration that stirred Jack's gut and danced on his nerve endings. From inside the train came waves of excitement, boredom, indifference, and sadness. The Fabric shimmered and flared and brightened the air around him. He stumbled and grabbed the handrail to steady himself. Louise turned, concern in her face, which was again framed by the fur edging of the hood of her parka. Jack nodded to her. He was fine. The gesture shook the world.

Down the other side and onto a path that followed the river. Past a marina where winter-abandoned yachts huddled in the grey water, made forlorn by the rain. Sutton Hoo, the last resting place of Saxon nobility, lay on the Deben's heavily wooded far shore. There was a large house over there on the shoreline, alone, lonely.

An apt metaphor Jack decided.

He grabbed Louise's hand. It was warm despite the coldness of the air. She glanced at him and smiled from within the depths of her hood.

They walked.

Someone followed.

Jack glanced round and saw a large, hunched figure several meters behind them. It was a man, broad, tall, wearing a heavy overcoat. This time he was hatless, his grey hair slicked down by the rain. He didn't look up, but he was closing in.

Lyle.

The Fabric rippled and twisted about him. The distortion rolled through its threads to rattle against Jack's consciousness. He felt a wave of heat, smelled burning flesh. He walked on. Faster despite the jarring pain of his footsteps.

There was a shipwright's yard on their right, the entrance to a small park, the clubhouse of the town's sailing club. Then they were in countryside, which was open, unsheltered, and bleak. To the landward, the coarse vegetation hid what looked to be treacherous marshland.

It was bordered by a wood from which a footpath emerged to join the riverside walk. A few isolated houses could be glimpsed between the trees. The rain thickened; the air cooled. The river shone through The Fabric, almost too bright to look at. From it came a million tremors and disturbances: animal, instinct-driven, hungry, living, dying. There were other echoes, those of the drowned and the desolate.

Lyle was gaining on them. Jack heard his fake breath, felt his fake heartbeat. His own body was on fire with pain, his skin burned, his mouth scoured by a million particles and flavours.

Jack and Louise entered a narrow strip of woodland. When they emerged on the other side, they found that the pathway terminated in a small beach overlooked by a cottage.

A rough, wooden ramp caught Jack's attention. It looked to be a slipway, an age-worn wooden structure set at a shallow angle, and which projected about ten feet out into the murky water. There was a boat beached in front of the house. It was covered by a green tarpaulin, made dark by the rain. The river smelled of mud.

Jack stepped up on the ramp and stood for a moment then used it to walk down to the river. He heard Louise warn him to be careful.

Then sensed, rather than saw, Lyle emerge from the trees.

Louise called out a name. "Richard!"

Louise was alarmed when she saw Jack step onto the ramp. It looked slippery and precarious. This must have been how Richard entered deep water. The edges of the river were too shallow and muddy for anyone to wade very far.

And then he was there.

Richard.

Louise saw him with brutal clarity, standing on the ramp. He turned to toward her and he looked angry and hurt. She had to go to him.

"Richard!"

It wasn't him. Richard was dead and gone. Richard was in the water.

Strength failing, Louise dropped to her knees and almost immediately the cold damp seeped through her jeans from the wet sand. She wanted to go to Richard. She wanted to follow him onto the ramp. She would even wade in to drag him back.

She began to crawl toward the river edge. The sand was cold under her hands. The hood framed everything in an oval of fur. As she crawled closer, she saw the foggy green of the river, its muddy bed and dark olive-coloured plants. She plunged her left hand into the water, and it was brutally cold.

How cold it would have been that day. How awful, the shock of it, the panic as he sank into the freezing womb of the river. How frightened he would have been in those last, frantic moments as he clawed for breath, as his lungs filled, as he choked and thrashed and panicked and begged aid from whatever god he might have found in those dying seconds....

"This is none of your concern."

Startled, Louise looked up to see a figure standing a few meters away. Lyle. He stared at her, his face a terrifying blank, a mask of nothingness. Then Louise returned her attention to Jack on the slipway. His head was bowed. He stared hard at the water. He looked broad and strong. He looked like—

Richard. It was Richard.

Louise scrambled to her feet and ran toward him. She clambered onto the ramp, which was slippery and dank. Richard didn't look round to watch her. He was drenched, his hair plastered onto his scalp, the back of his parka black with rain. Louise struggled for grip on the slipway's slimed wooden planks. She windmilled her arms and almost fell. In that moment she saw, again, that it was Jack.

Jack, Jack, Jack, *Jack*.

She turned about to face Lyle who now stood at the top of the ramp. The edges of his body had blurred. They had lost definition and boiled away in tatters of oily black smoke.

She heard the splash of Richard entering the water, behind her. She heard him gasp as he slid down into the icy murk. She had to save him. She had to turn round and go to him.

It was an illusion. It was a lie.

She had to stand fast here and watch Lyle. She would bar his way and to do so, she must not flinch or look away for a moment. According to Jack, he couldn't hurt her, because he was not here for her. Which meant that he could not simply shove her out of his way.

If Jack was right, of course. If not, then she sensed that Lyle could crush her like an insect.

Lyle was barely human now. Whatever lay at his core was concealed deep within the swirl of black he had become. As she stared at the hound, Louise saw something vast and indefinable hurtle toward her from the seething dark. She remembered the underground station, the burning thing that had erupted from the tunnel. She remembered its terrifying energies.

"You can't hurt me," she shouted. Her voice sounded small to her, weak against the machine-gun patter of the rain. "You can't hurt me!"

She heard a baby's cry.

The sound emerged from within the smoke. It wasn't real.

Esther was dead.

Esther was dead.

"Esther's dead!" she screamed the sentence. It burst out of her as an angry sob and carried with it every fragment, every shred, of her grief.

Dead. *Dead.*

She stood her ground.

"Louise," Richard said from behind.

She didn't turn round.

"Louise."

She could see him, vivid in her imagination, teetering on the edge of the water, which lapped at his feet. He was calling to her because he needed her to take his hand and draw him back to herself. Then she would hold him forever and take care of him.

She started as the water beside her boiled into white foam. A figure surged out to grab at the slipway, as if the river itself had rejected him and spewed him out of its belly. Richard coughed and gasped and clung to the wet, slimy wood and looked up at her. He wore his business suit, although it was now a sodden ruin.

"Louise, please help me."

She made no move to save him. His hands slipped and his head dipped under the water. Louise glimpsed his shirt cuffs, the cufflinks.

She spoke his name but the sound was lost in the relentless wail of her child. The cries grew loud and the illusion of him shattered into a star-scape of splintered light, scattered over the river's surface. When she returned her attention to the Lyle thing, she saw that he was human once more. Esther was in his arms, swaddled in a bright yellow blanket and crying as if from a broken heart. Lyle held the child out to her.

"She's yours, Louise. She needs you. Take her."

Louise took a step toward them.

Jack stared down into the water. The Fabric within it was a million skeins of energy strung between dazzling pinpoints of incandescent white. The lights acted as nodes, each one a tiny echo of some emotion or trauma. Jack felt his way along each one, weeping over the sadness he found there, flinching at the terrors and anguish. The rain had strengthened and beat at him. Each drop was a hammer fall, a burning impact on his face. He delved deeper into The Fabric, followed thread after thread deeper into the water.

He heard Louise cry out again, his name, then Richard's. He felt Lyle's presence enfold them, no longer slowed by Louise's resistance. A wave of searing heat slammed into Jack's back and burrowed through him and brought with it an exquisite, complete agony. Someone cried from deep within the flames that had sprung up around him. Barely able to stand, fighting the illusion back into his own memory, Jack returned to the search, desperate now, looking for that last echo, that last glimmer of soul, of spirit that would speak the truth to him.

Lyle was close, a dark swirl, his core black and unravelling. He was a well of terrors. A wall of flame and destruction.

Then the sky opened.

Louise's hands closed about the living bundle offered to her by Lyle. She felt Esther's warmth, she caught a waft of her milky scent.

No.

"You're not Esther," she whispered to the bundle. "You're not my child."

The baby vanished in a torrent of spray as Richard reared out of the water once more.

"No, no, no!" Louise screamed. "Go away, leave me alone!"

Richard grabbed at her ankle, then dissolved in a sudden eruption of dirty water and was gone. Again. And again. Louise held Lyle's stare. Held it. Fought it.

Then, suddenly, driven by an instinct she didn't understand, Louise looked up and saw the sky open.

It was glorious, terrifying, Biblical. Threads of blue-white fire danced about the torn edges of the clouds and burrowed into their swirling grey underbellies. The air rippled and distorted as though something was pushing its way through the thin membrane of reality. A wind blew up, sudden and cold, and drove the rain into Louise's face.

Something appeared in the gap. It was featureless, smooth, and pure white. Its surface, though solid, shimmered with light. Louise could see that this was a part of an unthinkably vast object. The miles of it exposed by the torn cloud were only a fragment of the whole. From somewhere deep inside the thing came a rhythmic booming sound that pulsed like a titan's heartbeat. It was impossible to tell how close it was.

Suddenly, the three of them, Jack, Lyle, and Louise, were not alone. Other figures stood on the small beach and on the rain-stippled water of the river itself. They were human-shaped but featureless, blank windows, through which Louise could see stars and the multi-coloured swirl of nebulae. The figures made no move to intervene.

She tore her attention away from them and saw that Lyle was gone. Then Jack shouted; "I've found him!"

He was an echo that rang up from the chopping restless surface of the water and shivered, clear and vivid, along the threads of energy from which the fabric was woven.

Richard….

…This is the only way, Louise, the only way to protect you from the darkness in my soul. When Esther died…at the heart of my grief, I could no longer love you. Can you forgive me for that? I hid myself from you and tried to care while you crumbled to dust, and I let the darkness come. I welcomed it. Can you imagine that? Can you conceive how much guilt that feeling ignited in my heart? Can you imagine how vile I felt and what that did to me? I had to walk away from you. I had to leave you to heal. The world is closing in on me.

But I can't do it. I can't….

"He's alive," Jack said. He looked up from the water and saw the beings. He tensed, expecting the end, overcome by a bleak resignation. He was tired and battered by the sensory overload from The Fabric. He also knew he had lost Louise because Richard was alive.

He forced himself to walk toward her. When the end came, he would, at least, be looking at Louise, or even have her in his arms.

Would there be a sound, would there be pain, some warning or would it be instant? Would he feel or know when it happened, and what about afterwards?

"He's alive," he said again.

"Are you sure? Can you be certain?" Louise sounded as if she was desperate for the affirmative.

"Yes, I'm certain."

"Where is he? Where did he go?"

Jack shook his head. "All I know is that he came here then walked away."

Without a further word, Louise crossed the distance between them, walking carefully down the shallow slipway. Jack waited. When she reached him, she came close and Jack took her hand. A moment later she was in his arms. He held her tight and there was a feeling of finality in the embrace.

Louise pulled away. "What happens now?"

"I don't know."

"I'll stay, until…I'll stay with you."

"You should go," he said and remembered the ending of Josephine Anderson. "I don't know what it will be like, what happens. It may be...it might be awful."

"I'm staying," Louise said. And took his hand again.

Jack looked around at the figures. None of them moved. Their passivity was agony. The wait was all-but unendurable.

"I'm here," Jack shouted at them. "Don't you want me, now? For Christ's sake, get on with it!"

A moment.

Then the figures rushed in.

Louise cried out and staggered back. Jack saw her struggle for balance and slip down onto her hands and knees, still on the ramp, not in the water. Safe.

The beings converged in a sudden explosion of movement and Jack shuddered from the electric shock of their touch. He heard the sum of their voices, silent yet deafening. He felt the absolute cold of space then the raging heat of suns. They tore at him. They dismantled him, scooped out all the memories, sensations, and emotions he had accumulated. They fed on what he was. The pain was immense. He wrenched himself away, the action mostly instinctive.

Mostly.

The violent movement unbalanced him and clawing at empty air, he fell.

Cold, shockingly, mind-breakingly so. It was knives. It took his breath. The world was suddenly icy, dark, filthy water. It was in his mouth, his throat. It suffocated him. He thrashed against it in panic.

All the while, as he convulsed and writhed and sought escape, his creators tugged and twisted like predators at the raw meat and bones of their prey. His strength dissolved. His body was failing. It could not self-heal now. It was dissolving, leaking, fading.

But he fought on. He wrestled the water and his creators. He stretched toward the surface, which glowed dimly in the winter light. He heaved himself upward, but the darkness was coming. He was melting. They were taking him.

He was almost done.

Louise...God, Louise....

She saw the vacant cold figures hurl themselves onto Jack and bear him down.

She saw him twist then overbalance. The splash he made was an explosion that drove a fountain of muddy water upward into a brief glistening mushroom. As it shattered against the slipway it threw icy splinters into Louise's face. She stood, for a moment, crushed by the size and weight of the thing that had appeared in the sky, exhausted from her battle with Lyle. Shocked at the ending of Jack Smith.

She stared into the turbulent patch of river into which he had fallen. She watched for him to bob upward, ready to reach out, to haul him clear.

The water calmed, closed in on itself. Sealed him in.

He wasn't coming back. He was drowning.

Louise tore at her coat. Impervious to the rain-sodden air, she wrenched her jumper over her head and kicked off her shoes. Wondering, at the last moment when it was too late, if this was as insane as her logic told her it was, she leaped into the river.

The shock of the cold water exploded through her, but it was a distant pain. She had to get to Jack. She had to find him and save him. She felt a current tug at her, trying to drag her upriver, toward the sea, away from Jack.

Her lungs already cried out for air. It was a dark nothing. A solid grey.

No, there, a deeper darkness. A sphere of pure black. She felt the soft, silt riverbed under her and forced herself on toward the blackness.

Jack fell.

Endlessly, into a well of light and dark. Its walls were titanic clouds of many-coloured gas from which stars burned blinding white and fiercely hot. He knew that he was inside the vessel. He knew also that the craft was both solid and fluid. It had structure, yet that structure and its dimensions enclosed vast swathes of the universe, both the physical and the invisible. Time and gravity flowed, intertwined, through a network of immense conduits to power its engines, if the galaxy-vast complexities that drove the vessel were truly engines at all. Jack sensed that the craft didn't move as he understood movement, but folded time and space about itself much as a human would turn the pages of a book.

There was light and he recognized it as the core of The Fabric he had seen during that opium dream eight decades ago.

The glow resolved into a seething, slowly pulsating heartbeat of raw energy that, with each beat, swelled to a burning sphere with a girth of a million lightyears then shrank to a speck the size of a grain of sand. Things moved in the boiling oceans of light that raged about its surface, beautiful entities that could have been angels, or gigantic butterflies, or machines whose components were gossamer-delicate webs of steel and glass, or perhaps cities that formed and dissolved then reformed in the blink of an eye.

Jack felt solidity under his feet, yet there was nothing, only the immense pulsing sphere a thousand lightyears below.

The creator(s) spoke in a whisper that was like the gentle trailing of silk over Jack's mind. There were other voices mingled into its voice. Lizzy, Marion, Alfred….

She cares about you. She fights for something she knows is not human. And you, you gave up the final moments of your existence, for an act of generosity. You gave up the fight for that puny match-flare you call love, even though you knew she may turn away from you when you uncovered the truth she sought. What does she gain from this? She has what she wants from you. She no longer needs you. We do not understand such selflessness. We need more. And you, you are malfunctioning. You are flawed. You confuse your humanity with your function. We need to recover you. Yet we need to know more. This random entanglement of souls is puzzling, perhaps even a redeeming feature of this world. We see so many small acts, so many pinpricks of light in the darkness.

Jack saw them too. The rough and ready character in the pub who had bought him a drink and took him under his wing, Lizzy giving him a home, acts of mercy on the battlefield, Alfred, tended and healed by

German doctors and nurses, courage in the Blitz where he saw the desperate need of frightened men and women who could not self-heal, to save those trapped in the wreckage of bombardment, Marion, loving him even when she came to understand that he was different, Louise even now, risking her own life to save him, on and on, small stars that glinted in a black and desolate firmament.

The random entanglement of souls, love of a thousand different kinds.

Redemption.

Redemption

Louise?

"This is my home." Jack's voice sounded loud and crass in the vast hush of this place/time. "Earth is my home. Louise is in danger. I have to get back. Let me go back—"

You have no home. You are what you gather to yourself and nothing more. Jack, release your grip on the sadness and tragedy and pain of that place. Swim The Fabric. Be The Fabric.

"You need more. I'll go back, gather what you want. I want to go home."

Shining weft and weave, The Fabric stretched out before him. It promised peace, fulfilment. Lizzy was there, and Marion. They were in The Fabric and part of the fabric. He felt them.

"Earth is...." he ground out through gritted teeth. "Earth is my...home."

You have no home but The Fabric. You have no place other than as part of its weft and weave.

Don't suffer no more, Jack, said Lizzy.

Come home, pleaded Marion.

"Earth is my *home*."

Jack....

He reached towards The Fabric and felt the joy of its embrace. He wanted to pour himself into it and let it bear him away to his reward. He whispered their names; Lizzy, Marion, Alfred, Josephine....

Give in old chap. Your job's done, said Alfred.

Give in....

No, Earth is my home.

Louise is my home....

"Louise is my home!"

You would rather suffer than take your rest and she would rather risk her life than walk away. There is no logic to what we built here. There is only malfunction and redemption, cruelty and mercy, an endless cycle of light and dark. Embodied in you, Jack Smith.

"Let him go," Lyle said.

Lyle?

"He's done enough and I'm tired of him. Give the fool what he wants. We offer him Heaven, he chooses Hell. So be it."

A hand. Jack's hand. She had found him, deep in the dark. Her lungs were on fire. She wanted to breathe. God, she wanted nothing more than to gulp in precious, wonderful, gorgeous *air*.

A baby wailed, on and on. She saw Richard, thrashing in the water, desperate, drowning. She ignored them and hauled at Jack instead, willed him to wake up and help her.

She reached out with her left arm and felt a weed-slimed leg of the slipway. She grabbed it and dragged herself and her burden through the water. She was almost out of strength now. Almost done.

Wake up. Wake up, Jack.

Unable to endure another second under water, she surged upward, broke the surface and sucked in a lungful of air. Her body was numb with cold, impaled by it. Almost paralysed by it. She still had Jack's sleeve in her right fist. She pulled at him. Used her failing strength to get him to the slipway.

"Louise is my home!"

The Fabric shattered and Jack was hurled outwards and —

Found himself buried alive in icy water, his lungs filled, unable to breathe. His arm was snagged. He thrashed and struggled then understood that someone had him. Driven by panic, by the need for air, he propelled himself upward and suddenly there was rain and air and Louise. He retched and gagged and spewed water.

"I'm all right," he gasped. "Out, we have to get out."

Louise swam a short distance then stood where the river was waist deep. Jack followed until he too felt mud under his feet. They staggered to the shore and collapsed on the wet sand, unheeding of the rain or the cold.

"Jack," Louise said, hoarse and panting for breath. "Look."

He rolled opened his eyes.

The sky was cloud-locked and empty.

"They've gone," Louise said. "Jack, they've gone. Does that mean that they're letting us live?"

"For a while longer. You…we confuse them."

"Did they let you go?"

"Lyle…Lyle advocated for me, at least I think he did." Jack laughed. He was cold and in danger of pneumonia and shivering uncontrollably, but he laughed. "They've abandoned me and I don't care. They abandoned me because they didn't understand why I choose this place over Heaven."

"Heaven? Was that thing God?"

"Whatever it was, they took what they wanted from me, but they didn't understand what I gave them or why I wanted to stay."

"Why did you want to stay?"

Jack rolled over, reached for her, and touched her face.

"Why do you think?" he said.

Louise was in his arms again. They held each other and shared what meagre warmth remained to them.

"How long have you got on Earth this time, Jack?"

"I don't know, and I don't care. I think they've only wanted me back to empty out my memories, after that they dumped me here because I didn't want to walk into the light. It feels different, though." He could no longer sense The Fabric. He felt weaker, tired. He suspected that his body would deteriorate and crumble just as Louise's would, just as all human beings did. "I'm just glad to be home." The laughter drained away. He had to tell Louise the truth. He hesitated. The next sentence he spoke could be the end of this.

"Richard is still alive, Louise."

Louise drew away. "I know." She struggled to her feet. "I'm sorry, Jack, I need to breathe. I need to think."

Jack watched as she descended the slipway to pick up her discarded coat and sweater then she returned to the beach and walked away into the trees and out of sight. She didn't look back. Jack was suddenly bereft and his grief turned to anger. Which was of no use. Louise and Richard belonged to each other. He had to accept that.

He should go home. He was cold, wet, and exhausted. Louise could have the car. There would be a train. He would find his way back to his flat and he would find his way through the next hundred years, or fifty, or ten, whatever remained to him.

He was alone once more and, as it always did when human friendship and love was taken from him, the wrench of parting felt harder to bear than whatever ending the creators would have given him. But he had faced this before and survived. That was what being human meant.

A while later, Jack walked through the trees and back out onto the bleak openness of the river path. He was once again alone here, just as he had always been.

When he reached the station, shivering and cold, he was surprised to see the car still in the car park. Louise leaned against the vehicle, arms folded, a blanket wrapped about herself.

"I can't help you find him. I'm sorry," Jack said. "The Fabric has gone...I've been discarded. I'm dying, the way you are, the way everyone is."

"There are other ways."

Jack nodded. "Can you take me back with you? I'll leave you alone after that. I understand if you can't. I'll take a train—"

"I don't want to search for him. Richard left. He must have known where I was, but he never came back for me. I hope he's all right and has found what he wants, but I have to let him go."

Jack nodded, shivered, but made no move. It was Louise who spoke next. "Come on, Jack, get into the car before you die of hyperthermia and let's go home."

Jack nodded and took her hand, no longer alone.

MEET THE AUTHOR

College lecturer, electrician, actor and musician, Terry Grimwood is also the author of numerous novels, short stories and novellas, including the British Fantasy Society award-nominated *Interference*. Three of his plays have been performed on the stage, Directed by the author. While most of his work lies in the science fiction, horror and fantasy genres, Terry often strays outside their boundaries, which he considers a must for all genre writers and a cure for writer's block. He has co-written a number of engineering textbooks for Pearson Educational Press, penned a romance for *People's Friend* magazine and his novella *Joe* is inspired by a true story. Terry lives by a lake with his wonderful wife, Debra. In his spare time, Terry is vocalist and harmonica player with The Ripsaw Blues Band.

He can be found at: https://www.facebook.com/terry.grimwood.9/

and https://www.facebook.com/the.ripsaw.blues.band

Curious about other Crossroad Press books? Stop by our website:
http://crossroadpress.com
We offer quality writing
in digital, audio, and print formats.

Subscribe to our newsletter on the website homepage and receive a
free eBook.

Printed in Great Britain
by Amazon

60688258R00139